COUNSEL OF RAVENS

To Michel,

Hope you enjoy Hugh's Route 66 Adventure!

Madeleine

COUNSEL OF RAVENS

M. M. Gornell

Champlain Avenue Books
Henderson, Nevada, USA

Published by Champlain Avenue Books, Inc., Henderson, Nevada
A Hubert James Champion III Route 66 Mystery

ISBN-13: 978-0-9855008-9-4
Library of Congress LCN: 2013909031

Cover by LAWRENCE

FIRST EDITION

Printed in the United States of America

Dedication

Marie Ann LaCour Boles

Acknowledgements

As always, my gratitude goes to my excellent editors--Mike Foley and Virginia Moody--and to my marvelous agent and editor, Kitty Kladstrup. This story would not be published without them.

To my relatives and friends, knowing you're there has meant the world to me. Thanks for your continuing words of encouragement. I'm also most grateful to my Route 66 and Public Safety Writers Association (PSWA) friends and business owners who always so graciously provide information on animals, politics, law-enforcement, and local lore.

And my regular refrain to my husband, *thank you Larry for being there*!

To my readers, here's hoping to meet many of you sometime, someplace, on the Mother Road!

Sequel to Reticence of Ravens

Preface

Topography, climate, scenery. When you think about all the different environments Route 66 touches as it forges westward from the Midwest to the Pacific Ocean—*the mind boggles.* From Chicago's sophisticated big city hubbub and bejeweled lakefront, to Los Angeles's movie-ambiance and sun soaked ocean beaches—*what a ride!* Literally and culturally.

Amongst all those locations—each offering myriad possibilities for intrigue, murder, and mayhem—this author's mind remains captivated by California's Mojave Desert. *Stark, heat-baked, wind battered, and in-your-face*—yet oddly comforting and sheltering. *How can that be?*

Hubert James Champion III continues to wonder…

Mors Vincit Omnia
Death Conquers All

Before Hugh Knew

If a starlit night could be called beautiful, she thought tonight was such an instance.

Mojave County Deputy Sheriff Melony Dibbs felt good. Not only had Chief Audrey Boyes thrown her an afternoon anniversary party—*one year on the job*—but afterwards, in her office, over a shot each of Ernie Stapleton's left behind "bottom drawer" whiskey, Audrey also complimented her on a job well done. Liquor on the job was a definite no-no, but today had been special.

Remembering again as she headed toward the Fort Cady freeway exit, Melony felt a renewed glow of pleasure. And it wasn't from the booze—she'd barely tasted her shot, then surreptitiously disposed of it in the restroom when she had a chance. Unfortunately, she could still taste their former chief's "rot-gut." *Nasty.* Not that she was a connoisseur, but hopefully, the bargain-basement booze would soon be used up—Audrey replacing it with something smoother.

Melony turned off I-40 onto National Trails, her Impala cruiser's 135 dB siren yelping her presence to sentient creatures for miles, and her thoughts remaining on her boss. She sure liked Audrey, and was glad retiring Chief Stapleton promoted her to Mojave County Sheriff. Melony was looking forward to learning a lot from Audrey over the next few years. She was also planning on becoming indispensable—*Audrey's right-hand deputy*. Like tonight, volunteering to work past her shift.

For sure, she was not going to pass-on or screw-up any opportunity coming her way. She'd eagerly volunteered to answer CHP's request for a Mojave Sheriff's Department

1

assist—*no overtime required, thank you very much*. It made sense. The call was on her way home, and she was clearly closer to the incident site than CHP Officer Rociana Bustamante who was still on her way from a meeting in Victorville.

Even her cruiser's roof-mounted strobes, which she often found annoying, hit her as pleasantly hypnotic tonight as pulses of light cut through desert night blackness. *Yep*, things were good. In fact, her fellow deputy, Neil Knight was also acting a lot nicer. In some respects, he seemed a changed man since that hospital stay. *Well*, almost.

Ahead to her right, Melony saw what looked like a dirty BMW parked on the shoulder—neither color nor condition yet determinable in the darkness; but with its emergency blinkers flashing. *Was that the car? The 10-46 call— motorist needing help?* Had to be.

She turned off her siren and pulled up behind the vehicle. Once stopped, she punched in the three digits of the Beamer's California license plate number she could see between mud splotches, checked her dash cam and her chest mounted microphone. *Yep*, both on. Everything needed to be according to "the book."

She got out, put on her jacket, and made sure she was "packing heat"—as they said in the gangster movies she loved to watch on TCM. Glock and taser. *Not a rookie anymore.*

It was Winter—the air felt and smelled fresh, dry, and familiar. She'd been born and raised in the desert, and here is where she planned to live out her life. *My desert*, she thought and smiled. And so beautiful at night. The sky, the stars, the smell—a wisp of a breeze brushing her cheek.

On this particular traffic assist, Melony figured she could be a big help—she knew all the tow truck numbers by heart, the closest tire-jockey—a lot of tire-piercing objects lay just below benign looking Mojave dirt road surfaces. But few muddy roads, she fleetingly noted—again taking in the

Beamer's license plate. Still, wouldn't be the first time a desert day-tripper got back on the highway and found —

Barely heard by Melony —*crack, crack, crack*—three shots pierced her Mojave night.

PART ONE
Days of Craziness

Chapter One

Startled into an awakened state by Hobo, Hubert James Champion III, sat straight up in bed. Hobo was already sitting erect and stiff on the foot of the bed, clearly sensing *something*—and whatever it was, Hugh immediately knew it was bad. *Awful, in fact.* Indeed, his canine friend's nose was pointed toward the ceiling, his neck stretched long, and he was howling befitting a banshee wailing across the Irish Heathlands.

Hugh shook his head to clear residual confusion from his abruptly-ended dream state. *That damned dream again about his father.* From his position in bed, all he could see out his curtain-less bedroom window was blackness—the time of night evading him. *Evening, midnight, early morning?* On the tails of Hobo's spine-chilling howls, his bedside phone rang—unmercifully slashing farther into his peace of mind and causing his stomach to lurch. Though he was feeling psychologically better than last Spring, Hugh instinctively wanted none of what Hobo and the sharp ringing were announcing. *Trouble is coming. Trouble* he wouldn't be able to avoid. *Not again. Not again.*

He flexed his hands. *No trembles, at least.* Then he tried to sidle back down into the safety of bed and pull the bedspread up over his face, but Hobo had somehow pinned him in. For a moment, all he could do was close his eyes, hold his breath, and pray the message wasn't Audrey was hurt.

How had I ever thought the Mojave would be a safe haven?

*   *   *   *   *

7

It was the worst night Sheriff Audrey Boyes had ever experienced.

Sure, she'd seen some horrific and gory crime scenes — but sweet Melony Dibbs splayed lifeless on cracked and lumpy asphalt, with the faded outline of a Route 66 pavement medallion vaguely framing her torso, a pool of blood seemingly spread in all directions from her midsection and drenching her uniform shirt—was nearly incomprehensible. Much less bearable.

She fought back waves of nausea as she stared at Melony's body, almost mesmerized by her multiple wounds that looked more like one gaping bloody mess. *A shotgun certainly. Oh my dear God.* Too much. Too painful to completely take in.

I just put a commendation in her folder this morning—Melony Josephine Dibbs, twenty-five years old, one year on the job—exemplary service. They'd even kidded about her middle name.

For a moment, Audrey felt like she couldn't breathe — on the edge of passing out—but she willed herself not to collapse. *No,* the Mojave County Sheriff would not lose control; especially not in these moments when her expertise was dearly needed. For the time being, it was *her* crime scene, *her* job to make sure nothing was missed. *I owe Melony to hold-it-together.* She mentally ticked-off crime scene protocol in an attempt to manage her emotions and the scene.

Save life was paramount. *Too late for that.* She fought back a gasp. *Still, I called for EMTs.* All the rest seemed so abstract, so cold, with Melony down. Think protocol, she commanded herself. *Arrest suspects, ensure safety of others, witnesses, preserve order*—logical thinking, however, was near impossible. She just wanted to cry out in pain.

Then—and even though she was able to remain standing—on top of her nausea and pain, a white-hot anger flooded her being. And it took every ounce of emotional strength Audrey could muster to keep from screaming a string of curses into the night.

She wanted to hit something, shoot something.

After several long moments, she gained enough control to only hiss "Jesus Christ," under her breath.

Compounding Audrey's pain, her Assistant Sheriff Neil Knight was standing a few feet away, and she couldn't let him—or any of the other cops for that matter—know how shaken she actually was. *And they're arriving in droves.* Indeed, the news of a fallen comrade was pulling them to this desolate spot like a magnet. Uniforms differed, cruisers differed—but "they" were one.

Officer down, 11-99, officer down, 11-99, officer down, 11-99... She had to force herself not to bring her hands to her ears—drown out the all-hands radio announcement she'd received earlier. The awful words wanted to repeat themselves in a hated mantra she couldn't turn off.

"Sheriff?" Someone approached her from behind. "We've started securing the scene, until forensics—" The unrecognized male voice faded. Had he moved away, or been overcome? Had her back told him something like, *not yet?* Maybe. She didn't know, and couldn't make herself turn around to look—*look into his eyes.* Indeed, *not yet.*

All around her the night was throbbing with strobes and approaching sirens. Circus lights and sounds as Melony's death knoll—right here on National Trails Highway and Fort Cady Road—just a few miles from her own home.

And oddly, all the while just underneath the awful hubbub, Audrey sensed an eerie, inexplicable, and separate layer of deathly silence weighing them down. Under the flashing strobes, layered an underlying sheet of silent horror.

9

She straightened her shoulders. *I have to do my job.* This was a CHP highway traffic stop, but in *her* county. Final jurisdiction yet to be called.

Somehow, within minutes that seemed like hours, she was able to debrief and organize the arriving officers. *Secure the crime scene, secure the scene.* There were tire marks that had to be preserved, brass to be located—if any. Nonetheless, and her steely resolve aside, with every second of "doing her duty," Audrey had to keep fighting back the pounding in her head, and the swell of emotion wanting to bring her to her knees in an angry blubbering mess.

Melony is still lying there on the ground—dead. Why doesn't she just get up?

Finally, Audrey was able to release a sigh under her breath without an accompanying cry of emotion. And in a few more minutes, standing halogen lights were in place and the scene was marked; she was even able to speak professionally to Neil, giving him instructions to notify her as soon as a CHP Sergeant arrived. Maybe they would even send a lieutenant. A lot of resources would be extended tonight—especially for a podunk county like hers. *One of our own is down.*

Some of her responsibilities taken care of, Audrey walked toward a CHP officer she recognized—Rociana Bustamante, disbelief contorting her otherwise lovely face— and this time when passing Neil, she gently touched him on the back. There was nothing she could say to him, nothing that would fix this. But he needed to know she cared.

Bad people were supposed to be murdered—not an innocent like Melony. Whatever organization ended up in charge of this investigation was of no matter. *I will personally find whoever killed Melony,* Audrey promised herself. *Maybe kill the bastard myself.*

For now though, all she could do was make sure nothing was compromised. With renewed determination,

Audrey stopped for a moment before she reached Rociana's stricken form and called Hugh on her cellphone. She needed a friendly ear, even if just for a stolen moment. Funny how often she now felt the need to talk to him, be with him, see him.

Neil Knight couldn't take his eyes off Melony's body; at the same time, he couldn't stop repeating today's events over and over in his brain. How she'd brought him a cup of coffee from the AM/PM Mini-mart this morning. *Then* during her anniversary party, she'd told him what a good job he was doing as Assistant Sheriff. *Then* she'd handled the phones when Audrey's FBI brother Ted and CHP Liaison Officer, Rociana Bustamante, stopped by to talk inter-agency logistics. Consequential stuff, he'd thought at the time. And now—*and now* he couldn't remember a word of what he and Rociana talked about.

Kindnesses. Melony hadn't needed to bring him coffee or boost his ego. He swallowed and inhaled deeply to keep his emotions in check. He didn't want Audrey to know how vulnerable he was at this moment—standing in the middle of the road mesmerized by Melony's lifeless body.

A forensics technician was placing paper bags over Melony's hands. Neil almost yelled out, *She didn't kill herself, you fool. For Christ's sake.* Of course he knew it was a crime scene evidence procedure.

Neil sucked in air to calm himself. When he'd left their department offices earlier—him eager to go home and change, then pick up Sally for dinner—Melony had offered, "I'll do the paperwork on that scrap-metal robbery." He'd looked up from his desk to see her standing in the doorway, a smile on her face. "It's time for you to go home," she'd added. Those

11

words, *her words*, so eager to please—would remain with him forever.

His final vision of Melony alive was also indelibly burnt into his psyche. As he was getting into his Audi down in the parking lot, something made him look up at his second floor office window, and there she stood, silhouetted by his desk lamp—giving him another smile, this time accompanied with a jaunty salute. Always so keen for the job, and oh, so naïve. Yet, he'd come to like her. More than he'd expected.

Melony is dead. Still impossible to comprehend.

For a moment, Neil thought his legs were going to give, and had to turn his eyes from the sight of her body. He knew his boss Audrey was just to his right, and sure, they were on good terms these days, but she couldn't see him fall apart. *And on the verge of sobbing? Never.*

The night was turning cool, yet he felt hot and clammy. In the past, he'd voiced his dislike of the sucking Mojave, while Melony loved it. He heard himself sigh far too loudly. But Audrey didn't seem to have noticed. Caught up in her own emotions, he guessed.

On more than one occasion in the past, he'd even scoffed Melony was an idiotic name for a cop. Tonight, his regret was huge. He even doubted there was a French or Latin idiom capable of capturing what he was experiencing tonight. *La culpa es mía, la culpa es mia*—at least Spanish hadn't deserted him. *The sin is mine.*

Then a slice of French did come, *Jeune fille innocente.* Innocent girl.

For a second, Neil was rather surprised at his thoughts—foreign phrases didn't come to him like before—not since the accident last spring when they'd solved the Turner Jackson murder. "Things" for him, had changed. To further mock him, and seemingly from nowhere, a mild French curse also came to him. *"Bon sang,"* he said under his breath. If he could just start today over—bring Melony back to life.

    Bloody hell.

Chapter Two

Monday morning

It was still dark when Hugh and Hobo walked across the deck between his double-wide and Joey's. It was much earlier than he usually opened—but after Audrey's call, he'd only "played" at being asleep. Stunned, horrified, and deeply saddened, he wasn't sure what he could do, and the only concrete action that came to mind was to open Joey's. Besides, he only had to traverse ten or so feet, and it was also an act in line with the concept of "going into work."

Even though his receipts remained dismal, and his stock sketchy, Joey's mini-mart was a business as far as the State of California was concerned. And as a business, he needed to keep business-like hours. *Okay,* he was rationalizing—or was it fantasizing? His hours were often variable and whimsical; if he wasn't in the mood, and Ruthie Chavez or Gabe Travers couldn't, or wouldn't relieve him, *so be it.* The "Closed" sign went up.

This morning, he needed to keep busy, keep moving. Think.

Melony murdered.

He could barely comprehend what Audrey told him. The Melony Dibbs he'd known was a lovely person, and he was having a hard time absorbing the facts that not only was she actually dead, but also—that someone would hurt such an innocent. He'd asked Audrey to repeat her words twice, but he'd heard correctly. Melony had been murdered.

Over the last half-year, he'd finally felt like he'd stepped forward "into" his life. A life he could almost imagine

15

being a good one. Admittedly baby steps, not giant leaps, but he was mentally headed in the right direction. Even letting a few new people and their concerns into his life. *Now this.*

Something always happens when you start caring about people. Clients had said that to him, and he'd said it to himself. Too often.

After Audrey's call, sleep had been impossible. *Melony was so young.* Mid-twenties he guessed. And Audrey, for the first time since he'd known her, had sounded deeply shaken. Of course she would be. Her deputy, a friend and protégé maybe—dead almost in an instant.

Murdered. Hugh could tell he was really struggling to wrap his head around what had happened.

He stopped for a second on his little wooden deck between home and work, and looked out past his rose garden—into the distance over the top of his fence. Had he seen a flash of light? *Headlights?* It was still dark, and the burst of light so quick, he wasn't sure what had caused the flash of light, but *yes,* he had seen something. There was not much human habitation down that way, just Gabe's place and a couple abandoned singlewides. No reason for anyone to be driving in that area this time of night. Morning, actually. *Probably nothing sinister.* Two kids looking for a make-out place probably. He took a deep, but quick breath of cold predawn air, and his mind and heart returned to Melony.

Murdered.

He shook his head, took the few remaining steps between home and work, then unlocked Joey's backdoor. Once inside, he reached for and pressed the start button on the thermostat. It was mounted just below the light switch on the wall, and not hard to find in the dark. Mojave winter nights were cold and his office felt frigid. He didn't turn the lights on, even though the sun hadn't officially risen—*thank goodness*—for neither was he ready to face artificial illumination.

16

Besides, he didn't need lights to navigate his office in the back of Joey's; like a mouse in a familiar maze, Hugh easily walked over and dropped like a lump of lead into his desk's wooden swivel-chair. His chair was old and hard, but still gave him emotional comfort. Something he needed this morning. He couldn't yet see his round-faced black and white schoolhouse clock on the wall above his window into Joey's proper, but guessed it read around 5:00 A.M—and for a second or two, he thought fondly of his mother Eloise, who'd given him the clock as a Joey's opening-present. In the background, he heard the low hum of the propane furnace start up. It wouldn't be long before the morning chill was gone.

He rubbed his hands together and was surprised at how cold they were. *My second Winter.* He leaned back and stared up toward his ceiling fan—a habit he'd developed over the last few months—and found it mentally restful, whether the fan was on or off. It's outline was still vague, but he could see the antique contraption was motionless and mute. He sort of remembered there was something he was supposed to do to it for winter—reverse the blades or something like that so it would push hot air down. Gabe had explained the maintenance procedure in detail, but he hadn't listened. Just being "off" for winter was enough for him.

As expected, his thoughts quickly returned to Melony. Sure, he knew motorist pullovers were dangerous. But this was different. Someone had deliberately called in asking for assistance, *then* cold-bloodedly shot Melony. *Personal? Maybe.* Or just plain old-fashioned evil indiscriminately rearing its ugly head?

Even though it was still dark, inside and outside, Hugh closed his eyes, and for a second, wished for Della, or Gabe, or Ted, or even Neil. *Someone* to talk about this with. Hermit that

17

he sometimes wanted to be, Hobo and Black-Jack just weren't sufficient companionship to deal with Melony's murder.

As if conjured up by his desire, headlights appeared at his special garden's back wooden-gate. Two quick horn beeps. Gabe Travers.

How the heck does he know about Melony already?

Special Agent Ted Fletcher was showering in his state-of-the-art multi-jetted shower when he internalized the fact he loved Rociana Bustamante de Reyes. He turned his face up toward the ceiling jet and let the sharp spray pelt his face. Ted liked his showers hot, intense, and lengthy. This shower contraption, he decided, was an engineering marvel.

He wasn't surprised he was in love—just that the opportunity and circumstances had come together so quickly and easily. It was an added bonus she was also a cop. CHP in fact—there was definitely cache in that. She'd only shared a little about herself, and he was planning—unashamedly and illegally—to check a few databases. He needed to fill in some details. His protective urges had already started to kick-in, and he figured Rociana had likewise done some background checks on him. She had yet to bring up his one quickie marriage and divorce, but figured it was coming—one day.

Though he knew Rociana's personality didn't lean toward prying or recriminations. Yep, Rociana was one of the "good" people in the world, of that he had no doubt. *She's also very good for me.* In fact, he bought his new upscale condo in Claremont because of its proximity to Route 66—one of Rociana's passions. And now, he was becoming quite fond of the college town at the base of the San Gabriel Mountains.

Ted could hear his phone ringing in the bedroom. He turned up the temperature on his digital shower panel and

18

mentally closed his ears to the annoying sound. *They'll leave a message.* Anyway, it couldn't be Rociana. She'd pulled the night shift and had no doubt hit the sack as soon as she got home last night.

"I'm guessing your Honey's department, CHP, and even the FBI are gonna be on this hard and heavy," Gabe said, more asking than telling.

"I'm going into Yermo and talk to Audrey first thing." Hugh was glad for Gabe's company, so he didn't give him grief for calling Audrey his "Honey." He glanced up at his clock—but it still wasn't light enough to be certain of the time. He loved that clock, and loved his mother for giving it to him. Fleetingly, he again thought of her, and this time chastised himself for not calling her for almost a year. Regret, ashamedness, and another emotion he couldn't quite place washed over him—then disappeared just as quickly. *I'll call her next week,* he vowed to himself.

To Gabe, Hugh added, "Their shift doesn't start until eight." He let his head drop backwards, again staring at his ceiling fan. "Is it cold out?"

Of course he knew how cold it was, and he knew Audrey often came in at six, though neither she nor Neil were officially on the clock until eight; he also knew they didn't pay much attention to "officially." Couldn't have their jobs and be nine-to-five clock watchers. Ten, even twelve hours on the job was more the norm. Heck, after last night, they might not have gone home yet.

"Of course it's still cold out." Gabe eyed Hugh suspiciously. "You're not opening this morning? 'Cause it's cold, or 'cause of what's happened?" He made a disparaging

19

sound through this teeth. "And why don't you turn on the dang lights?"

Hugh ignored his question about the lights, but answered Gabe's first question easily. "No, I'm not opening." After a short silence, he added, "It just doesn't seem right." His voice faded into sad nothingness, and after another moment of silence, he sighed. Sure, he'd walked over to "work," but now realized talking to Audrey was far more important than opening Joey's. Besides, it wasn't a Wednesday morning when Gabe's cousin Leon Travers stopped with his tour bus on their way to Vegas. "How did you know about Melony?"

Murdered. The word kept screaming inside his head.

"Scanner." Gabe got up from Hugh's singular visitor's chair, an aged and uncomfortable wooden slat-back at the side of his desk, and walked over to Hugh's inside picture window with its view into the mini-mart. "Everybody's got 'em you know."

Hugh didn't, but refrained from pointing out the fact. He'd learned it was often easier to just "go with the flow" when conversing with Gabe.

"Place looks funny with the lights off, you know," Gabe continued. He looked thoughtful for a couple seconds before saying, "I could open for you and hang around until Ruthie shows up. Think she really likes running the place." Gabe shook his head as if mystified by what he'd just said.

"That would be great." Despite his ambiguity over this morning's priorities and his laissez-faire opening attitudes, Gabe's offer was a relief. Oddly, it wasn't right if *he* opened, but okay if *Gabe* did—some kind of goofy rationalization.

Monday mornings sometimes had a few customers leaving Vegas and returning to LA, and he knew his housekeeper Ruthie was bored just cleaning his doublewide. And even though his customers were few—Monday mornings

20

included—Joey's offered his well educated jewel-of-a-housekeeper an opportunity to interact with a few people.

Hugh pushed himself up with a groan and walked over to stand next to Gabe peering into his mini-mart. He guessed his friend to be about 5'5," and his protruding belly made Gabe look even shorter—knowledge that left Hugh often feeling like a giant when standing at his friend's side.

Oddly enough in the past, Hugh hadn't paid much attention to how Joey's looked without the lights on—much less given it thoughtful consideration. But this morning, in predawn illumination, his modest little place exuded a museum-like aura of a bygone era. How that could be was a mystery. *I'm just tired*, he thought.

"It'll be light soon," he said to the world in general. The import of his statement was emotional—he'd have to face the realities of the day soon.

"Yep," Gabe echoed. And Hugh wondered if Gabe had similar thoughts about facing the day. And grief.

With a sigh, Hugh turned his back on Joey's, leaned his butt against his narrow inside windowsill, and next took in his office from a different perspective. The schoolhouse clock he knew was on the wall above him, and along with his desk and two chairs, after a year-and-a-half, remained his office's only embellishments. His walls were still generic cream, and he hadn't added pictures or photos. He did now have a lovely five-by-seven Sino-Tabriz rug between his desk and window into Joey's.

Somehow, Audrey had figured out his birthday, September nineteenth, and had given him the rug as a present; perversely, he thought, she refused to offer him her own birth date. He wasn't holding a grudge however, and thought the rug quite nice. Like-mindedly, it had become Hobo's favorite snoozing spot when forced to be in the office. Another recent addition—smack-dab in the middle of his side wall surface—

21

was a Bob Waldmire Route 66 Poster Map Ruthie had presented him from the Barstow Route 66 Museum.

Clearly, if office adornment revealed anything, he hadn't settled into the Mojave, or even Joey's yet. *Still a wayfarer.* "You know," Hugh said slowly, "Melony's murder could be someone local." He hoped he was just logically examining all the possibilities, no matter how unlikely. *No,* he didn't want to actually believe someone in the area had murdered Melony.

Gabe was still gazing into an empty Joey's illuminated only by several nightlights. "Nah," he said. "Sure, we got some dopers, some scrap metal thieves too." He turned his head to look at Hugh's profile. "But a murderer—heck no." He clicked his teeth. "Foreigner."

Despite the horrible tragedy of Melony's murder—for a blink-of-a-second, Hugh wanted to laugh. Gabe's tour bus driving cousin, Leon, had confided Gabriel Travers actually had a lot of education initials after his name. Since that time, Gabe's "ah-shucks" inbred backwoods persona was not only amusing, but he now knew, was an act.

"'Foreigner' as from another *country*, or 'foreigner' as in not a desert rat?" Hugh asked for the heck of it, guessing he knew the answer.

"Back East foreigner."

"Could be," Hugh said. And now that Gabe had brought it up, truth was, he did remember seeing on cable news a story about someone murdered on the highway in Oklahoma. Or was it St. Louis? Whether under similar circumstances, he couldn't remember; but Audrey would know. "You may be on the mark."

Gabe turned his whole body toward Hugh, his tone and body language demanding Hugh's full attention. "You know something I don't?"

22

Instead of looking at Gabe directly, or acknowledging his question, much less answering him, Hugh stepped away from his window and back toward his desk. Remaining non-communicative, Hugh walked all the way to his other window, the one looking outside into his rose garden.

First light was finally touching and changing the horizon. His garden was indeed charming in the early light—this morning, this moment in time, starting to sparkle from winter-light touching the leaves of rhododendrons sharing the small garden-space with his dormant and limp-leafed roses. Finally he sighed. Soon he would have to see Audrey's face, share her grief.

It's going to be a really horrible day. One of the worst.

From a distance, a raven called out, "Krawk, krawk." Maybe all the way from the clump of Athols he'd dubbed Poe's Condo? More likely he thought, though he couldn't see a bird for sure, the raven had given counsel from the telephone pole at the end of his garden. Only twenty-or-so feet away.

"Well?" Gabe demanded. "A sigh doesn't answer my question."

Finally, but still without turning to look at his friend, Hugh said, "I sure hope it's not a local." The thought of Melony's murderer being someone they knew was doubly disturbing, even frightening. "But I don't know anything you don't know."

Finally Hugh turned around to face Gabe directly, his tone also demanding. "What's this about scrap metal thieves?"

"She'll be here any moment," Neil said from behind his desk. They were in Audrey's old office—*Neil's* new office.

"Thanks," Hugh said. He was standing at his favored spot, at the second floor window looking down along the

23

sleepy town's streets, and alternately out at the rolling hill backdrop to the world of Yermo. Audrey had been forced to take Ernie's vacated office at the back of the second floor; but Hugh was addicted to at least a couple moments of "Yermo time" whenever he visited the Mojave County Sheriff Department. The building remained the only two-story in town, and there was still an aura surrounding Yermo that intrigued Hugh. He steadfastly remained fond of the town even though Gabe insisted on disabusing his fascination whenever the topic came up.

Without turning from the window, Hugh sighed, he hoped too softly for Neil to hear. The newly appointed Assistant Sheriff's tone sounded lackluster, flat. Hugh hadn't thought about having to deal with Neil's grief too. *This is going to be even worse than I thought.*

"She was standing where you are now," Neil continued, *his* tone so soft, Hugh almost missed hearing him. "That was the last place I saw Melony alive."

Jeez. Hugh didn't know what to say; what *could* he say that would change things—or even start to make it better? He knew he should be offering the right words; *I'm a psychologist for Christ's sake.* Yet he remained silent, and like he'd done earlier with Gabe, didn't attempt to turn around and see Neil's face. And for a moment, Hugh was taken aback by his un-psychologist-like behavior. He should be there for his friends. Instead, he was focusing his attention on the barren scrub-desert spread across the rooftop horizon north of the freeway. *Escaping.* So much easier to focus on the pale coloring and illumination of the Yermo-Calico hills in early morning light.

He heard Neil's chair-legs scrape against tile and guessed he was coming over to stand next to him. He held his breath, but after a few seconds, he instead heard Neil walk out of his office. *Down the hall to the unisex employee restroom?*

24

Neil gone, Hugh allowed himself a louder half sigh, half moan. Then he heard himself say Melony's name out loud. He hoped Deputy Dibb's empty office door was closed — she'd been so excited when Neil advanced. She would have an office to herself. He didn't want to see it when he headed back to Audrey's rear office.

The vague and barely audible sound of an auto engine pulled Hugh's gaze away from the horizon, compelling him to look down into the parking lot. In line with his fascination with Yermo, the Mojave County Sheriff's Department parking lot was also oddly compelling. Remarkable because of how lumpy its concrete was, and at the same time endearing because the corner-marking California Fan Palms were doing so well. Death and renewal at the same time, *yep,* that was MCSD parking lot. *A metaphor for life?*

"Jeez," he said, and shook his head. Melony's death was dragging him back to a maudlin mental state he was hoping he'd moved past.

Audrey was pulling in below, and he forced his attention to the very real logistics of everyday-life being lived. And in line with that reality, Hugh knew he needed to mentally keep moving forward also. If only to keep up with the passage of time. *What a time to turn philosophical.*

For some reason he didn't know, she was driving a CHP black-and-white, while her Impala sat unoccupied and looking a little dusty next to its twin- cruiser — a patrol car that used to be shared by Melony *and* Neil. *Now only Neil.*

She was in uniform — unusual since her promotion — and carrying several manila envelopes. Maybe news on Melony's murderer?

He wondered where Neil had parked his Audi A-4. Out back, he figured, and probably under the protective cover he carried around in the trunk. The thought, like Gabe's camouflage "ah-shucks" persona, almost brought a smile — but

25

didn't. Not even humor at Neil's expense could make this "all better."

He wanted to *see* Audrey, *talk* to her, *be* with her. *I need her.* It was a startling admission, and its intensity took him quite by surprise.

Neil and Hugh sat in matching wooden chairs in front of Audrey's desk while she read something on her computer screen. It seemed to Hugh like it was taking ages for her to finish, and they were school boys patiently waiting for their teacher's attention. On top of that, an unnatural silence seemed to have encapsulated the room, producing what he could only categorize as an otherworldly feeling. *Except* for the tapping of Audrey's long fingernails on some unopened folders she'd brought in—now sitting enticingly on her desk. That irritating sound was very "this world," unnaturally penetrating an otherwise veil of silence. *Mocking us.*

In the grand scheme of things, he'd not yet summoned the courage to tell Audrey how irritating her nervous tapping was. He forced himself to take a barely audible long slow breath, managed to relax his back, and sought the patience to wait.

In a flight of fancy, he imagined the place itself was holding its breath, while a giant Alfred Hitchcock-like clock ticked in the background. All in all, it was awful, and for a second, Hugh wanted to stomp out of the room. But his wanting "to know" held him suspended in time, a prisoner in front of her desk.

God, do I wish she wouldn't do that nail thing. To circumvent his irritation, Hugh took in with counterbalancing pleasure, Audrey's pristine and angular face, her large brown eyes that somehow managed to sparkle when she was pleased, then transform into fireballs when not—and then there was her red hair. He'd never been attracted to redheads—so for him, Audrey was a glorious exception.

Finally, Audrey blew out a breath herself and looked at Neil. "There's an FBI-issued APB out." And to Hugh's great relief, she stopped tapping her nails.

"FBI?" Neil murmured.

"Just out on NLETS." She turned to Hugh. "That's our national law enforcement communications system."

"This has to do with Melony?" Hugh leaned forward. "FBI means," he paused, not really sure what their involvement meant, but guessed, "this has happened before. In other states. Is it a nationwide APB?"

"Yes." Audrey's voice was cautious. "Similar incidents. But sketchy descriptions. I'll call Ted and see what he can tell me. Evidently, the incidents have all been near or along Route 66." She rubbed her hand over her mouth and made an unpleasant sucking sound underneath. "He and I are flying up to Sacramento together."

"Your brother knows about Melony?" Hugh asked.

Audrey looked at Neil, moved her hand from her mouth to rubbing her eyes. Then she dropped back into the padding of her swivel desk chair, nodded toward Neil, and said. "You tell him."

Hugh was surprised to see Audrey look so dejected, and act so fidgety. On top of that, her handing off an explanation to Neil caught him by surprise. *This is not good.* He realized his own hands were clasped tightly in his lap. His "trembles" hadn't returned for months— still, he remained on guard. Audrey was becoming a stabilizing factor in his life— and now, maybe the tables were turning. He needed to be as solid as he could for her.

Neil cleared his throat. "It seems Special Agent Ted Fletcher," he inclined his head slightly toward Audrey, "the

Sheriff's brother, has been 'seeing' CHP Officer Rociana Bustamante de Reyes on a regular basis."

"She goes by *Bustamante*," Audrey said, and Hugh thought he heard a slight irritation edging her words. *At Neil, Ted, Rociana—or all of the above?*

"And," Neil finished, "it was Rociana's 10-46 Deputy Dibbs was answering."

His first thought was, *Ted's been dating?* They'd just had a poker game a month ago and he hadn't mentioned a word. *Sly bugger.* But quickly, his thoughts jumped to the serious implications of Neil's words.

Melony had taken Rociana's place on Route 66 asphalt last night.

With that realization, Hugh felt the start of a churning in his gut, and he clasped his hands together even tighter. Something very bad was going on, and he knew that *once again*, he was about to be in the middle of "it"—whether he wanted to or not.

Audrey fell back in her chair and said, "This is not good."

What was not good? Hugh wondered if Audrey was talking about Melony possibly dying in Rociana's place, or that there was a nationwide manhunt for a roadside killer? Neither sounded positive to Hugh. And once more, his unconscious flippantly and irreverently marveled, *Ted's been dating?*

What he said was, "How come you're not driving your cruiser?"

"Transmission died. I'm driving a CHP loaner." She shook her head miserably. "Transportation is coming out this morning to haul mine away."

Hugh was incredulous, and impressed. "Mojave County has a Transportation Department?"

She made a face and laughed. "San Bernardino County is assisting on the repair." Her laugh turned to a sigh. "And we're going to have to reimburse them for the loaner."

Neil mumbled, "No free lunch."

Hugh wondered why Neil hadn't come up with something "Frenchy"; then ironically, and much to his surprise, he heard Audrey murmur, *"Pas de repas gratuity."*

Mid-morning, and before finally calling Hugh, Ted sat in his newly issued Chevy Suburban with his motor idling for almost ten minutes. He pressed button number five on his cell. While he waited, he rubbed his right hand slowly, almost caressingly along the ridge of the dashboard. It was a mannerism he'd acquired in his early days as a teenager with his first car.

My first car, a hand-me-down Chevy Camaro. To this day, memories still came with the touching—the feel of the dash board leather, the smoothness of the custom sunken-in steering wheel, the retro-look of the circular hooded gauges. A feeling of rightness.

Ted sighed, and brought himself back to the present.

He was only minutes away from Joey's, parked on the shoulder of the mini-mart's poorly marked and seldom used off-ramp. A quiet place to think for the moment, he'd figured—and was right. Only one truck and one sedan had pulled off; Vegas bound Monday morning drivers feeling the need to stop at Joey's were few, almost non-existent. Of course, it wasn't his special "favorite spot"—it had taken him a long time to find that little bit of Mojave Desert isolation.

This morning, *for once,* he thought, *no wind.* It seemed like he'd never driven out to Mojave County without gusts whipping at his SUV, or at a minimum, sand and dust

29

blowing across the freeway. Fortunately his heavy vehicle was a stable ride, even though it provided a large surface for wind. Rociana had told him stories of semis and RVs overturned on I-14 in the Ridgecrest area—another driving tidbit now stored in his mental *Hazards of the Road* file.

No one was answering Champion's phone. Ted knew Hugh was there, saw his Altima pull in awhile back. Knew he'd been to his sister's office and returned. He'd also seen Gabe leave. He shook his head and smiled, remembering what a sharp poker player Gabe had turned out to be. The man definitely wasn't what he looked like. He didn't see Mrs. Chavez's truck, however, and wondered if she was due today. He couldn't remember the housekeeper's first name, but he'd heard her story, and was surprised she was still cleaning Hugh's house and minding his shop. His smiled turned bemused, and he shook his head in wonderment.

The absent winds were also noisy buggers. He lowered his window a few inches—the air was cold, crisp, and quiet—even with the proximity of the interstate's continual traffic hum. The Mojave was definitely not LA—or any of the East Coast. He'd yet to find it inviting. Besides the occasional awful weather, there just weren't enough people.

Hugh, though, seemed not to mind the isolation, lack of amenities, and weather. The man remained an enigma. Once again, he shook his head, as he often did when thinking about Hubert James Champion III. He'd initially thought attending his periodic poker games would give him some insight into the man.

Well, he now felt comfortable with Gabe and Leon Travers, even felt he understood Neil Knight a little better. But Hugh—*no,* the man kept his emotional and psychological cards close to his chest. Far more interesting than his plain "everyman" looks would lead one to believe.

Nonetheless, he liked Hugh, and thought him trustworthy. How much of that came from the fact his sister Audrey liked the man, he wasn't sure. But since the LoraLee Jackson and Toby Portson incidents, he'd felt some kind of bond developing between them. Maybe he was just intrigued? Or was it his FBI inquisitiveness leading the way?

He sighed aloud.

The call Ted had returned this morning when finally getting out of the shower was to Rociana. Her message had been curt, almost cryptic; he'd immediately been on alert and immediately called. He wanted to tell Hugh about Rociana, about how he felt hearing her voice this morning—knowing he could have lost her—and about how Melony's death was impacting them—hell, how it was impacting all law enforcement in the area. A Blue Alert had been declared—this was serious business.

To share those kind of intimate feelings must mean he liked Hugh? Or maybe, he just needed an impartial sounding board, and Hugh was convenient?

Joey's phone went to message, and Ted hung up.

Convenient. Now that was a joke. Nothing in Mojave County was convenient. Emotionally convenient because of Audrey? *Maybe.* Audrey was as tight lipped as Hugh when it came to their improbable and most probably romantic relationship.

Should he call again? "Hell no," he declared aloud. Instead, he shifted into drive and pulled away from the shoulder back onto pavement, heading toward the interstate overpass. *You're just going to have to talk to me, Hubert Champion. Willing or not.*

The pulsing sirens of law enforcement vehicles peeling down the interstate startled, but didn't surprise him. Blue Alerts were big deals. Looking quickly, he managed to catch sight of a pack of cruisers from the rear—CHP he thought—

didn't know how many—but the lights in their cruiser bars were rotating, and sirens were on yelp even though traffic was light. For a moment, the emotion which he'd yet to find the perfect name for swelled within. An emotion that swept over him whenever he thought about the brotherhood of law enforcement. A shared camaraderie and willingness to put oneself in harm's way for others. One day, the perfect word would come, but for now, this moment, on hearing the sirens—all he could do was experience, not name or explain.

Ted cursed vehemently and loudly given there was no one to hear, letting his words take his anger from inside and dump it into the world. A good agent couldn't carry that kind of baggage around without ending up doing something stupid.

"I'll find you." He was thinking about Melony's murderer and was surprised to hear he'd also voiced the words. Ted turned up the volume on his Mobile Data Terminal, his two-way radio, his GSM communication system, and glanced at bulletin alerts. One was about getting up to Sacramento, but he'd read that earlier. He wished for a basic and lowly CB; Truckers were a great source of info—they'd know what was going on.

He wasn't looking forward to Sacramento and having to fly in a Cessna. Hell, flying in any kind of airplane was not his favorite activity. But he couldn't miss this meeting.

Hugh's office phone rang. He ignored it.

Instead, he continued to stand motionless at his rose garden window, hands stuffed in his pockets, looking out at sparrows jumping around and chattering at their feeders. Winter, and pickings were slender for his feathered friends— but this time of the morning, the sun was at its warmest.

Perfect time to chatter and eat. Hobo was stretched out on the small deck between his doublewide and Joey's, his eyes closed; while Black-Jack, Arnie Bellow's left behind cat was also motionless—but wide awake, clearly also enjoying the sun and intently watching the birds from his own window into Hugh's rose-garden.

Indeed, Black-Jack, his cousin Della's murdering ex-husband's cat—*now his cat*—loved looking out at the birds in Hugh's private garden, his vantage point now, Hugh's doublewide. He was strictly an inside cat. Hugh thought there were too many predators for him to make it very long otherwise, and to accommodate his inside status, Hugh had put a solid glass-paned storm door on his doublewide's backdoor, and replaced his smaller kitchen side-window with a garden-window. Black-Jack had several choice views of the outside world. Hugh also caged in a three-by-five area on his front deck so Black-Jack could watch the sunsets with him and Hobo in safety.

Audrey had chided him during his kitty-remodeling efforts, "Who knew you were such an animal lover? And a carpenter too..." Her comment was followed with a kiss he'd easily accepted.

"Grandmother Todd's influence—" he'd started to explain. But she kissed him again, and their discussion changed.

While Hugh pondered and remembered, still gazing into his garden, the sparrows suddenly disappeared, and in their stead, a large raven stood in the center of his wintering-roses—almost as if the bird had appeared from nowhere. And in harmony with Hugh, Hobo, and Black-Jack—the raven was also momentarily motionless—facing directly toward Hugh, small black eyes seemingly lasered-in on him.

His ravens, alone or in consort, were usually "talkative." But this morning's solitary visitor was clearly giving silent counsel about something. Then, and quite startling in their import, Hugh heard police sirens yelping in the background.

On the highway he was sure. Loud and moving fast. He blinked and turned his head slightly toward the fading piercing sounds. Sirens and ravens, harbingers of something. When he turned back—his raven was gone.

How odd. And for a few fleeting seconds, Hugh wondered if he was having a vision—hallucinating? A new symptom in his residual craziness? Maybe he should rehire his shrink, Dr. Charlotte Lincoln. She'd sent him a Christmas card, *as all good doctors should.*

He turned from his window and sighed heavily. Another Christmas greeting, a card from his sister Murphy had been a surprise. Her return address was still in New York where she'd lived for years—near their parents. In fact, only a couple blocks away from them.

January was more than half gone, and he had yet to open Murphy's card.

All his *opened* holiday cards, ten in total, were still on display on Grandmother Todd's antique Early-American sideboard-hutch. The holiday display gesture was Ruthie's doing. Ironically, it was the same hutch where he kept his B&B, Glenlivet Scotch Whisky, and Sheesham box on the bottom shelf. Holidays and booze—*oddly fitting.*

His box was empty now—signifying that maybe that part of his life was now closed. *No, I will never forget Lewis.* It didn't make any difference Arnie Bellows was rotting in jail—he would never forget his cousin Della's first husband. Lewis Jenkins's memory would be with him forever.

Now there was Melony pulling on his emotions and psyche. He was going to have to deal with this present horror, no matter how much he hated it. Before Hugh could further indulge in melancholy thoughts, or his need to adapt to current circumstances, Joey's front door buzzer went off.

"You don't live through a cop killing," Ted said, "without a lot of bottled up emotions bubbling to the surface, looking for release." He was now staring out into the rose garden, while Hugh was settled into his familiar desk chair. "And with Melony, she was so young and —" Ted left the rest of his thought unsaid.

Hugh had swiveled around from his desk toward Ted — but his view was of Ted's back — and he couldn't tell exactly what bottled-up emotions Audrey's brother might be experiencing. He did intuit these were special moments for Ted and himself, and most assuredly delicate revelations from Ted. Even though he was no longer a practicing psychologist, he needed to "be there" for his friends. Neil and Audrey's grief had earlier brought that point home quite clearly.

"Sure hope they catch the bastard," Hugh said. "That would probably go a long way toward healing." Then with a barely audible sigh, he turned back to looking at what he could see — an empty Joey's. It was the first time he'd voiced his own opinion, and Hugh was surprised he had. Not only was he revealing more of himself than he should, but he was also opening up to Ted of all people. Audrey's brother.

"It's a brotherhood, you know," Ted said, then walked around Hugh's desk, turned his visitor's chair around backwards, and straddled it. "For good, and even bad sometimes." He looked Hugh straight in the eye and said, "And this time, we'll come together for good. We'll get whoever did this."

Hugh wondered why Ted often turned his chair around. A habit he thought spoke of an image integral to

35

Special Agent Ted Fletcher's persona—a man he was beginning to actually like. But *now* wasn't the time to explore personality issues. *Now* was a time to commiserate. Ted wanted to talk, and he needed to listen and make appropriate responses.

"And," Ted said, "nobody is taking any chances. I hear CHP has its road-units on two-officers per cruiser, and requiring full particulars on stopped drivers before initiating engagement." He made a sound of dismay. "Really should be standard procedure these days. All the time."

"You're alone this morning."

"I'm FBI, remember? No directive to us—yet." Ted held his breath, and looked away for a second. "But I am meeting up with Audrey, who you know is Sheriff's Department, then heading to Victorville and hopping a CHP Cessna for Sacramento."

Hugh thought Ted's look a bit chagrined, and asked, "That's not good because?"

"Hate flying in those little contraptions."

Hugh laughed despite their somber mood. *Macho FBI Special Agent hates to fly in propeller planes.* But he didn't press further. Again, not the time. Audrey had already told him at her office they were headed to Sacramento, but still, he asked, "How come the trip up north?"

"Law enforcement confab."

"That was pulled together fast."

"Yep." Ted hesitated a second, then continued, "I'm guessing you're wondering about Audrey?" He waited a few more seconds, but when Hugh didn't grab the bait, he said, "Meeting is tomorrow morning. We expect to be back by afternoon."

"Have you heard anything about scrap metal thieves?"

36

Ted looked surprised. "Yeah, if you're talking about moving industrial and construction stuff by the truck load across interstate lines. Is that what you're talking about?"

"No. Talking about closer to home."

Ted shook his head, and they fell silent for several moments. It was a silence Hugh didn't find uncomfortable—in fact, he considered their ability to just sit and think together, a good thing. Male-bonding didn't come easy, or often. Deceased Lewis Jenkins, and surprisingly, Julian Bogard—LoraLee Jackson and Marsha Portson's new "protector" in New York—were recent exceptions. Julian in particular since their acquaintance was so short—but even with the mileage and environment differences—they'd actually talked several times.

"Rociana hasn't called me all day," Ted eventually said. "I stopped leaving messages."

"Rociana?" Hugh feigned surprise. *About time he mentioned his girlfriend.* "Who's she?"

Poor Melony.

Rociana Bustamante de Reyes didn't cry often, and when the tears rolling down her cheeks reached the corners of her mouth, their salty taste was not only unpleasant and emotionally distasteful, but also a huge surprise. She was on duty, heading west on I-210 to meet up with two fellow officers at Southern Division's office in Glendale. From there, she was scheduled to drive up to headquarters in Sacramento for a meeting early Tuesday morning. Day shift—no night duty for a couple days at least.

Good thing, she thought. Rociana wasn't sure she could handle patrolling that area so soon after what happened last night. Another emotional weakness added on top of the tears; she'd thought she was made of sterner stuff.

Stretching her back, making herself sit tall in the driver's seat, Rociana took a long, deep breath, and tried to relax a bit. Sure, she was miserable, but she needed to loosen her taut muscles.

I'm a CHP officer for Christ's sake.

It was a clear-blue-skied winter morning, no major accidents, light traffic, and she loved this area of Southern California. If time wasn't so short, she would have taken Foothills Blvd. Indeed, she loved old Route 66—one of the reasons why she's picked Victorville—Apple Valley actually—to live. Easy access to LA environs to the west, the High Desert to the north and east—and two Route 66 museums close—Victorville and Barstow. And getting stationed at Barstow Station in the Inland Division was a godsend. Rociana was also thankful she was still patrolling alone. Some of her compadres were already assigned to pair up.

And now Ted's moved to Claremont. She felt her face warm, but refused to pay attention.

The "The Highway Killer"—already acronym'd THK—was on the agenda; actually, THK *was* the agenda. She expected to see San Bernardino and Mojave County Sheriffs, CHP Officers, Barstow Officers, and FBI Agents. Many she knew, some were even friends of a sort.

Rociana glanced in her rearview mirror. Two cars back, a black sedan—*Mercedes-Benz?*—pulled out, then quickly pulled back in. Not that unusual a maneuver from motorists unpleasantly surprised to see they were about to pass a cruiser. But there was something about this car, like she'd seen it before—or someone had told her something about a black Mercedes-Benz. She couldn't remember, which depressed her even more.

38

Keeping one hand on the wheel, she swiped several remaining tears from her cheek.

Nonetheless, her thoughts quickly returned to Melony. *One of our own down.* She sighed loudly, the sound of her anguish oddly echoing front to back in her empty cruiser. Rociana felt a catch in her throat, wanting to become a sob. She pushed it down.

I'm going to have to face Ted and Audrey in the morning. She'd avoided their calls all day—afraid she'd do just what she was doing now—riding a rollercoaster of emotions. But even though they hadn't talked, Rociana was guessing Ted and Audrey would be getting up to Sacramento together if they could. Everyone was coming. She'd heard a couple CHP Cessna T206 Stationairs were heading up out of Victorville. Easy for both of them to catch a ride.

"Damn." On purpose, she banged her fist repeatedly on the side of her steering wheel until it hurt like hell. Physical pain she could manage—guilt, now that was something else.

Though, it certainly was better blubbering *now*, rather than at the meeting with her brethren. They all knew by now it had been her traffic-call, and Melony had possibly taken a bullet meant for her. Sure, they'd be sympathetic; but everyone's main focus would be on catching the bastard —not keeping her from falling to pieces.

Once again Rociana inhaled a deep long breath, then let it out slowly—controlled. Ten or so minutes and she'd be in Glendale, and needed to have her act together. Which included deciding what she was going to reveal, and what she wasn't on another, more personal front. *Am I going to tell them about Roberto?* She hadn't even told Ted she was married and divorced. *Of course he's a nosey FBI agent, so he probably knows already.*

Rociana knew of instances where personal business of the wrong kind destroyed careers. On the other hand, if

39

Roberto did show up, she could be in trouble for not letting her bosses know.

"Damn straight I'm going to tell them." He was a bastard and didn't deserve special consideration. But did she really think he was involved? Robert "Roberto" Reyes was still in Puget Sound last she'd checked. *Yep,* she'd checked alright. He still had an apartment in Tacoma—paying rent regularly. And besides, the man she saw dressed like a desert-rat in Barstow couldn't be him. Her ex-husband always looked like he'd just stepped off the pages of GQ.

No, Roberto was no longer part of her life.

She noticed in her rear view mirror the black Mercedes pulling off at the Haven Avenue exit, and simultaneously noticed that three cars ahead, a red Corvette pulled up inches behind a minivan passing a truck in the outside lane. The Corvette driver flashed his lights at the minivan, then blew his horn.

Though her eyes might be a little puffy, her tears had completely dried up, thank goodness. "Don't know I'm back here do you?" she whispered. Then without looking, Rociana reached over to her MDT, switched on her sirens and lights, and pulled out into the passing lane.

Duty calls.

Ruthie's eyes were wide, her breathing rapid and shallow "My neighbors could have gotten killed, you know." She stopped talking long enough to start pacing back and forth. Her quilted carryall bag was sitting on the counter in front of Hugh, and even Whiskers's doggie-expression as he peeked out from between the handles of her bag appeared equally shocked.

Hugh was watching her from behind Joey's main counter, and figured his own eyes must also be wide—he could hardly believe what she was telling him. He also couldn't push down a strong feeling of *déjà vu*. Then he remembered Ruthie telling him about that awful drug lab explosion last Spring. Fortunately, Crazy Campie, like Arnie, was also in jail. And here Ruthie was *once again* bearing local *news*. And once again, news that was probably part of something bigger than him, and horrible in the making. Events that would eventually involve him.

"Cleo and Bob Thomas," Ruthie said, without looking at Hugh, and for the moment, seemingly unable to stop her nervous walking. "Have been so nice to Justin and me." Finally she stopped, grabbed hold of the counter in front of Hugh, and looked into his eyes. Hers were moist, appearing ready to overflow.

He reached out—couldn't help it—and patted, then held both her hands. "They are okay, though? Right?" Hugh didn't want to believe home-invasions had come to his little piece of the Mojave. "The intruders didn't hurt them, did they?"

"Oh, Mr. Champion—" She sniffed, paused for a few seconds, then stiffened her jaw. "You're right. They *are* okay, and that's the main thing. They weren't home, down in Covina for the night staying with their granddaughter." Her voice sounded stronger, more in control. "Justin says we need a shotgun."

"I don't want you to worry." He heard a hollow ring to his words. *Have I completely lost my ability to empathize?* He gave her hands another little squeeze, released them, and tried for a more sincere tone. "From what you told me, they weren't after your friends. Cleo and Bob weren't actually *supposed* to be at home, right? And other people knew they were gone?"

She nodded.

41

"They were just looking for stuff to steal." *Just,* he thought. *What a way to rationalize away a crime.* Hugh wasn't much worried about Ruthie. He'd met Justin, a kind man for sure, but a former Marine before his job as an engineer at Fort Irwin, and not someone to be trifled with.

He'd heard Hobo bark outside while comforting Ruthie, but had paid no heed. Now as he looked out toward the parking lot, he saw Gabe's Toyota Camry peel in, flying dust and gravel in its wake before finally coming to an emphatic stop. He hadn't guessed Gabe's three-hundred-thousand-mile vehicle could achieve such a speed, or that its brakes worked so well.

It was turning into a very long day—Gabe first thing this morning, Ted having just left, now Ruthie with her news, and unbelievably, Gabe again. Hugh could feel his jaw, the back of his neck, and his shoulders tighten up. *I need to relax.* He massaged his jaw and watched as Gabe jumped out of his car and came running in. *More like waddling fast,* Hugh mused at his friend's expense, and almost smiled.

Gabe made a beeline to where they were standing at the counter; then after a quick nod in Ruthie's direction and a murmured, "Glad your neighbors are okay," Gabe demanded at shout-decibel level, "Why is your backdoor locked?" His question was clearly rhetorical, and contradictory to prior admonishments to Hugh to keep that same door locked. "This scrap metal crap has gotten out of hand. I've known Cleo and Bob for years. Something like this happening to them ain't right."

"You know about it too?" Ruthie asked. "It's horrible." Whiskers barked his agreement.

Hugh hadn't seen Gabe quite this excited since his protestations over LoraLee's innocence almost eight months earlier. Once at the counter, his friend spread his hands out flat and locked Hugh in a squinty and piercing stare. "I think I know who's behind all this." He looked from side to side conspiratorially while waiting for Ruthie to move in closer. "We're pretty sure it's that lowlife G-Man."

Hugh felt like his jaw had literally dropped—but was pretty sure it hadn't. "An FBI agent?"

Gabe sighed, rolled his eyes, shook his head, and blew out a long stream of air. "Of course not." He looked to Ruthie. "You know G-Man, right?"

She nodded.

A vague memory came to Hugh, "You mean the birdfeeder man?"

Gabe nodded. "Exactly."

Hugh felt like the last man in the race dragging himself across the finish line. "I have a wrought iron birdfeeder I got from a guy named Griffith," he explained for Ruthie's benefit. "You mean him, right?" He vaguely remembered and retained a mental impression Griffith had been tall and handsome. *Can't be talking about him.*"He's stealing scrap metal to make birdfeeders?"

"Dang it, Champion, don't you know there's *metal*, then there's *metal*." He shook his head. "What the dopers are stealing right now is *copper* wire and pipe. Like that pile of mismatched pieces and the rolls you got out back. You need to cover it, not advertise what you got." In conclusion, he crossed his arms across this chest, took his trademark wide legged stance, and squinted his eyes even tighter. "We need to get to the bottom of this."

"We?" *Another complication Gabe is trying to drag me into.* All Hugh wanted to do was hang out—more like hide out—in the Mojave.

Unconsciously Hugh brought his hands together and squeezed them tight. While Ruthie and Gabe were talking, somewhere in the back of his consciousness, tiny warning bells started going off. He was again being *pulled into*

43

something he didn't want to be involved in, *into* the lives of people he didn't know, and *into* emotions he wasn't sure he was ready to deal with. Sure, he was better, *but still.*

He broke away from Gabe's glare and looked past his two friends out into the parking lot. He could see airborne sand swirling lightly around his defunct pumps. A wind had come up out of nowhere. In early Fall, he'd planted five sizeable Pindo palms near his Joey's sign as one more attempt to tame the untamable Mojave. He watched as the wind was starting to whip his palm fronds like they were ribbons.

A storm was coming, he knew that—and he wasn't thinking about the weather kind. *If I just had somewhere else to run.* Maybe one day he would realize the Mojave was where he needed to take a "stand." Maybe one day.

Not today.

Nonetheless, despite his impulse to flee and bury his head, Hugh experienced a sudden and intense urge to talk to Audrey—be with her. *Escape* with her. He pushed his irrational notion and ill-timed desire down, reminding himself he was a middle-aged psychologist—and Melony had just been murdered.

Still ignoring Gabe, Hugh held his gaze on his parking lot, lamenting his current predicament and the building weather. Seemingly out of nowhere, he caught sight of a small dark-blue pickup truck driving forward slowly, moving out of a blind-spot on the west side of Joey's. He hoped it wasn't a motorist in trouble. He hated telling folks he couldn't fix anything, that he didn't even have gas.

As the truck came into better view through Joey's front windows, it quickly sped up and headed across the freeway overpass—tangentially reminding Hugh he hadn't seen his cousin, Della, in several weeks. She had a pickup about the same size as the one he was watching hightailing it out of sight—only hers was red.

Della. Yes, he would go see her in Oro Grande today. He'd drive her stretch of Route 66—try to wrap his mind around Melony's murder, think a bit, figure out how he could avoid getting embroiled in scrap metal thievery. A much better alternative than bothering Audrey with his neediness.

Maybe he'd even stop at the Route 66 Museums in Barstow and Victorville, pick up a present, or two, for Della. She was becoming fond of Route 66 memorabilia. He could almost feel his spirit buoying as he thought about his escape. He'd drive into Barstow down I-15, get off on Old Highway 58, stop at the Harvey House, then take the back road out of town to the National Trails light, pass Della's and hit Highway 18 to the Victorville museum, then back to Della's with presents. His little circular and backtracking tour idea almost deadened the sadness aching in his heart. A good dose of his cousin Della would keep him going. And taking her Route 66 gifts was definitely a good idea.

Hugh knew Gabe was still looking at him, trying to stare him into submission. *But hell no* to whatever mess Gabe was trying to drag him into. Even though Hugh knew deep down, his little excursion wouldn't even make a dent in moving him past Melony's murder, going to see Della would get him out of Gabe-radar-range. Heck, he couldn't remember if Della had even met Melony. But if she had, he would now have the added burden of telling her; the thought almost brought a sigh of pain, even with Gabe and Ruthie there.

"You hungry?" Gabe asked, his eyes still boring in on him.

Ruthie immediately offered, "I can make you both sandwiches."

Bless you Ruthie.

"Or we could go to the Community Center Café and I can tell you about G-Man and Don." Gabe finally broke his eye-strangle-hold and actually entertained a half-smile.

45

Hugh wasn't buying, Ruthie had given him an out, and he readily jumped at the chance she'd offered.

Nonetheless, and regardless of his immediate and compelling desires to both avoid getting involved in scrap metal thievery, and to head south to Della's, Hugh remembered to take his time to be polite. "Thanks, both of you." He didn't have many friends, heck; he could count them on one hand. Certainly didn't want to offend the few he'd made. "I just remembered I was supposed to see Della this afternoon," he lied. Actually, he planned on calling her as soon as he got in the car—hoping she'd be at home. If she wasn't, he wasn't sure what he'd come up with.

He looked first to Ruthie, then to Gabe. "Can either of you watch the shop?" He knew he was being unreasonable with Gabe, he'd already done a stint this morning, now he was asking again.

Ruthie looked enthusiastic, but Gabe, not so much. She quickly offered to Gabe, "I can make us sandwiches like I already said. We can watch the shop together." She smiled her most charming—youth and optimism wrapped into her twinkling eyes. "And I brought some potato salad and apple pie for Mr. Champion. I'm sure he won't mind sharing."

Gabe's eyes lit up. "Maybe me and Ruthie can figure out how to trap G-Man." He rubbed his stubby little hands together.

Hugh wanted to smile, but didn't—Gabe now had a willing audience, plus potato salad and apple pie in his future. He was free to escape.

"I just happen to have some leftover spinach quiche we can have for lunch." Della got up and headed for the kitchen before Hugh could verbally agree or object. "And a bottle of

Chardonnay," she said over her shoulder, "is already chilled." His *stomach* certainly agreed.

Her dog Jasmine remained in the living room, keeping a watchful eye on Hugh as he stretched out in the puffy cushions of one of Della's matching armchairs. It was his favorite chair, favorite spot, and favorite viewpoint from her house—facing west with a view of National Trails Highway and the Mojave riverbed.

"It will only take a minute," she called out, her voice fading as she started preparing lunch.

He figured Della could no longer hear him, but nonetheless answered, "Take your time, I'm enjoying the view." To Jasmine, he said, "Not to worry, Jazz. You don't have to watch me every second. You know who I am."

He stretched his neck, and allowed a smile and sigh of relaxation to come. Truth was, he was very happy the border-collie-shepherd stray and Della found each other just over a year back. Jazz now weighed a whopping ninety pounds, and it was clear she had the intelligence and loyalty of Rin-Tin-Tin and Lassie combined, and a fierce sense of protectiveness for her mistress. Unfortunately, Jasmine also displayed a disposition to be a cranky prima-donna.

"You're good protection for your mistress." It was nice talking to Della's dog like he did with Hobo—as if she understood. And *relaxing* was an emotional and mental state he'd been working on since finally catching and shooting his nemesis—Della's murdering ex-husband, Arnie Bellows. If he was going to get better, *he'd* have to work on "mellowing out" as Gabe called it. No shrink alone could make him well; he needed to also be part of the solution. Somehow, talking to dogs helped.

Admittedly, he also enjoyed driving what he thought of as "Della's stretch of Route 66," along National Trails Highway from D Street in Victorville to Barstow. It was an old

47

two lane section of Route 66 that still retained its olden-days feel. Indeed, no matter how many times he traveled it, driving that piece of history, he was taken back to a time when travel meant experiencing people, places, and scenery.

He liked it the most when he could take the drive easy, rolling down his windows in warmer weather, savoring deep breaths of Mother-Road-air—as he liked to call it. For sure, another way to relax a bit, order his thoughts.

Indeed, as he hoped, the drive down was nice, but not as relaxing or laid-back as other times. In giving himself a little time to think, last night's event and this morning's aftermath were even more vividly horrible. Fortunately, only once did he feel overwhelmed; he'd had to catch his breath when a Victorville police cruiser passed and emotionally slammed him with a fantasy-picture of a living and vibrant Melony behind the wheel.

She was much too young to die.

He'd diverted his thoughts and replaced Melony imagery by revisiting a familiar fictional reverie—*in sepia tones no less*. It was the improbable scenario of his mother and father driving the Mother Road—actually cruising down this section in their chauffeur-driven Bentley. Of course Hugh was aware his "could be" fictional journey for his parents was a way to think about them, without having to formally think about them. It was a childlike and obviously immature fantasy, *craziness actually*, but emotionally helpful. *I should call Mother.*

The thought of his mother, Eloise Todd Champion, brought back his broken waking-up dream from this morning. He couldn't remember all the actual details, but an emotional hangover was still with him. It was beginning to bother him— particularly since he was a psychologist, and if there was some hidden meaning there, it should jump right out at him.

"Good thing I don't have clients anymore," he told Jasmine.

48

He closed his eyes and was partly able to bring back the image that was so vivid when Hobo had started his woeful howling. He and Julian Bogard were sitting in side-by-side matching chairs—only their backs visible in his dream-eyed-view. The two of them were looking at a tableau of the backs of four people standing in front of them and looking out floor-to-ceiling windows. Somehow he thought there was a city vista beyond the windows. But then, and in remembering, the picture would not refine itself. And now, within a few moments, even that picture disappeared from his mind's eye.

For a second though, *something* did jet through his synaptic connections—something he couldn't grasp and visualize. *Another image? Another memory?* But he just couldn't mentally grab it.

Hugh opened his eyes, turned his head sideways, and once again said aloud, "What the heck?" He looked down at his hands, they were calm, but he thought maybe his whole body had shuddered, and he hadn't noticed. He took several calming breaths, long and slow, and felt some of his remaining anxiety release itself into the world.

Unfortunately, and quite suddenly, that anxiety was replaced with sadness.

Then came anger.

He was *angry* there was so much evil in the world, *angry* some of that evil had again touched someone he knew, *angry* his friends were being hurt in the process, and *angry* there was nothing he could do to make it better.

Sitting in Della's living room, Hugh thought he heard a train in the distance—almost like a low timbre, low volume hum—and he felt that somehow, the train's steady and rhythmic progress down the tracts could take some of his anger with it. *Yep,* he decided, being here with Della in her wonderful little world was the key to making it through this afternoon.

Her house sat in the middle of an eight acre plot in the low hills east of Route 66 and afforded several views Hugh liked. His favorite being the vista now visible through her living room picture window. The train he was hearing but couldn't see, he knew to be the Union Pacific-Atchison, Topeka, & Santa Fe railroad line as it ran along the Mojave River.

He could feel a smile trying to insinuate itself. *Good.*

"Coming soon," he heard Della call from her kitchen.

Hugh also liked her easterly view from the dining room and wrap around deck—where uninhabited desert hills rolled to what he fancied were unknown destinations. He *did* know I-15 was to the east, but no direct roads accessed it, and it was a pleasant thought to envision a different scenario. Again, like with his parents, fiction preferable to reality.

He heard Della call out again, and breaking from his introspection, he got up to go help her. His cousin was a treasure for many reasons. One being her looks—more exactly, her aura. When he'd first tried describing her to Audrey, all his modifiers and descriptive phrases came up short. Physically, she was medium height, on the thin side, had a large mouth, prominent nose, soft brown eyes, and almost identically colored brown hair.

But most importantly, Della had a way of looking at you, most definitely kindly, but with a pensive directness that demanded your attention, revealed little, but said she was interested in what you had to offer. On top of all that, Della was intelligent, strong willed, and amazingly self-sufficient.

As children, she had often been his sister substitute. He and his actual younger sister, the colder more self-centered Murphy, were never close—though he wished that could turn into a different story someday. *I haven't even opened Murphy's Christmas card. Who's the cold one here?*

Once in the kitchen, he asked, "Where are we eating?" He smiled, forcing himself not to be so gloomy. "Still a little chilly to go out on your deck, don't you think?"

"How about in the living room so you can continue to enjoy your favorite view."

That was Della, always considerate, always thinking about *your* point of view and comfort. He thought, *how can I hang on to anger in my cousin's presence?* Hard to do.

Today she was wearing her typical long shirt and loose pants, and seemed more flyaway looking than usual. He knew from experience, however, Della's mannerisms and wardrobe prompted misleading impressions. Underneath, and behind her inherent kindness, there was a layer of Todd-toughness.

They settled in eating quiche and sliced tomatoes from huge plates balanced on cloth napkin-covered laps. Crumbs were not relevant—Jazz clearly saw it her duty to be their walk-around-food-vacuum. And while they ate, talk was light—what they were starting to like about the Mojave, and what they both still hated. Wind and flies were high on both their *bad* lists. Della had more Mojave years than he, but Hugh no longer felt like the ignorant newbie he was a year earlier.

This is nice, he let himself accept while taking a sip of wine. The Chardonnay wasn't great, but pleasant enough not to ruin the moment. Actually , the perfect tonic to counter balance Ruthie and Gabe's outrage and his own anger without getting soused. He blew out a long releasing breath, looked over to Della, and was surprised by the cast of seriousness he saw on her face.

Before he could comment, she put her wineglass down on the lamp-table between them, and said, "You know, I had lunch with Melony a couple times."

"I didn't know you two—" Hugh was surprised she knew about Melony. He hadn't yet built up the courage to tell her.

51

"Audrey called me. The three of us like," Della's voice caught, but she recovered quickly, "*liked*, Thai food."

He didn't know what to say, so he waited, and his thoughts were in limbo for a tiny speck of time. Sure, he knew the right words, what psychologist wouldn't. But this was, Della—and somehow different. Even Jazz, now sitting beside Della's armchair, seemed momentarily motionless.

Della sniffed, then said, "Melony loved her job, loved working with Audrey."

Hugh looked away so as not to see the tears streaming down her cheeks.

More silent time passed while Hugh finished his drink and Della went wherever her emotions were taking her. He didn't know how long, but when he finally felt brave enough to look back at her, she smiled, and he saw Jazz had surrendered to a nap.

Della asked, "Did you receive a Christmas card from Murphy?" Her voice was calm, back to normal. "I was surprised to get one. Haven't heard from her in awhile."

Surprised, Hugh blurted out, "Yes, but I haven't opened it."

"You know, it'll soon be February. Don't you want to know what she said?"

"Not really." He hoped his tone was neutral.

Hugh pondered on many an occasion how different the worlds of his mother, father, and sister were from his. *Even when we lived in the same city*. And now, miles and their vastly different environments emphasized and highlighted how wide and deep the divide between them had become. Yet, he knew Della crossed back and forth with ease, aplomb, and with what appeared to be enjoyment between both worlds.

Murphy. He rolled his sister's name over in his mind. Just what he needed, more ghosts, memories, and haunting past emotions. His one past love, Serena, had been Murphy's best friend.

"Well," Della was saying, looking at him. "She's coming for a visit. Staying with me."

Hugh remained silent, not sure of what he wanted to say, should say, would say. But his face must have revealed *something*—because Della said, "You should open your mail when you get it."

Della stood on her westerly desk, almost motionless as a breeze caught her long shirt and flowing pants. She watched Hugh's Altima wind down her road to National Trails; then unconsciously, she sighed as he turned north, heading toward home. Indeed, with Jazz at her side, more than several pensive moments passed watching her cousin's car navigate her meandering and lump-pocked dirt road, then turn toward home on Route 66.

She was concerned—but not for herself. Murphy's visit and how Hugh would handle her arrival was worrisome. Scared her, actually. There was a strong likelihood her visit would be emotionally cataclysmic for Hugh. She, like his prior shrink Charlotte Lincoln, doubted Hugh was ready for the truth.

And to be perfectly honest, Murphy was a nasty piece of work. It was a phrase her Aunt Eloise, Hugh's mother used to use. Of course never directed at her daughter Murphy—*but if the shoe fits.*

Eventually, Della took in a deep breath; the air seemed moister than usual. Funny weather this year. The afternoon was getting cooler, damper, and windier. Della had a clear view across the valley and past the railroad tracks, and her eyes were sharp enough to see rolling dust devils starting to move through the riverbed.

And besides Champion family ghosts, there was Serena--"Fair and Bright One" in Latin. She'd never forgotten that, though she couldn't remember her last name. "Did I ever know it?" she asked Jazz.

A quick bark from Jazz told her not to worry about it.

With a sigh and half smile at her anthropomorphic interpretation of Jazz's response, Della left the past, turned around, and along with Jazz, headed inside. Over the last year, she'd come to believe Jazz actually understood much of what she said. *And who is a widowed and divorced lady living by herself in the middle of nowhere supposed to talk to anyway?*

Before they got inside, both woman and dog were strangely compelled to look to the west across the valley one more time. A solitary raven soared, then dipped across the horizon—its black wings luminous and iridescent in the sun. It was an eerie replay from six months earlier—almost exactly.

"Krawk, krawk," it screeched.

Oh dear. Ravens did not much come her way, and the last time one visited, and so loudly pronounced a warning was right before she found out her ex-husband Arnie had killed her first husband, Lewis. *And Hugh had almost killed Arnie.*

She straightened her shoulders, and told Jazz, "Whatever is about to happen, we can deal with it." *I'm a Todd, for heaven's sake.* Then Melony's smiling face flashed across her mind's eye—and directly mocking her assertion of toughness and strength, Della felt tears rising again.

Gabe was waiting for Hugh when he returned to Joey's, pacing back and forth in front of the counter. His friend was happy to inform Hugh he'd sold thirty-dollars worth of merchandise, mainly Cokes, candy bars, and water. What Hugh considered the staples of life. Coke being *numero uno*. Sales of any kind above twenty bucks was an event to be celebrated, and Hugh tried to give Gabe adequate basking-in-glory time. He also formally and effusively, thanked him for watching the place twice in one day.

Gabe's other big news was he'd seen several cop cars driving around. None had stopped, but still, it meant the Thomas' incident was being taken seriously—at least for today. But police involvement or not, Gabe was not going to let scrap metal thievery go unchallenged.

"I want you at Drifting Sands Café no later than eight, you got that?" Gabe's words and phraseology were bossy and insistent, but his tone was more in the line of pleading. "We'll have breakfast, then head out to his place."

"Sure," Hugh agreed without really thinking about what he was saying. His mind and body were in the present; he just wanted to check everything was okay, lock up Joey's, then go sleep the rest of the afternoon away. *If Hobo will let me.* He'd missed taking his pal for their morning walk.

"Want me a witness when we go to G-Man's place," Gabe said over his shoulder before closing Joey's front door emphatically behind him.

Hugh wasn't listening. He'd moved on to checking if his Ruger .45 was still safely under the counter. Ruthie and Gabe knew where it was and how to use it. The Super Redhawk Alaskan was his favorite gun—if one could have a favorite "killing machine."

The semi-automatic was where it should be, and there was a note on the counter from Ruthie. *Changed Black-Jack's litter before I left.*

Only then did his brain take the time to register what his friend Gabe said. However, when he looked up, Gabe was already getting in his Camry.

He wanted a witness for what?

As Hugh feared, Hobo, usually a fairly laid-back canine, campaigned aggressively for a walk. He barked, whined, went down on his front paws—finally he took a stiff legged stance in front of his leash on its hook by the back door, then let out a low but hefty howl.

Resisting was impossible, especially when Hobo next lowered his head and looked pleadingly out the top of his eyes. With a resigned sigh, Hugh grabbed his cell phone, Hobo's leash, his Glock from the bedroom, then headed out the backdoor quickly, so he wouldn't be tempted to crash despite Hobo's protestations and pleading.

It was cooler than earlier at Della's and the wind was still building, toying with the trees and swirling sand more aggressively. But it wasn't too terrible *not* to walk. Man and dog had developed a comfortable walk routine down a well worn path inside the fenced area of his property—which stretched generally north and east to form a square-shaped chunk of terra firma.

At the halfway mark of their walk, near the northwest corner of his property, stood a thick stand of self-sustaining Athols. One tree stood as a giant among the others, and in its flowing higher branch perches, an unkindness of ravens often gathered. Quite early on, in a flight of literary fancy, Hugh had dubbed the tree, "Poe's Condo." In fact, he liked the spot so much, he'd even snuggled a teak bench in amidst the trees. It was their *special* and rather hidden spot.

This afternoon, he and Hobo walked briskly toward their bench, Hugh having to hurry Hobo along—shortening the canine's favored trail-mail stops. But when they actually reached their bench, despite the building weather, Hugh stopped, sat a bit. Since he hadn't seen any breaches in the fence line he also let Hobo off his leash to "nose" around.

He'd grabbed a hooded jacket before leaving and was now glad as he pulled the hood over his head and stuffed his hands in his pockets. Even though protected amongst the Athols, the chilling winds were swirling enough to find him.

His ravens were used to man and dog, and often did not stir. That was the case this afternoon. And in those moments of mental quiet—oddly induced by pressing Mojave winds—for the first time, Hugh progressed his thinking from what had been a fanciful and otherworldly feeling, to the real notion that he and his ravens were connected.

Rationality and common sense almost immediately made him denounce such silliness, even causing him to smile at the ridiculous conclusion. Still, *somewhere* in the recesses of his psyche, he knew *something* existed between them, and he shivered.

Suddenly, there was no sound of wind stirring Athol branches, no dust devils dancing among the scrub-brush, no sparrows singing, no trains clanking along the BNSF line, no cars humming on the interstate. He looked down, and Hobo was lying quietly at his feet. Was this the eye of the storm? And his little corner of the Mojave was protected for a few moments?

In that vacuum of quiet, whether real or emotionally manufactured, thoughts and images of Melony flooded his being. He *remembered* her smiling face, *remembered* the naïve lilt of her voice, *remembered* her always offering him coffee— *remembered* the moment she escorted Julian and Timothy Bogard into Audrey's office and his life—all less than a year ago. Then there was the picture of Melony rushing into his hospital room after the capture of Crazy-Campie—childlike glee spread across her face.

57

She'd made him feel simultaneously wonderful—and old as dirt. He dropped his head in his hands—and in tune with his eye-of-the-storm reality, Hugh's tears were eerily silent ones.

Once back home inside his doublewide and refilling Hobo's water bucket, Hugh knew he'd also passed some kind of psychological milestone on his walk which didn't have anything to do with grief over Melony's murder. *Am I finally getting well?*

On the down side, he also couldn't shake off a sense of dread he was being pushed once again into something he didn't want to deal with—and was unsure he could handle. *Continuing fears and doubts?* But that shouldn't be—now that Arnie was dead, his guilt and remorse should be fading.

Canine-water-duty completed, Hugh rubbed his forehead, as if he could physically start his thinking anew. As Hobo noisily slurped up his fill, Hugh stared out his kitchen window without really seeing anything.

Okay, Melony's murder and his response to her tragedy had stirred up "things." *But what?* Something else hiding in the dark shadows of his mind? For a second, he thought maybe he should call his shrink, Charlotte, but quickly rejected that idea aloud with an emphatic, "No."

As he turned from the sink, he caught sight of a dark colored pickup moving slowly down the road on the north side of his property. *The same one from earlier?* He wasn't sure, but he certainly hadn't noticed it during their walk. Traffic on his side of the road was scarce, not many properties except his and Gabe's big chunk of desert. He sighed and shook his head at his lapse in visual attentiveness.

After that shake of the head, Hugh headed toward his bedroom—Hobo at his heels. He hadn't heard from Black-Jack for awhile, but in passing, found him curled up on the couch in the living room.

He needed a nap. Once undressed down to his boxers and Wal-Mart-issue T-shirt, Hugh stretched out on his back—pulling a section of quilt up to his chest. Within seconds, Hobo jumped up and claimed his spot on the right corner foot-of-the-bed.

Hugh closed his eyes, and tried to *will* himself to sleep. He could hear the wind blustering again outside. The eye of the storm was no more. Mojave wind-hell had returned. Inside, the air on his shoulders was surprisingly comfortable—moister than usual. As expected, his mind took control, flashing back to his former twilight sojourns to retrieve his Sheesham wood box. It had been a horrible time—*just a few months back*—but now his past demons should be gone.

Nonetheless, and to his surprise and dismay, his mind continued to force him back to those days, and instead of drifting off Hugh found himself getting up and walking into the dining room. Black-Jack was sound asleep, and evidently didn't hear his almost silent footfalls in passing. And as he'd done so many times in the past, Hugh squatted in front of Grandmother Todd's hutch, his hands easily finding what they sought at the back of the bottom shelf behind his booze.

Why am I doing this? And why tonight?

Even now, he still handled his box with reverential care—even though time and events had moved him forward. Indeed, it was late afternoon, not like before in those ephemeral moments 'twixt night and day' his ex-shrink whimsically referred to as the human body's twilight-zone. Nonetheless, Hugh carried his box into the kitchen, placed it precisely on his kitchen table, then sat down in front of his prize.

Just like before.

It was slightly bigger than nine-by-twelve, made of Indian Sheesham tree wood, with the darker "heartwood" used for the box itself, and the whitish "outer-ring" wood used for the inlaid Asian design on top. Hugh still thought the piece beautiful. He smiled slightly, remembering his father, a shrewd man and not blind to beauty. He had chosen this particular box as a gift based upon his son's esthetics, and *as always*—to influence.

So long ago.

Still, it was nice holding the box once more, running his hands over its top surface, then along the sides, slowly, almost lovingly. The wood was smooth, cool—indeed, the box was a lovely piece. He could almost feel his father's presence, relive those moments when he'd received this special box.

Hugh raised the lid. Impeccably crafted—it was precisely fitted, perfectly weighted, and attached by small but ornate brass hinges. It was empty of course—Arnie, Lewis, and "death" on the steps of a Chicago brownstone were relegated to memory status.

All that's over now.

So why was he again sitting in his kitchen—albeit late afternoon, or was it early evening already? So moved and captured by this possession, he wasn't quite sure. He did know he was looking into an empty box. What did he expect to see—the face of Melony's murderer?

Hardly.

Still, he sat, silent and again near motionless—didn't know for how long. Just like at Poe's Condo. Several of his "friends" had evidently followed him home, for the silence was quite irreverently broken by a screeching convocation of raucous ravens—sounding like they were in his rose garden. He could only hear, not see, but his inner eye imagined them, rising, circling, and fussing their way as they rose—jet black figures against a fading late-afternoon Mojave sky. He'd experienced a similar moment, just six months earlier.

He wanted to see, and got up. Once at his kitchen window and able to bring them into view, Hugh was overcome with an unshakeable sense of *déjà vu.*

"How odd," he murmured.

An unidentifiable pickup truck, an empty wooden box of memories — then ravens again. Would a nap be possible?

His home phone rang, and he answered it at the kitchen desk. It was Audrey.

"Where are you?" he asked, guessing she was calling from Sacramento.

"At CHP headquarters on Seventh."

Her voice was comforting, and he smiled. "You know anything new yet?" he asked, hoping she'd say something like *"We've caught the bastard."*

"Meeting's not until tomorrow morning." He heard her blow out a wisp of air, and her voice suddenly sounded tired and sad. "I can tell you there's a lot of long faces around here."

"Do they think the killings are random?"

"That's one theory."

"And the other?" He knew what she'd say, but he really didn't want to believe it. *Melony, Rociana, someone local — all connected.*

"Someone wanted either Melony or Rociana dead."

Hugh couldn't tell which way Audrey was leaning. So he pushed. "And you think?"

"I think," she said with more venom than Hugh had ever heard her express, "I want to kill the bastard myself."

Hugh was overcome with an intense desire to immediately drive up to Sacramento and fold Audrey into his arms. The urge scared him. *Too soon.*

61

Then he saw that damned truck coming down his road again. In the same direction as earlier.

Who the heck was he? And what was he doing going down his road?

After talking with Audrey, Hugh wasn't able to go directly to bed. Sleeping would be impossible. Instead, he headed for his miniscule TV room and stretched out in the recliner. Hobo jumped up on the small daybed underneath the window and immediately closed his eyes.

Hugh's doublewide wasn't large, but this room—billed as a second bedroom—Hugh didn't consider much more than a spacious walk-in closet. But there was a window, and room for a recliner and a rocker—another of Grandmother Todd's treasures he'd had the good sense to keep and bring along into his forced exile. Black-Jack had already claimed the rocker and was curled up fast asleep on the quilted and tattered seat pad of Grandmother Todd's heirloom rocker.

The second bedroom was the only room in the house he'd made a point to hang blinds, but he hadn't bothered closing them this afternoon before plunking-down in his recliner. He was amazed to see sunset colors were already filling the sky. *Where has the day gone?*

Not overly fond of Winter, whether the New York, Chicago, or Mojave variety—Hugh knew his body was also not yet in tune with the shortened days, and this afternoon's transition into evening was not an exception. Consequently, with his day waning and unable to sleep or do something more constructive, Hugh spent the evening in his recliner, watching shows he'd prerecorded, but not really paying much attention. And before he finally called a finish to this longest-of-days and trudged off to bed chasing after elusive sleep—

62

somewhere between watching the evening news and the end of a Thin Man movie starring William Powell and Myrna Loy—his grief for a life lost, turned back into the same burning hot anger that flamed on his way to Della's.

This time around, Hugh's rage was more intense, more encompassing—burning even hotter at the injustice of it all. He knew he was still a man limping along on emotional crutches, wanting to continue to hide out among the creosote bushes and Palo Verde trees—*but this just isn't right.* He wasn't sure how he could help, but from resolve born in sadness, revulsion, and anger, Hugh knew he had to be part of avenging Melony's murder.

Revenge.

He could taste it. First Lewis, now Melony.

When the actual time "twixt night and day" did come, Hugh found himself startled and waking abruptly. Instinctually, he slid his hand under his pillow and wrapped his fingers around the surprisingly warm grip of his Glock 9mm. And within what felt like milliseconds, he was sitting straight up in bed, adrenalin flooding his body.

Like Hobo Sunday night, he sensed *something* was amiss. *Something* or *someone* had triggered an alarm. *Danger.* It was like he could taste "it" in the air.

Hobo was only seconds behind in recognition, and from somewhere in the darkness at the foot of his bed, Hugh heard his friend emit a low deep growl. An ominous canine warning.

The night outside his window was black. Of course it was late January and he knew the moon was sliver-size. Still, the stars usually provided a miniscule glow. *Clouds?* Sure, there were building winds during his walk, and he and Hobo had sat in the eye of "something"; but he hadn't really noticed a cloud bank moving in. He also knew weather sometimes changed rapidly in the Mojave, maybe some clouds had moved in and were causing the blackness.

He heard Black-Jack meow softly from somewhere in the house—probably from the guest bedroom where he last remembered him curled up in the rocker.

Hugh now heard *someone* or *something* outside bang against his bedroom wall siding, then he caught a hissed curse.

My firewood and bathroom remodel supplies. Hugh felt Hobo leap from the bed and charge the window—this time with a full throated growl. He could vaguely see the outline of Hobo, but thought his ears were erect and the hair along his back standing on end.

Hugh wanted to reach over and turn on his bedside lamp, but his Quantico training from way-back-when kicked in. Instead, he lunged forward on his bed, making himself flat, then rolled off onto the floor, all the time holding his gun with both hands. His body hit cold tile faster and harder than he expected, and a sharp pain shot through one knee. His instinct was to yell out, but he managed not to—biting his lip instead and managing to hold back a yelp of pain.

Hobo's growl turned into barking and Hugh could no longer hear what was going on outside. He crawled the few feet until he was underneath but to the side of his window, flattened himself against cold plaster wall, tightened his grip on his Glock, and took a deep breath.

"I have a gun," he yelled out, "and I WILL shoot." Hobo quieted back to a very low timbre growl. *Smart dog.* He hoped Black-Jack was also smart enough to stay out of harm's way.

He heard, almost felt, a bang against his siding, followed by several thumps, bumps, and footfalls—all of which Hugh interpreted as a person falling against the house, stumbling and knocking over his remodeling supplies, then running away.

Rolling to a semi-sitting position, Hugh scooted on his butt closer to a more centered spot underneath the window, then stood up. His finger was still on the trigger, his gun still gripped firmly and ready. He felt adrenalin continue to race through his body. He was excited. Also scared.

His heartbeat pounding in his ears, Hugh finally raised up and hazarded a look outside. Within seconds he caught sight of headlights on the road—moving past him and Joey's, then on toward the freeway. *A small dark pickup truck?* He wasn't sure.

He ran barefoot through the house, Hobo at his heels, and barely reached his living room windows in time to see taillights moving away. He still couldn't determine the make or color for sure, but thought it was indeed a small dark pickup. Hugh expected the vehicle to make a right, and head west on the freeway. Instead the lights continued south, straight across the freeway overpass. *A local?* Or heading to the eastbound entrance on the other side of the freeway—he couldn't tell or hear.

It was indeed a dark night, and starless now that he took the time to look. How that could be, he did not know. Hobo stood at his side in the living room, motionless, his stance, if not aggressive, definitely firm. *My fearless protector.* Hugh almost smiled at what must be the sight of him and Hobo at that moment. He did look down at his hands—*no trembles.* And he felt his heart slowing down, and his grip around his Glock relax a bit.

Then he saw the second car.

No lights, but somehow his eyes—*or senses*—caught "sight" of a black sedan-shaped object creeping along the same road outside of Joey's, also heading toward the freeway.

Following the other car? He didn't think so, though he couldn't say why he thought not.

Unlike the pickup, the sedan turned on to the freeway entrance ramp, keeping its lights off until near where he was forced to merge.

If the sedan wasn't a tail—then who, what, and why?

Outside the temperature had dropped at least twenty degrees, and the winds had returned, even more blustering and nasty. Prudently, they watched from Hugh's kitchen window—both men, Neil and Hugh standing in front of the sink, peering outside. Not that Hugh could see much, except for right around the portable flashers Neil had set up; but he *felt* like they were "guarding" the scene while waiting for the Barstow Police, or CHP. He wasn't sure whose jurisdiction this fell in. Neil wasn't sure either, and Audrey was out of town.

So far, Neil hadn't shown signs of wanting to take over. "I've called it in, and those flashers should guide them here." His tone was subdued. "Everyone's on around-the-clock manning until the bastard who killed Melony is brought in."

Melony's murder has changed us all.

"CHP's looking at almost everything," Neil continued. "They'll probably log this in. And Forensics will take maybe half an hour to get here."

Hugh didn't point out he thought there was no connection between "his" incident and Melony's murder, just accepted Neil's statement *everything* was being looked at closely right now. He could see Neil's reflection in the window as they both squinted and peered into the darkness. He didn't look particularly concerned.

"Coming from Riverside," Hugh murmured about the Forensic team's arrival time. He wondered if the twin CSIs he'd met at Turner Jackson's house last Spring, Leonard and Leopold Phelan—most confusingly going by Leo and Leo— would be assigned?

His emotions were calmer now a little time had passed, mainly because Neil was on the scene. Nothing against Hobo, but having an armed Sheriff's Deputy watching-your-back was reassuring. He looked at his clock over the refrigerator. Three-forty-five. "Terrible time to be called out. Middle of the night." Of course they could have a forensic nightshift, just like on TV.

"Usually don't come out *here* for something like this," Neil said. "But..."

Hugh didn't take offense at his words or tone. Neil had already intimated if it weren't for Melony, law enforcement would normally look at his little incident as just another run-of-the-mill low level attempted burglary. Under normal circumstances, a forensics team investigation would be highly unlikely.

He was getting special treatment. *For a horrible reason.*

It was an odd moment, both men looking at each other via their reflections in the window, while Hobo lay contently in the center of the kitchen. Hugh fleetingly thought, *we're an Edward Hopper painting.* What he said was, "Your doing, you know, getting them out so fast." Easy situation to give Neil credit for, regardless of actual circumstances. Then Hugh tipped his head and clicked out the side his mouth before saying, "Thanks." He felt like a cowboy caricature, but was indeed thankful for his connection to the Mojave County Sheriff's Department, if only in a peripheral way. Audrey— and the Turner Jackson affair last Spring.

Neil nodded an acknowledgement. "For a second," he said, then paused, and squinted more intensely. "I thought I saw movement way down the road."

Hugh narrowed his eyes also and stared into the darkness as hard as he could. *Nothing.* "Usually it's brighter than this. The stars—"

"No moon."

Something is happening. "Yeah—"

Once again in the same night, Hugh sensed *something* yet unseen was going on. *Something* awful. *Something lethal.* He dived for the floor, taking Neil down with him—just milliseconds before what sounded like his kitchen window had exploded. His rational mind thought it had been a high-velocity round. Whatever the projectile—he realized after the actual happening—flew through his kitchen into the dining room, and crashed the glass front of his dining room hutch. *Grandmother Todd's Hutch, damn it.*

And Neil, even though smashed against kitchen cabinets by Hugh, still managed to curse, "*Merde.*"

Somehow in just a second of time, Hugh's mind somehow formed and relived a slow-motion picture of the bullet—more like a missile—projecting itself through the space until oh-too-recently occupied by Neil's head, then flying through the archway between kitchen and dining room, before finally exploding the glass front of Grandmother Todd's hutch.

In just a few more seconds, Hugh rolled away from Neil who then jumped to his feet, un-holstering his Glock .375 in the process. Next, the deputy rushed toward the light switch by Hugh's back kitchen door and flipped it off, then tried the door knob.

"Locked, right?" Hugh whispered, still on the floor and hoping he'd hadn't been fool enough to leave his back door unlocked.

68

"Yeah." Neil was also whispering, but Hugh thought his tone surprisingly calm. "We were sitting ducks, you know. One of the first things you learn—never backlight yourself at night." He blew out a breath, revealing he wasn't as nonplussed as Hugh thought. "Targets, clear as day."

"I know," Hugh agreed. "But who would have expected *this*?"

Slowly Hugh propped himself up on what turned out to be sore elbows. "Must have hit myself against the sink." His voice was a whispered complaint, and he couldn't actually remember what his exact movements had been. What he *did* remember was seeing the slightest flash in the distance. But that wouldn't have given him enough time to duck. *A premonition of a flash?* He sure hoped not. *Pre-sight?* Another craziness-symptom he did not need.

All he really knew was, for the second time in the same night he found himself on the floor in pain, combating danger from persons unknown. And for reasons also unknown.

Hugh's instincts now told him immediate danger had passed. Whoever had shot at them—*no*, shot at Neil—had packed up his rifle and headed out. He knew little about rifles, but figured only a sniper rifle could have produced that velocity and range. He visualized, admittedly pretty much out of whole cloth—a shooter leaning against his car fender: his rifle probably footed and supported on a quilted-like blanket on the car's hood; taking his time; aiming through a night scope; waiting until he had a perfect bead on Neil's head; bracing himself for the recoil—then slowly pulling the trigger.

He couldn't know that, and figured his picture of the event was based on TV dramas, and not real experience. *Or*, had some part of him actually seen what happened? Without thought, he shook his head and almost laughed out loud before catching himself. He'd never had such a second-sight kind of experience before, and figured this wasn't one either.

Nonetheless, he felt himself rather discombobulated as he got up enough to peek outside and check for danger. He wasn't about to rely on whatever insights his brain *thought* it was having.

The second time in one night, peeking out my own window.

On cue it seemed, Hugh thought he saw a black sedan moving down the road, but wasn't certain. And there was no sound of an automobile motor he could detect. Was this car, if it actually existed, connected to the earlier one? Some part of him certainly thought so. But why? The same sedan had returned, but that didn't make any sense.

Through the darkness, he could hear Neil breathing, and thought him still to his left.

"Hobo," he whispered, and was rewarded with a hesitant bark from where he reckoned was underneath the kitchen table. *Thank goodness.* Clearly, this time Hobo had decided taking cover was the best part of valor. *And thank goodness again,* he'd locked Black-Jack in the guest bedroom when he'd called the Sheriff's Office and Neil had answered. *Seems like an eternity ago.*

Hugh sighed with relief over his pets' safety—loudly, and not caring if Neil heard. He let himself fall back to the floor and lean against his sink cabinet doors, trying to force himself to relax. He needed to put things in perspective. Neil, his best friend Hobo, and his new feline companion Black-Jack were safe. Not much more mattered. Several deep and long breaths helped. Indeed, this was one of those nights that put "things" into perspective. "The shooter is gone," he said.

"I think so too," Neil answered from the darkness near his backdoor.

Hugh pulled himself up once more to peek out the window. This time, and for certain, he saw taillights on what looked like a black blob heading toward the freeway. Fast. He reaffirmed his guess it was the same sedan that had left earlier. *Probably went down to the next exit earlier, then circled back.*

None of it made sense, though, and Hugh thought his hands must be trembling, but when he looked down — nothing. He had moved on to a different psychological plateau, higher or lower, still unknown.

After calling for another assist — this time with a code-3 emergency tag — Neil had turned the lights back on, but not done much more. In fact, the deputy had cautioned they didn't want to disturb anything outside. Hugh expected to hear sirens within minutes. Maybe even the FBI. A sniper with a high powered rifle — even if state lines hadn't been violated — probably set off a few alarm bells.

"Why don't you have any darn blinds or curtains?" Neil asked, heading for the kitchen table.

Hugh opened the refrigerator door. He needed a Coke. "Who's going to be looking in?"

"A sniper, that's who." After pointing out the obvious, Neil sat down stiffly at Hugh's kitchen table where Hobo was still reluctant to abandon his position of safety underneath. Hugh thought Neil on edge — or maybe just very vigilant. Well, a sniper was serious business.

"You're right," Hugh said. But before joining Neil to commiserate, he grabbed a bottle of Dos Equis and two glass bottles of Coke from the refrigerator, and popped the top on one soda with an opener he dug out of a kitchen drawer near the sink and window. In passing, he glanced outside and saw the flashers Neil put out after the break-in were still going. He offered Neil both beer and Coke.

"No thanks on the beer, I'm technically on duty." He smiled weakly, apologetically. "And sorry, not a pop drinker."

71

"No problem, two for me then," Hugh tried for a joke—but could hear how forced his tone was. "That's right, you don't drink sodas at poker." Giving up on levity, he dropped in the chair opposite Neil and sighed while shaking his head. "None of this makes sense. First somebody tries to rob me, *then* somebody tries to kill you." He looked back at the window. "And one person being a thief and sniper in one night—just doesn't sound right."

"Yeah. I'm guessing two different people."

"Your flashers are still on out there." Hugh took a long and slow swallow of soda. "The guy who tried to kill you had to be a good distance away when he made that shot. Otherwise those flashers would have silhouetted him, don't you think?" He tsked, then blew out air. "At least that's my guess from the sound."

"And have a night-scope," Neil murmured. "You certain it was me he was after?"

How could he tell Neil how he knew? *Impossible,* in that he didn't really understand himself why he knew Neil was the target. "I just know it was your head he was aiming for."

Neil didn't challenge his "knowing," just stood up abruptly and cursed. This time, *"Sacré bleu."* Then he turned and headed into the living room where he stood for a few moments grimacing in front of Hugh's hutch. "Damn shame." Neil sighed, as if he genuinely appreciated Hugh's loss. "I know someone. As soon as forensics says it's okay, I'll send him over to fix your hutch. And your kitchen window."

Hugh didn't want to look at his hutch. Too much to deal with in one night. Tomorrow he'd face repairs. He took a moment to get up from the table, and consequently lagged behind Neil. But even from his room-dividing archway, he was surprised by the expression on Neil's face, and was quite taken with the level of caring he'd heard in the deputy's voice.

72

Indeed, over the last few months his opinions about Neil had evolved, and though he still wasn't really fond of him, more and more he thought Neil a "good" man.

Sure wish I liked him more. Of course he wasn't about to reveal his inner thoughts to Neil. Instead, he asked, "*Sacré bleu* means 'holy cow,' right?"

Neil was now inspecting all surfaces of Grandmother Todd's hutch carefully, taking care to avoid glass or touch anything. He even stooped to look at the bottom edges. "Yeah, it's an idiom. The words 'holy cow,' actually translate as *vache sacrée*. There's a story behind..." his voice trailed off as he tried to see into the space between the hutch and the wall. Without looking at Hugh, he asked, "You have any latex gloves?"

"Ah..." Hugh remembered Ruthie's cleaning supplies under the sink. "Hold on."

He found them with little effort, and when he returned, Neil was knocking on the wall just around the corner from the hutch.

He handed Neil the gloves, and the deputy straightened his shoulders, cleared his throat, then looked at Hugh straight on. "Mr. Champion," he said, his tone somber and his body rather stiff, "I've been remiss in not thanking you right off. *Mea culpa.* Thank you very much."

Hugh was momentarily at a loss for words.

"I'd be dead right now," Neil added, "if you hadn't pulled me to the ground."

For a second, Hugh thought Neil was going to tear up, but *no,* Deputy Neil Knight was evidently made of sterner stuff.

"I'll never forget." Then, in a quite formal and ceremonious way, he offered his free hand to Hugh.

Hugh—fittingly he thought—returned Neil's firm and emphatic handshake with appropriate solemnity. "Appreciate

73

the sentiment, Neil." He cleared his own throat, released Neil's hand, and said, "What the heck are you doing?"

"What's behind this wall?"

"Inside of the visitor's closet—" He caught up with Neil's thought process. "You think the bullet's in there?"

Neil nodded. "I can see it went right through the hutch and penetrated this wall."

He followed as Neil went a-hunting. Indeed, there was a large bullet penetration hole behind the closet door, with the surrounding plaster splayed almost perfectly. After quickly slipping on the gloves Hugh gave him, Neil stuck his fingers in the bullet hole, and in seconds pulled out the largest bullet Hugh had ever seen. Admittedly, he'd never trained with or even seen a sniper rifle bullet, but the one Neil retrieved from his closet was immense by any standard.

"Jeez." Hugh stepped closer to get a better look. "Are you supposed to just pull that out of the wall like that? Isn't it evidence, and what will Leo and Leo say?"

"Oops," said Neil making a comical face, and again Hugh was surprised—the Neil he knew was one of the most humorless men he'd ever met.

He couldn't believe the size of the bullet Neil was holding. The shot, the bullet, the velocity—they had survived an unbelievable shooting event.

Hobo had come out of hiding, curiosity about what they were doing evidently overcoming fear. And when he saw the bullet in Neil's hand, he whimpered uncannily.

"Even Hobo's impressed," Hugh said. "You know about these bullets?"

"Not a lot, but enough to know how far they'll go, and the damage they'll do." He held the bullet up like it was a rare jewel. "Fifty caliber—guessing a Barrett M82 rifle or the like."

Who would have a rifle like that?

Neil answered his thought. "This was probably somebody with military training. Marine maybe."

Hugh shook his head. Before he came to the Mojave, except for Lewis, Della's deceased husband and his Quantico training, he'd never been around or been involved in shootings of any kind. There were his counseling experiences. Indeed, one in particular, during a volunteer prison program, he'd found emotionally horrendous.

And now, his little High Desert piece-of-escape was turning into the Wild West of yesteryear—especially if he included the Turner Jackson affair.

What next?

It was a scene illuminated by two sets of cruiser lights. Shadows stark and hard. Rookie CHP officer Collin Boyle tried to keep his voice calm as he called in repeated 11-99 emergency requests. One was enough, of course, but he couldn't stop repeating the numbers—and unfortunately, he could also hear the note of panic in his voice, and see his hands weren't as steady as they should be.

Collin was on his knees on the ground, rough shoulder-gravel-dirt digging into his kneecaps, his one hand pressing his own crumpled up CHP jacket against what he'd immediately seen was a gaping hole in Officer Gideon Will's chest—Collin felt like he was holding his fellow officers life inside his body. He *dared not* stop the pressure, *dared not* move his jacket away. If he did, Gid would die. And it would be his fault; his fault because he hadn't kept the pressure on. Collin's other hand was shakily holding his portable radio close to his mouth as he repeatedly called for assistance, He was kneeling in blood. Warm and sticky even through his thick uniform pants.

Kathie Marie Hoffman was kneeling on the other side of Gideon, her one hand holding the fallen officer's, her other hand next to Collin's on the jacket, and like him, clearly trying to also contain and hold back the maroon deluge that wanted to spill into the night. Collin could see her knuckles were taught—he'd only looked her in the face a couple times. Barely audible, but oh-so becalming, he could hear her repeating Hail Marys at a feverish pace.

Twenty-year veteran Fred Johnson was standing to the side behind Collin, his CHP brimmed hat in his one hand, wiping his brow with his forearm, then rubbing his neck with his other hand, then sighing—then all over again. "He'll make it," he said with a strength his nervous actions didn't support. "He'll make it."

Collin couldn't see, but he indeed "felt" Fred's nervous movements behind him. But it was Fred's words, his intonation, that Collin internalized. He'd barely looked at his mentor, yet his presence and words of assurance were a point of strength for the rookie officer.

"The meat wagon will be here soon, Gid." Collin doubted Gideon could hear him, but he wasn't dead. *No he's not dead yet.* He wasn't sure if the ambulance would be coming from Needles or Barstow. *Either way, only a few more minutes.*

He saw and felt—almost simultaneously—Gideon's hand closest to him reach over and grab the wrist of his own hand pressing down on Gideon's chest; the pressure the injured CHP officer was exerting surprised Collin. Even more amazing, Gideon turned his head toward him, and though he didn't actually open his eyes, his eyelids flitted rapidly for a few seconds as he managed to murmur, "White Toyota, hand-gun..."

His voice had been low and faltering, but Collin heard him quite well. In the far distance, Collin also heard the

76

distinctive wail of ambulance sirens, and said a prayer of his own.

PART TWO
Islands in the Desert

Chapter Three

Tuesday morning

"The Highway Killer" woke up happy and glad to be alive even though he worked into the night. He loved mornings, loved doing what he did, and was liking what he'd seen of the desert so far. Especially enjoyable was cruising I-40—low traffic, only truckers to possibly notice him. Downside—the winds sucked. He'd staked out his new hunting ground for over a week now, and he thought the stretch from Kingman Arizona to Barstow California was perfect. Though the California part was really beginning to grab him. And the *CHP*—always liked the sound of that. He'd loved the TV series.

He also liked the new handle he'd been given. Up till now, he'd just been a run-of-the-mill serial killer. Out here, near the rarified air of La La Land, he'd finally gotten his own acronym, "THK." Yep, The Highway Killer, was a great handle—but the THK acronym was even cooler. Had a nice ring to it. Almost as nice as CHP.

First off, after doing his morning exercises, he left the motel and headed for breakfast at the Ludlow Café—their pancakes were damned good by his way of thinking. And he'd eaten his share of pancakes at a lot of joints. After breakfast and two cups of coffee, he headed back out on the road, down National Trails toward Amboy, and somewhere before Klondike, turned off on a seldom used dirt road and drove back about a mile until he was on ground higher than the road—but not too near the railroad tracks. THK didn't like trains. Scared him. Then he turned his car around so he wouldn't be surprised by some yahoo coming his way, though

81

he doubted anyone would be driving down this piece of crappy potholed dirt road. Still, he prided himself on thinking ahead.

There seemed to be swirls of sand crisscrossing the freeway out in front of him. He thought he'd better make a note of that in his little book. Weather conditions were important, especially when you're talking about getting away. Last night hadn't been bad, weather-wise.

And that's why they couldn't take him down—*he* paid attention. On top of that, his mission was righteous, now wasn't it? He pushed a button on his dash and two telescoping antennas rose, one from each fender. His new replacement car, an older compact white-colored Toyota, had been so easy to retrofit. He was planning on a long and enjoyable run before they realized he'd switched cars and some stupid cop got lucky and took him down. That cop last night hadn't seen a thing.

Maybe, he was actually invincible? Especially if he kept thinking ahead.

And that was just what he was doing this morning, thinking ahead.

No more nights; last night was his last evening hunting job. And no more shotgun. Though he sure had loved his sawed-off break-open Lupara. It had been hard to part with that baby—but it had always been tricky opening his door, turning, and firing with precision. The shotgun spray pattern had helped, but still damned iffy, even for him.

Now in bright all revealing morning light, THK looked at his new handgun on the seat next to him, and smiled—a Smith and Wesson Special Hogue Bantam .44 with a 3 1/8 inch barrel instead of his Lupara. The pawnshop guy had assumed he was buying the S&W for his girlfriend—small, light, and easy to hide. Had worked damned well last night.

Yep, he was always a step ahead of them. And that crazy murder with the Sheriff's Deputy Sunday night, well that was just an added distraction for them. It had swelled his pride a bit. Someone copying him—but she wasn't CHP, now was she? Couldn't they see it wasn't a Highway Patrol cruiser? Cops should know by now it was the Highway Patrol he hated. Though the copycat did use a shotgun like his. *Weird, that.*

Well today was a new day, a new way of doing things.

"They'll never catch us," THK told his Hogue Bantam .44—and his smile broadened. "And with my always monitoring the police bans, well hell, I'm not stoppable."

Then he let his seat go back, stretched out, and relived the parts of his life he enjoyed. *Ha,* he thought. All those sessions, all those shrinks, all the reasons and excuses why he couldn't fit in—school or anywhere else. So what if he'd been suspended, expelled, then written off from school—and finally from an ordinary life.

But he neither made nor needed excuses. They just never understood. His childhood had been perfect by most standards—no traumas, no mistreatment. THK laughed out loud for several long moments, letting his head fall back, and the sound of his voice joyfully encompass his Toyota world. He hadn't opened his windows, too much dust, and the desert smelled different from the Midwest, even different from Arizona and New Mexico. *Funny that.*

His thoughts returned to himself, his nature, and what made him happy. Yep, *Evil* ran in his veins, and THK cherished the joy that knowledge brought him. And now, he had new toys and a new playground.

He felt an even larger smile spread across his face. And running into those cops taking a break at the Dairy Queen bar last night, well that had been pure gravy—actually, more like an ice cream sundae with a cherry on top. One of his favorites.

So easy to watch until they were almost finished, then pull out ahead of them. Go a couple miles, then pretend to breakdown on the side of the road, quickly call in an emergency. They'd had to stop. *So easy.* And they were all supposed to be on alert. Hadn't helped them one bit, now had it?

He closed his eyes to further enjoy reliving those moments. Yep, he was a special man, a man with a purpose, an island of his own making. A new island. A desert island.

What next? Yep, he was a man who thought ahead.

"I guess I better get back," Sally Meliano said. She glanced at her wristwatch. "Do you spend much time with her?" Their waitress had just cleared their breakfast dishes and topped off their coffee mugs. They were sitting in a booth at The Summit Restaurant at the top of Cajon Pass.

Even though they'd been dating over six months, Neil still found himself on unsure ground—in this case wondering for a second if Sally had been jealous of his CHP Liaison Officer. *No,* he decided, her question just sounded like idle curiosity.

"We have a few minutes still," he said, not bothering to check his watch. He could see the wall clock from his side of their booth, and knew they each needed about forty minutes to get off the summit and to their respective work locations in opposite directions. "Not really," he answered about Rociana Bustamante.

Truth was, he wished he saw more of her, in fact, hoped to maybe connect with her today. He was dying to hear more about THK, and figured she was his inside connection. They were both designated Liaison Officers—Rociana for CHP, and him for Mojave County Sheriff's Department.

84

As if she could read his mind, Sally leaned across the table and lowered her voice. "Has she given you any inside information on that maniac who killed Melony?"

Neil found Sally's occasional intuitive side both disturbing, and endearing. He also found it an incongruous trait for an ME. But all in all, it sure was nice she wanted to know what he was thinking, even participate in his thoughts. "Well, we've met to talk several times." He closed his eyes and leaned his head back for several seconds before saying more, trying to re-picture their meetings.

"Maybe three times altogether now that I think about it," he continued. "In Yermo. She likes Peggy Sue's on Yermo Road. And you know, she's stationed in Barstow." He brought his head forward, opened his eyes, and waited for Sally to nod. "But that was before Melony—" his voice caught, surprising him. He rushed on, "I do know she drove up to Sacramento yesterday, they're having some big meeting about THK today at CHP Headquarters." He glanced at the clock again. "Audrey and her brother headed up there too." He smiled slightly, forcing himself to get past thoughts of Melony. "Flew. I get the impression neither of them liked that very much."

Sally leaned back against her red upholstered booth back, her eyes wide and dancing. "And they're leaving you here in charge?" Her intonation was one of pride, and a smile spread across her face.

Neil was wearing his uniform, he knew Sally liked it, and the look on her face intimated his decision had paid off. Also good to be in uniform today, since he was going to be pulling "take care of everything" duty most of the today. He didn't clarify it was just Audrey's decision—Ted was FBI, and had nothing to do with him. Instead, he just basked in the warmth of her praise. *À bouche ouverte*. Another thing about Sally that brought forth mixed emotions. Sometimes she was a

85

little gullible, over-eager—again, especially for an ME who cut-up and sawed on dead bodies day after day.

After a long moment of what Neil felt were shared emotions, he cleared his throat, then said, "I need to talk to you about last night." His tone turned somber, and his words came slowly. "I almost got killed."

The look on her face endeared Sally in his heart even more; but before he could fill her in, his cell vibrated. He pulled it out of his deputy's jacket, looked at the screen, then sighed slightly. "I have to take this." He pressed the return call button. "Audrey just texted me there was another cop shot last night."

"Jeez," Sally said. "Who's next?"

He didn't have an answer for her.

After breakfast, driving from Cajon Pass to Yermo, Neil spent the piece of his driving time on I-15 between Victorville and Barstow trying to figure out why there was a target on his back. *More like on my forehead.* Indeed, something instinctual to his cop experience told him the shots at him and the THK-thing were not one-in-the-same.

The stretch he was cruising through was usually a non-eventful section of road with plenty of lanes. Consequently, he could slide in behind slower-moving vehicles like campers and trucks—especially in his A4—and think.

He hoped he hadn't scared Sally telling her about Audrey's call and last night. After he'd told her about going to Champion's, then getting shot at, she seemed genuinely afraid for him. Even suggested he needed police protection. Sally was funny that way, inured to dead bodies, but real police work, that was something different. He'd countered her concern with a smart-aleck quip accentuated with an off handed laugh, "I *am* the police."

Truth was, he probably wasn't going to have a choice on a protection-detail if he and Audrey didn't get last night's incident sorted out fast. So far, it wasn't common knowledge his head had been in a sniper's gun sight at Hugh's. You don't shoot at cops without consequences, including podunk county Deputy Sheriffs like himself. His being a target was circumstantial and not yet publicized; but Melony—her death had already started a full-court-press.

Why me? Clues were minimal, motivations were minimal. It wasn't like he was a big city cop and had been putting a steady stream of bad-guys behind bars. Except for last Spring and the Turner Jackson affair, he'd spent most of his career investigating B&Es, vehicular pileups, check-bys, and dee wee stops—*a lot of those.* Especially when he'd pull a weekend night shift. *Drunks leaving bars must think all cops are in bed by then.* He smiled for a second before remembering how much Melony had hated DUIs.

"Cars are loaded weapons," she was fond of saying. Then without fail, she would modify her condemnation with, *"I think."* Neil looked out his side window, forcing down a lump in the throat. It just wasn't "manly" getting choked up every time he thought about the deceased deputy. *I need to get-a-grip.*

Traffic-wise at that moment, he'd tucked his sleek little Audi in behind a gigantic mobile home—worth around half-a-mill he figured. He was near Wild Wash Road, and on cruise-control at about sixty-five miles-per-hour. When he looked out his side window trying to banish his mental picture of Melony, a woman in the passenger seat of a passing Lexus LX gave him an inquiring and rather superior look.

"Yeah, lady," he said, "I know I'm slugging-it." Of course she couldn't hear him, but he liked voicing and hearing his sass aloud. "Just be glad I'm not in my cruiser. I'd be flipping my sirens on about now." He didn't have a radar gun in his sports car, but Neil guessed the driver was hot-footing it at well over eighty.

He forced his thoughts back to murder and attempted murder. As early as last night Neil hadn't thought Melony's murder, scrap metal theft, and an attempt on his life could possibly be connected.

But what had he come up with to explain all these events? *"Rien du tout."* And having nothing made him angry. He felt his hands tightening around his steering wheel just thinking about his lack of clues. His steering wheel was covered with Wheelskins custom perforated two-toned leather, and he rubbed his right hand along the side of the wheel. The tactile experience of rubbing the leather made him immediately feel better. He knew from experience it would. He'd watched Ted do a similar motion along the edge of his dashboard and had immediately liked the Special Agent a little more, even though he was his boss's brother. He'd understood the motion, understood what it meant.

Next Neil took a deep breath, tried to relax, and brought Sally's face into focus. The living, replacing what was no longer there. It was a relaxation trick Champion had told him about; force your thoughts to what's good in your life, or a past pleasant experience. Claimed it lowered your heart rate immediately.

On their first meeting, Sally's almost black hair and her contrasting hazel eyes had caught his attention. Sure, her nose was too small for her generous month, but he especially liked her default expression of cheerfulness. With the memory of her face smiling back at him, Neil felt his hand and arm muscles ease.

Unfortunately, he wasn't sure what to do next in the evidence-gathering department. Forensics was doing what they do—but what about him? He could at least work on motivations. *Cui bono?* But it was hard to attach a money-motive to killing cops. Had to be something other than money. But without anything, no leads, no hunches, no clear motives—Neil realized all he could do was wait. And that thought replaced his anger with the lesser emotion, irritation.

After a sigh to himself, an aberrant and perplexing thought did cheer him up a bit. Even though he'd been shot at, he wasn't afraid. *What kind of lunacy is that?* Maybe he needed to talk to Champion about all this.

He sighed again, this time long and loud. *Who's to hear me or care?* He could be himself inside the luxury cocoon of his A4. The mobile home's right turning blinker came on, going off I-15 to CA Highway 58. Neil hadn't realized how far he'd come already. He was almost entering Barstow. All that time thinking. And he hadn't come any closer to one positive nugget. *Nothing.*

"Dial," he said to his wireless voice-activated cell phone. He'd promised Champion he'd get his window and hutch fixed, and a promise was a promise, especially to a man who'd just saved your life. First he'd call his friend, then he'd call Champion; this was something practical and real he could do. Of course when he got hold of Champion, he wouldn't be talking about fear, and his apparent lack of it. *No,* not on the phone. That would have to wait until another time. Maybe at the next poker game.

A CHP patrol car whizzed by him, siren wailing, lights flashing. Before he had time to speculate further or state a number for his cell, his handheld police ban came to life, then his cell phone rang.

*   *   *   *   *

89

Hugh pulled his vibrating cell phone out of his jacket pocket and looked at its screen. *Neil.* He ignored the call and dropped the phone back in his pocket.

Gabe leaned in toward him. "You see that couple coming through the door?"

Hugh nodded. For once, Gabe had taken off the wool knit hat he wore year round and exposed his bald head. Up close like he was, Hugh noticed for the first time Gabe's head was covered with dark spots—*freckles*. His white beard had always been an interesting contrast of colors against his olive-colored skin, and the freckles were an added touch to the "Gabriel Travers" look. Hugh liked the man and the picture he presented to the world.

Even though their oval table was large, he and Gabe were sitting rather close to each other. *Breakfast conspirators,* he thought, and almost laughed. But he was too tired to muster up the energy to even smile. He did manage to follow Gabe's gaze, albeit from underneath drooped eyelids. Unfortunately, the eyes behind his weary lids were also barely functioning, very hard to focus; but he was able to make out the elderly couple as they entered. They walked slowly, but had eager looks on their faces as they headed toward a group of seven or so people sitting around a table across the room. *Eager,* Hugh guessed, to tell what had happened to their friends. It was the only fully occupied table in the place.

"That's Cleo and Bob," Gabe whispered.

"Are we going over to talk to them?" Hugh thought his words sounded mumbled, and his mouth felt dry, not working as it should. *I'm probably dehydrated.*

"I already know what happened to them." Gabe nodded emphatically and gave Hugh a knowing look. "News travels fast around here."

The Community Café was spacious, with large round tables capable of serving a sizable crowd. Hugh didn't exactly count available seats, but figured it would take a lot of folks to fill the place. *A place* only a few miles from Joey's, *a place* he'd never been to since arriving in the Mojave. A good, or bad fact, he wasn't sure; but he did remember when he'd first arrived in the desert, seeking out other human beings was not on the agenda. *Maybe now?*

He and Gabe were huddled at a corner table in the rear of the center waiting for their orders to arrive. Water and coffee were already in front of them. Their backs were "flanked and protected" by shelves filled with used books on sale for the hefty price of fifty cents each.

The morning light outside seemed unusually bright to Hugh, especially since he hadn't slept yet. And it wasn't just his eyes and mouth weren't working well, but his uncooperative facial muscles made it even hard to smile, and *any* physical movement or brain usage was taking an immense amount of effort. Still, he'd promised Gabe he'd accompany him. *So here I am.* Besides, no matter how he felt, Hugh doubted he could have slept anyway. Last night was a shocker he still hadn't completely taken in.

Fleetingly, he remembered Neil's call, and wondered where he was calling from. Work probably. Or maybe he'd taken the day off and was at home sleeping—like he wished he was doing. Unlikely though, didn't fit his personality, especially after getting shot at for goodness' sake.

The deputy's calls for assistance last night had garnered responses from a San Bernardino County deputy and a City of Barstow detective. Of course Neil was already on the scene, trying to do his job; but then after everyone arrived there were a lot of personnel he needed to assist. Mojave County's remaining deputy was on his own—Audrey involved in Sacramento concerns.

Melony was dead and everything had changed.

No, Neil wasn't home sleeping. On his own, probably needing someone to talk to. Hugh was immediately ashamed he hadn't answered Neil's call, and had to force another unwanted picture of Melony's smiling face from his consciousness.

In its place, he tried to bring up a picture of the forensic specialist from Riverside who was still supposedly nosing around his kitchen. *Not Leo or Leo.* Hugh couldn't remember this technician's name, but the eager young man had said he could go ahead and repair Grandmother Todd's hutch. "Just a go-through," he'd reassured Hugh, as if he expected him to realize the significance of such a fact and know what to compare "a-go-through" to.

Hugh suspected he was still there, working under Hobo and Black-Jack's watchful eyes scrutinizing their every move. Even Gabe had quipped, "Don't need to worry about nothin', 'cause Hobo and Black-Jack are on the job." Remembering, Hugh wanted to smile, but couldn't quite muster up the emotion or energy. At least his mind was waking up and clearing a bit. Nonetheless, the whole event last night remained perplexing, and had left him drained. Scrap metal thievery was one thing, but a sniper-attack was a whole different animal.

He managed to give Gabe a skeleton account of what happened on the drive to the center restaurant, and for once his desert-rat friend was rendered speechless for several moments. Not only was his personal scrap-metal incident big in itself, but when he also dropped the info-bomb Neil had been shot at — with a sniper rifle no less — and nearly killed, Gabe's jaw had dropped, leaving him completely speechless.

And now, as unbelievable as it was, *we're having breakfast at the Community Café.* As if it was the most ordinary of mornings. Hugh thought he heard a train go down the BNSF tracks to the south, and the clickety-click sounds were oddly reassuring, reminding him of the trains humming through Yermo behind Audrey's office. He looked down, his hands were still, but the minor act of moving his head left him slightly queasy.

Again, he wondered if maybe he was dehydrated? Hugh tried to remember when he last drank anything, and couldn't. *After Neil left?* Maybe, but he wasn't sure. He now forced himself to drink some of his ice water, and thought it odd he had to force the liquid down. If dehydrated, shouldn't he be lapping it up—not almost choking to drink it? Indeed, he suddenly felt awful, and wanted to snap at Gabe—ask him why the heck were they there if he had all the answers already?

But it *wasn't Gabe's fault* he'd been up all night. And it *wasn't Gabe's fault* he wasn't twenty-something anymore, with stamina to both study for exams and party all night. Indeed, now that Hugh really thought about it, he was amazed he hadn't dropped over prone by now. In fact, for a second, he felt a little swell of pride at his "old man" stamina. *False pride,* he quickly amended, *wouldn't take much to topple me over right out of this chair.*

"So what exactly did happen to Cleo and Bob?" he asked, trying to exercise a few brain cells. "Their last name is Thomas, right?"

"Yep, Cleo and Bob Thomas." Gabe leaned in even closer. "They were supposed to go down to Covina for the night and stay with their granddaughter. But Cleo thought she was coming down with something, and thought she shouldn't go." Gabe smiled wryly. "They've been married fifty years. And Bob don't go nowhere without Cleo."

"So they *were* at home." Ruthie's initial story had been wrong. "But the thief was expecting an empty house?"

"Yeah," he brought his finger to his lips, "but Ruthie don't know that yet." He gave a knowing look. "I'll give you

93

that though, thieving bastards didn't think anybody would be home to notice them ripping 'em off." Gabe made a sound of disgust through his teeth, then his look turned curious. "You weren't supposed to be somewhere last night, were you? And didn't tell me?"

Hugh ignored Gabe's question and accusation, keeping his strained and wobbly gaze on the couple. Everyone at their table seemed to be talking *at* Bob and Cleo not only with words, but also with sympathetic body language, indicating the Thomas couple was well liked. Hugh continued to watch as Bob pulled a chair out so Cleo could sit down. He was a large man, tall and broad-shouldered, even with age having taken its toll. His face however, seemed strained, and maybe a little angry.

"Bob doesn't look like the kind of guy a snatch-and-grab thief would want to meet up with," Hugh murmured. He could certainly imagine him noisily chambering his shotgun at a would-be thief in the night. Could even see him firing it. Especially if he felt Cleo needed protecting. "Where was the stuff the thieves were trying to take?"

"Only one thief," Gabe said. "And it was copper wire he was after. Out in back of their shed." He smiled. "Bob heard something, then headed out there with a shotgun. Must have pulled up a round when he got close, 'cause the guy took off running."

He thought it amazing Gabe now knew so many details about what happened—it had only been yesterday when they'd heard. Suddenly it hit Hugh *how much* had happened this weekend, Cleo and Bob, Melony's horrible murder, then his place last night and Neil being shot at. For a few seconds his tired mind and body told him these events weren't real. All a dream. *Some kind of horrible nightmare.*

Gabe was giving him a strange look, and Hugh realized he better say something. "Did Bob give the police a description?" Even though he had no idea what the Thomas place was like, his mind drew a picture of Bob in a nightshirt running out into a dark desert night, shotgun in hand, ready to protect his ladylove—and copper wire.

"Thin." Gabe stroked his full white beard. "And I heard tall." Gabe lowered his voice to where Hugh had to strain to hear. "Tall and thin." He squeezed his already slits-for-eyes even tighter. "Fits G-Man perfect." Even without the whites of his eyes visible, Gabe managed a challenging and demanding look. "And, just found out last night, G-Man's behind on his mortgage." He crossed his arms across his chest and leaned back in his chair.

Hugh didn't respond, didn't want to humor the man or add fuel to his fixation with G-Man.

Gabe, however, was not to be deterred. "After we eat, I'm taking you to G-Man's place. We need to have a look around."

Hugh was too tired to object, though some part of his brain was still functioning, and he asked, "Where were you last night?"

Gabe looked puzzled. "Me?"

"Were *you* supposed to be somewhere?"

"The American Legion."

"There's only two houses down that road. You and me."

"You think they were after my stuff while I was out?" Gabe's eyes widened farther than Hugh had ever seen them.

An amazing occurrence, Hugh thought. A half-energy chuckle even popped out at the sight of his friend's current eye movement, combined with the picture of Gabe's piles of helter-skelter stuff. "All that crap you've got all over."

"My stuff isn't crap."

He sounded slightly offended. So Hugh quickly modified his statement. "All the treasures you have out there."

95

Gabe smiled. "Yeah, I do have some special stuff." Then he cursed under his breath. "So that no-good G-Man was trying to rip me off..." His voice trailed off, and his smile was quickly replaced with a menacing scowl.

Unfortunately, Hugh speculated, if the scrap metal thief was just looking for an easy target. *Who the heck shot at Neil? And why?*

Hugh knew where they were *supposed* to be, and what he expected to be seeing. Consequently, he just couldn't quite take in the actual scene before him. Especially looking through Gabe's dusty Camry front window. Indeed, it felt like he'd been dropped from space into an alternate reality and was seeing the "new" world through a hazy lens.

Overly tired. Still, what he thought was unfolding before his eyes just didn't make sense—unless maybe he was hallucinating. He rubbed his aching forehead and eyes, then stole a glance at Gabe next to him in the driver's seat; his friend looked just as mesmerized, *or was it awestruck?* His eyes were wide, his jaw hung loosely, and there seemed to be a faint halo around his head. The beatific glow, Hugh knew, was an after effect of rubbing his own eyes, and it quickly evaporated.

"What's happening here?" Gabe murmured.

At least it's not just me. Hugh hoped their drive to the center would have cleared his head and stopped his eyes from jumping around. To the contrary, he now felt worse—like he'd stepped out of the real world into a Technicolor movie scene and been hurled into a story line he knew nothing about.

Then Hugh saw the back of an officer that fit the general proportions of Neil, and for a second felt reconnected to reality—*he knew Neil*—though he doubted it really was Neil standing a few feet ahead of them. What would Audrey's deputy be doing at Griffith and Don's place? Especially after last night. Though Neil was probably made of stiffer physical "stuff" than himself. *But Neil here?*

It was still early morning, a clear sky hung over them, painted a bright and heavily saturated blue that made its own statement, not just a canvas for the sun and clouds. The sun was high enough he couldn't make out its orb, but bright enough to flood every visible corner of the world he could see. There were no shadows anywhere. Weird, and nice at the same time.

Here at the location where they'd arrived, Griffith's place, Hugh still assumed, the horizon line in front of him seemed long, straight, and endless. What he'd expected, based on Gabe's pre-loading ramblings on the way over, was a vista of rolling desert hills. He'd also expected to see a doublewide, out-buildings, several workshops, a couple pickup trucks, a few dogs, feral cats, chickens; indeed, Gabe had rambled on effusively.

Maybe all those items *were* there, *behind* the surreal happenings they were seeing. *Behind* the clashing combinations of a crystal-clear sky exuding limitless brightness; flashing cruiser strobes, accentuated and intensified by attention-demanding sirens; and what seemed like a multitude of unexpected scurrying players. Many of them in uniform.

He rubbed his eyes again—to the point of pain. Nothing changed.

When Gabe finally turned off the car motor, Hugh took a slow steadying breath, then whispered to himself, "This can't be real."

"Something bad has happened." Gabe didn't hurry to disembark his little car.

There were three police cruisers—two marked with Barstow logos, another set back from them, and the third car bearing Mojave County's Raven insignia. *Neil's cruiser.* Who else could it be?

Hugh's mind could no longer deny the truth of the scene before them. *Yes,* sirens were *really* yelping, strobe lights were *actually* flashing, and officers and technicians were either rushing hither-and-yon like a fast-forward button had been pressed, or contrarily standing near-motionless, fixed in a stopped film frame.

And *yes,* Neil was indeed on the scene—standing wide-legged, twenty-five or so feet away from them—in uniform, hands in his pockets, his back to them, and *somehow* the only being or object silhouetted in the morning light. *How odd.*

Suddenly, Hugh realized his own hands, legs, and feet now felt funny—like they had a mind of their own. Fatigue, he guessed. Fortunately, he still had the energy to pull himself up and out of Gabe's Toyota to get a better view of everything going on around them. And for a few seconds, again thought he must be dreaming, or had stepped into some alternate reality. What he was seeing remained just too bizarre; he shivered as an accompanying eerie feeling slid down his back. *Oh no,* Hugh thought he knew what was going on—*you're a psychologist for goodness sakes*—his brain screamed at him. Cleary, he was having some type of psychotic episode. The possibility scared him to death.

"What the hell?" Gabe was seemingly also still stumbling to take in the scene, and clearly wasn't rushing to face what was before them—though both car doors were open and he could hear Gabe clearly.

Had there been hallucinogenic mushrooms in their omelets? Hugh forced his mind to straighten up. *Drugs in our omelets, good grief.* With a repeat deep breath, Hugh felt himself "come back." Sure, there were still discordant patrol car light bars

98

flashing, and sirens were screaming—set against an uncompromising crystal-clear-blue. But the Felliniesque nature of the world around him and his odd physical reactions subsided a bit. He looked down, his hands were still.

But my brain—a breakdown? "Not good," Hugh said aloud.

"Sure ain't," Gabe agreed, taking Hugh's remark at cross purposes. Then he finally got out of his side of the car. "That's Neil over there." Not waiting for Hugh, he started walking toward the deputy. And almost as if choreographed with Gabe's decision to enter the action, the lights and sirens suddenly stopped.

Hugh followed his friend, relieved his limbs and physical coordination were still functioning normally. *Legs steady and walking in a straight line.*

Audrey's Deputy Sheriff must have heard them coming toward him, for he turned toward them, and Hugh was surprised how haggard he looked.

Neil nodded his head to Gabe and said, "Travers." Next he gave Hugh an obvious once-over and shook his head. "You look horrible, Champion." His voice was tired and lackluster—no emotion, no spin. "I sent a guy I know out to fix your hutch. Left you a phone message." He shook his head again, this time also making a sucking sound through his teeth. "And how come you guys are here?"

Hugh neither explained why he hadn't answered Neil's call, nor acknowledge he'd heard his repairman message. Instead he forced a smile, and said. "I guess we're not used to all-nighters."

Gabe cleared his throat with emphasis, then came up to Neil's side, but Hugh didn't let his friend intrude and take the lead. He wanted to get a handle on what was going on—fast, and in his own way. "We wanted to talk to Mr. King," Hugh added before Gabe could say anything.

Nonetheless, Gabe forced his way into the conversation. "Yeah," he said, "where is the G-Man, anyway?"

"They're over there." Neil pointed to an area to the side of a massive manufactured home.

Why didn't I see that before? Hugh also now saw two men, both tall and thin, standing by a large workshop that was either right next to or attached to the house. *And how did I miss that huge workshop too?*

Neil said, "That's where the stuff was stolen from." He gave Gabe a pained and weary look. "*Une fois de plus.* Again, tell me why are you two are here?"

"Huh?" Gabe demanded. Then he put his hands on his hips and went into his trademark wide-legged bulldog stance, including narrowing his squinty eyes.

Hugh said to Neil, "Thought you'd given up with the foreign phrases." He forced his smile to broaden, congenially he hoped. Though he felt way past tired—just wanted to go home. "There's no mystery. Gabe thinks Griffith King might be the guy stealing metal around here. We came over to talk to him." For some reason, he felt he needed to clarify his position in their current situation. "Actually, Gabe thought we should come over and discuss the matter, and I came along for the ride."

Neil grunted, giving the impression it was an effort. "Well, your theory doesn't hold up, Travers," he said, then gestured with his arm. "The reason we're all here is Griffith King and Baddon Giles got robbed this morning. Right before dawn. They even heard shots."

"Shots?" Hugh mumbled. "Is that a road over there?" He was looking toward the eastern side of the property.

Neil turned to look, and after a moment, agreed, "Yeah, I think so."

In the bright glare flooding this particular version of Hugh's reality picture, he thought he saw the outline of a dark

100

colored sedan moving slowly down what looked to be some kind of access road. *Something familiar about that car.*

First, Hugh caught the flash of sunlight on metal, *then,* and for the second time in less than twelve hours, he suddenly and instinctively tackled Neil to the ground—while simultaneously yelling at Gabe, "Dive."

Once more, *une fois de plus,* Hugh's mind unconsciously mimicked Neil's pretentiousness, a bullet had shot through the space Neil's head had been occupying. Hugh twisted his body to follow what he thought was the bullet's continued trajectory—and thought it was probably heading to the side of G-Man's shop. He could also see, even from his distance and awkward position on the ground, almost on top of Neil—Griffith King and Baddon Giles were also now on the ground and crawling toward what they evidently saw as a safer spot.

Still down, Hugh took a moment to look around as best he could without raising his profile. Relieved, he blew out a stream of air. Gabe was safely on the ground next to him and Neil, and it didn't look like anyone had gotten hurt, especially Neil who was scrambling to rollover and get from under him. Hugh could see guns were drawn, cops rushing to take positions, and hear yelling of commands all around them. A second attempt at killing a Mojave County Deputy Sheriff—*a particular sheriff*—had unbelievably just occurred. A *failed* second attempt, thank goodness.

"Jeez," Hugh bemoaned sotto voce as he watched Neil go into cop-mode. Unbelievable as it seemed, his little desert island had yet again turned very dangerous. *What's going on?* Melony killed, Neil shot at twice, several local attempted robberies, an interstate serial cop-killer rampaging around the area…

Cleary he was in the middle of something. *Une fois de plus.* As incongruous and inappropriate as it was, Hugh couldn't hold back a chuckle at his homage to Neil. Mimicry had turned to homage—due to a sniper's bullet.

Hugh found himself still coughing and spitting sand particles long after the Barstow officers took their statements. Seemed like hours, but it was still morning, though barely. Physically, he was beyond tired. Emotionally, he felt a little better. Gabe must have seen something in his face or demeanor and insisted Hugh immediately drink a sixteen-ounce bottle of water without stopping. *No psychotic episode,* Hugh quickly realized with relief, and consequently wasn't as worried about his mental state. Most probably, he was simply suffering from dehydration and advanced fatigue.

Police presence remained high on King's property, including forensic techs scouring the area along the side road.

Neil had pleaded with him, "Don't say anything about last night, okay?" And Hugh agreed. Once it was out this morning's bullet was most probably meant for Neil, and a second one at that, his life would no longer be his own.

"Force me into protective custody," Neil had further explained.

Hugh didn't care, he just wanted to go home and go to sleep. If Neil didn't want to be guarded, so be it. Nonetheless, during their official question and answer periods with two Barstow Police detectives—peppered with wonder and outrage by all concerned—Hugh forced himself to listen. Payoff, he picked up quite a few details about Griffith "G-Man" King, Baddon "Don" Giles, and what happened this morning. As spent as he was, his curiosity was piqued, and Hugh found himself wanting to meet the men. Baddon for the first time, and a more thorough visit with Griffith. Thinking back to when he'd first purchased his birdfeeder, there was something about Griffith he couldn't articulate and even now tickled his intellectual fancy about the man. *Yes,* tired or not, he needed to buck up and talk to Griffith again.

Besides, Gabe had taken his wide-legged stance just feet away, trying for one of his intimidating squint-eyed stare-downs. For a second, Hugh almost laughed. But *no,* now was not the time. Too many peculiar things going on for him not to take the situation seriously.

Hugh was sitting on a surprisingly comfortable wooden bench on the south wall of Griffith's well equipped, seemingly climate controlled, neat, and spotless workshop. He and Gabe had already been given a tour of his welding equipment on an attached veranda. The air inside smelled clean and fresh, and he was hard-pressed to see a dusty surface. And he could hear a low level hum coming from somewhere he couldn't identify.

Griffith was pacing around his shop—and watching, Hugh thought him an impressive looking man. Tall, thin, and sturdy looking without being "thick" in his build. "You know we all live in our own little worlds," Griffith said, stopping for a second and turning to look at Hugh directly. Then he looked around his workshop as if to confirm his thought to himself. "It's my little place on earth." He chuckled and looked for a second toward Baddon sitting across the room on another bench with Gabe. "I should say, *our* little place on the earth. You've been here for what, Don, two, three years?"

Baddon smiled. "Five years, and that's my trailer out there." He inclined his head to the right indicating an area outside and east of Griffith's doublewide. "G-Man has let me crash here." He smiled and looked at Griffith with gratitude.

There's something else in that look, Hugh thought.

103

An awkward few seconds of silence passed before Hugh commented on Griffith's "my-little-place-on-earth" train of thought. "Well, some people *do* like to travel." His comment sounded inconsequential to his own ears. But Griffith had taken him by surprise. *A philosopher welder?* And quite likeable.

"None of this makes sense." Griffith returned to pacing back and forth between the bench where Hugh sat, and the one where Baddon and Gabe sat. Hugh figured this walking routine was Griffith's way of dealing with this morning's events.

Baddon, on the thin and tall side like Griffith, seemed to tower over Gabe, even as they sat next to each other. Especially since Gabe's sitting posture put Hugh in mind of a bewildered dove, not sure what next to do, or where to go—stuck. He was also uncharacteristically silent with a dumbfounded look stuck on his face.

Shock, Hugh guessed. *He can't take it all in yet.* He further speculated that neither was this the situation Gabe had envisioned, nor was Griffith turning out to be the lying, thieving, crook Gabe had mentally and verbally painted.

Hugh was most disappointed with himself, given his numerous counseling sessions with others on how to "roll with the punches." Indeed, *he* was the psychologist. But as with a lot of other happenings this last year, his mind and emotions were not performing with the flexibility he would have liked—or expected.

"Well, maybe the stealing part makes sense," Griffith amended, still walking, but this time, expanding his sweeping hand gestures and looking all around. It was as if he needed confirmation there *was* a darned lot of metal—mainly wrought iron—hanging around his workroom. "Though," he tilted his head slightly as if momentarily confused, "I'd heard they were mainly after copper pipe. Hadn't really worried that much."

Griffith's physicality was much as Hugh remembered from when he'd first met the man at Newberry Springs's annual Pistachio Festival, and now the welder's movements brought back the picture of Griffith that early morning—not very long after he'd plunked himself down in his new Mojave environs.

On that morning, Griffith had stood in back of his wrought-iron-creations display under the sweeping branches of an old and large pine tree. Trees were few in the community park, and Hugh had wondered at the time if Griffith had deliberately chosen that spot. Or had it been the-luck-of-the draw? *The* man, *the* tree, and all those wrought iron bird feeders and patio furniture had hit just the right note to create an iconic "snap shot." Norman Rockwell like—*almost*. There was an edge Hugh felt emanating from the man that wouldn't have been captured in that period's wholesome cover renditions.

Now, with his back to Hugh, Griffith said, "And that deputy being shot at..." his voice dropped off and he looked to his friend Baddon. "Don, do you have any idea what's going on?"

Baddon shook his head, his expression just as stupefied-looking as Gabe's.

"So, both of you live here full-time?" Hugh asked, not looking at Gabe who'd already filled him in. Since Griffith and Baddon had already offered information on their living arrangements, Hugh didn't think he'd come off as too nosey.

"I'm in the house," Griffith answered flatly, seemingly uninterested in such a mundane question. "And like Don said, he's got that single-wide to the west. It's sort of hidden behind all those trees."

"But you share this workshop?" Hugh smiled at Baddon. "Are you a wrought iron artist too?"

105

"Wood," Baddon said, nodding his head toward a corner worktable.

Hugh hadn't paid attention to the carved walking canes, bird houses, and bird sculptures. *My mind's been on metal.* "Wow," he said, but quickly returned his attention to Griffith. Instinctively he knew this wrought-iron artist was the key to *something*. But he wasn't sure it had anything to do with theft, murder, or snipers.

And this time around, he didn't see or feel the same stylized imagery with Griffith he'd experienced that Pistachio Festival morning. *No,* if Griffith was sending him any "messages" today, it was of a confused man, clearly bewildered by what was happening.

Silence descended on them, and after a couple moments, Hugh walked the few steps over to one of Griffith's work-in-progress creations clamped to a workbench almost in the middle of the spacious room. Subliminally, he noticed the background motor noise had gone away.

Hugh said casually, "You're still making bird feeders I see." His body screamed to go home and collapse, yet something inside was simultaneously pulling him not only to find Melony's killer, but also to nab the local scrap metal thief. The picture still hung in his mind from the Community Center that morning of Cleo and Bob Thomas. A nice couple, with nice friends. *Then there's a sharpshooter out there taking cannon-like shots at Neil's head.* Exhausted or not, he needed to forge on. "You know, I bought one from you last November."

Griffith stopped, turned and stared at Hugh for a long moment before a smile spread across his face, turning what Hugh had seen as confusion and agitation, into pleasure. He nodded, and pointed his finger at Hugh. "I remember you." He looked around, then made a dismayed face. "Don't have one of them around now. But I remember, with the humming birds, right?"

"Yep." Hugh said, and smiled himself. Then his eye caught a feeder in the corner, and without thought, took the few remaining steps toward it. "My, that is nice." His eye had caught the base of another work-in-progress bird feeder with a large bird, wings beginning to spread, perched almost miraculously on its edge.

My, my, Hugh realized. *A wrought iron raven.*

Audrey hated landings the most. Looking down out her window, she guessed they were closing in on about five hundred feet or so—getting close to approach and touch down. Soon, she'd be standing on mother earth again. *At last.* Fortunately, their CHP pilot was making a courtesy landing at Barstow-Daggett airport for her and Ted before heading back to their CHP home base hanger at Apple Valley Airport. A positive way to look at this flight—it wasn't as long as it could have been.

The terrain she saw out her tiny window was tan, tan, tan—with splotches of a variety of dull-green Mojave plant varieties. It was very bright, glaring almost; she'd even expected to see heat rising like in summer, but didn't. Her heart was a desert-heart, but even she sometimes despaired at winter's very limited and dull desert-pallet. Which brought her thoughts back for the millionth time this morning, to Melony. Oh how her deputy had loved the desert, seen beauty in almost every aspect of its landscape—in all seasons.

Audrey quickly banished the emotional lump in her throat, a lump she'd fought all morning. *Sorrow, grief, even guilt.* She certainly didn't want to think about Melony anymore—envision her lifeless body splayed first on asphalt, then wrapped in sheets—cold and alone on a table in the "tombs." She shivered involuntarily and wondered if Sally

107

Meliano, Neil's "lady friend," was involved in Melony's autopsy? Maybe she'd even met Melony, eaten Thai food with her like she and Della had.

How awful. Covering her mouth with her hand, she took a surreptitious slow and deep breath, hoping Ted wouldn't notice. She needed to get her emotions under control.

Though Audrey was apprehensive about touching ground in once piece, thinking about Melony was not preferable to facing up to her fears in the world of the living — her flying hell. Focusing back on herself, she noticed her heart was racing and her stomach jumping erratically. She almost brought her hand to her chest in an archaic and archetypical feminine-like gesture she wouldn't have wanted Ted, or the pilot to see. *Good grief.* Hopefully she wasn't also perspiring — another giveaway to her fear.

Though not succumbing to Victorian "vapors," she did bring her right hand up to her cheek and found her skin hot and clammy. She stole a quick glance at Ted before returning her gaze to what seemed like too rapidly approaching *terra firma.* She saw her brother wasn't looking out his window and his face was expressionless. *No,* more like stoic. Fear, or Melony's murder getting to him too? Since he'd never mentioned a "fear of flying" phobia, she guessed Melony's murder was affecting him harder than she'd realized. They hadn't talked much this morning, and in the airplane, it was almost impossible.

Rociana. Melony's death was most horrible, but piled on top of that loss was the quite plausible possibility Rociana was THK's intended victim. She wondered if her brother might love the pretty and competent CHP officer? He hadn't told her so, and he could be a very private person when he chose to be. But the unavoidable truth was Melony's murder

108

was not only a sad tragedy, but the radiating effects of her death were clearly awful for everyone.

Audrey had to pull away from looking at the rapidly approaching runway, focusing straight ahead at the back of the pilot's head instead. *Stay calm, stay calm.*

She tried going over the day's events to occupy her mind for the next few moments until they touched down. At least they'd gotten a smidgen of new information this morning—no paper reports—but a verbal briefing to everyone gathered in the auditorium. Evidently, all the coroner's office personnel and Riverside forensics folks were working their butts off. Sally flitted through her mind again. Surely, she *must* have declined the autopsy duty herself, assigned it to someone else.

Then we heard about the shooting last night. She even remembered the CHP officer's name who was in the hospital. *Gideon Will.* "He was still alive," she and Ted had been told by an officer before takeoff. *Barely.*

Last night Gideon had been shot with a handgun, but Melony was taken down by a shotgun blast to her midsection—several vital organs immediately hit. And trying as hard as she could not to, Audrey again saw Melony lying on pavement, and this time, she had an even harder time forcing the picture away. She prayed Melony had died instantly, no waiting painfully in semi-consciousness between life and the hereafter.

None of them were there with Melony Sunday night, like Collin Boyle was with Gideon. *None of them* knew what her last seconds of life had been like. Her deputy had been alone, and for a second, Audrey came the closest she'd been to losing it—barely keeping from releasing a sob into the confines of their little Cessna.

She felt and heard wheels hitting runway. *Almost over.*

109

Also at the meeting, the Assistant Commissioner for Field Operations had been direct. The message—we're a family and we need your help. But everyone knew that already, and everyone also knew by now there was not only an APB out, but a Blue Alert. Everyone wanted THK. New, was a very vague description, but a description nonetheless of the bastard. There was also the detailed allegation he was responsible for four known deaths, all police professionals of some kind. Three Highway Patrol, and then Melony, a Sheriff's Department deputy. All the murders occurred on interstate sections of Route 66 from Chicago to California. They also knew what kind of shotgun THK used, knew his car was a dark sedan, and that he was agile and a good shot. The handgun was new. CHP officers had stayed for a second meeting.

She and Ted actually talked a little about THK in Sacramento, but there'd been so much going on, a personal chitchat regarding his feelings hadn't materialized. And oddly, they spent most of this flight in silent contemplation. Now, as they sat on a bench seat behind the pilot and co-pilot, they still weren't talking. She couldn't, too scared.

Audrey reached out and took Ted's hand, causing him to look at her. She thought he had to force a smile—but smile he did. In that instant, Audrey realized her brother was also afraid of flying.

Oh, Ted. She squeezed his hand tightly for increased fortitude—both hers and his. She looked back out her window. Their Cessna had almost come to a stop, and the emotion and accompanying thought, *I don't have a good feeling about all this,* presented itself out of the blue. Audrey wasn't thinking about their Cessna landing. No, that was finally ending. She was remembering the rushed call she received right before take-off. Two attacks on Neil. *Craziness everywhere.* Hopefully Hugh could fill her in. Someone trying to murder her other deputy was not something she could tolerate, and she almost cursed out loud.

Well, she'd thought it earlier, but now, her resolve was clear and firm. She declared all out war on this man, or men, who had taken Melony's life and was now trying to kill her remaining deputy. THK's days were numbered—and she was going to be the one to take-him-down.

I need to talk to Hugh. She may have been lost in her own thoughts most of the morning, but she was not living on a desert island, and talking to and seeing Hugh would be living, breathing proof of that.

Ted still hadn't come to terms with the desert; but he thought he was beginning to feel more comfortable in his Southern California FBI environs. At first, over a year ago now, he also wasn't sure he liked the work. Back east he'd mainly worked robberies, jewelry heists and such, often by himself or on a very small taskforce. But out here on the West Coast, he was slowly coming to terms with different faces of criminality prevalent in the area, such as drug and gang issues; he was also beginning to accept the interdepartmental coordination required working drug and gang sweeps. It helped he liked his co-workers. Hadn't been able to say that everywhere.

All that being said, during this trip to Sacramento, he found himself spending most of his flying time revisiting his attitude on both fronts—the desert and work. On the very personal level, winter in the desert was gloomy and his personal life was becoming more *personal.* He couldn't forget his morning shower, his realization about Rociana.

Falling in love had not been on his short-term agenda.

111

He did spend some flying time thinking about his recent actions. One item in particular—his indiscretion this morning. *Ha.* More like illegal activity. *So hypocritical on my part.* Ted deplored fellow brethren taking advantage of their positions; now, he'd succumbed. Justifying his actions by telling himself it was to help Rociana. *Ha,* again. Ted fought back a self-berating sigh. He didn't want his sister to know what was going on in his mind. Never had.

Yep, ethics notwithstanding, truth was, as soon as they'd arrived at CHP Headquarters after leaving the hanger at Jacqueline Cochran Regional Airport, he'd hunted down his college roommate, Ty Redlin. *Amazing,* they were still connected. Fortunately, they were both now on the West Coast and had met a couple times in San Luis Obispo for lunch.

Earlier today in Sacramento, Ty committed to complete the search Ted requested without his name, ID, or FBI affiliation being involved. He promised to go through DMV, vehicular, arrest, and firearm registrations in two states. Anything else, he needed a warrant. *At least I still have limits.* Even though "Love" had clearly not only made him a fool, but also unethical.

He forced himself to look out his window for a few moments. The pilot was dropping altitude, preparing for landing, and the subtle tans and greens, the modest hills, the endless expanses of openness, for the first time impressed him with an unusual beauty. What he'd thought as uninteresting at a minimum, had morphed. *Another effect of love?* Indeed, Barstow-Daggett airport wasn't in what he considered a spectacular desert scenery area, but this afternoon, there was something comforting about it. Maybe because it was winter in early afternoon light, not summer Hades-hot yet.

He pulled his gaze from outside, deciding on a straight ahead focus, and though he didn't want to look directly at his sister, Ted thought Audrey might be doing the same. They would be back on land very soon, and he would be extremely happy when that moment arrived. He forced a normal inhale and exhale, making sure he wasn't holding his breath.

He thought he could feel ground heat actually rising all the way up to their little plane. But it was winter, he reminded himself. No, that was not heat, more probably fear was playing tricks on him, his nerves heating him up. *What a pansy.* He knew nothing about the physics involved, but certainly knew he was being ridiculous—*but damnit*—he hated flying. Landing in particular.

Pride kept Ted from admitting his fear to Audrey, and he figured this was not the time to publically claim this shortcoming. Special Agents had to fly all the time—he should have overcome this silliness a long time ago. *Funny I admitted my fear to Hugh yesterday.*

He forced another look out his door window and saw desert terrain now washed in almost blinding sunlight, and seemingly rising up to meet him. They were heading south-easterly, and pilot and co-pilot were wearing heavy-duty wrap-around sunglasses. *They can see fine,* he scolded himself. And *terra firma* was close. *No need to worry.*

If he could, he'd sigh, release his nervousness. But guessing Audrey's discomfort level was equally high, he wanted to remain unemotional for her. Hopefully, his facial expression was not revealing his fear. In his opinion, small propeller planes were large tin cans with wings, motor, and gas tanks. A fellow agent who once worked as a Boeing engineer had patiently explained—*more than once*—why planes were statistically the safest way to travel.

Phobias however, could not be rationalized away, and he was glad Audrey was holding his hand—tightly actually—as touchdown became imminent. By reassuring her, he was reassuring himself. He closed his eyes for a second and let his mind go free, and in that little snatch of time, Ted found

113

himself reliving his earlier conversation with Rociana. They'd finally talked in the hall before the all-agency briefing, and she admitted avoiding his calls. Stating quite candidly Melony's death had thrown her for a loop.

"It could have been me, Ted," she said, almost as a whisper. "*Should* have been. It was my call, you know."

At the time he hadn't known what to say, how to comfort her. He'd wanted to take her in his arms; but of course they couldn't do that then, and especially not there. "It's not your fault," he finally mumbled. "You were on your way."

"She was being kind—" Rociana's voice caught, but she recovered quickly. "Not that I think her murder was personal."

He'd thought that an odd disclaimer, but knew she wasn't thinking coherently yet. However, maybe was she inadvertently voicing support for his crazy inkling? "So far, there hasn't been a connection made between any officers, right?"

She'd shaken her head, and handed him a small handwritten piece of paper. He'd only read their names once then, but in the course of rereading all day, they became indelibly etched in his brain.

Now as he held his breath, still waiting to feel airplane wheels touching runway tarmac, Ted brought their names forward again, back into his mind's eye, making them real people. ISP Trooper Marjorie Thomas, OSHP Trooper Tamara Lions, Arizona HPD Officer Marsha McBride, out of Holbrook District 3—a place he'd visited. *Then Melony.* All State Patrol, except for Melony. Were these important people to THK, gender, and police department? *There was no way THK could know who would arrive.* Or was there?

He couldn't pull his mind back from Rociana this morning, from picturing her face. She'd looked so distraught, so sad. *And something else* had been there, but he couldn't yet articulate what. His instincts, as poor as he thought they were when it came to women, told him Rociana was holding something back. *Another man* in all likelihood. Certainly would be par for the course for him.

He felt the bump as landing gear wheels touched runway, and he sighed softly with relief. *FBI agents don't hold hands and sigh.* Even if it is with his sister. Yet, he'd just done both.

Out of the blue, for some inexplicable reason, he wanted to talk to Hugh. *We aren't that good of friends, now are we?* Truth be told, the man remained an enigma, a person he thought still driven by demons he was yet to recognize. *He is likable, though.* But definitely not similar to any of the other friends he'd made throughout his life. Yes, Hubert James Champion III was an odd sort. But, no man was an island, even if he'd isolated himself out in the middle of the Mojave.

He still wanted to talk to him. *Odd, that.*

Also odd, Ted suddenly realized, he'd barely said a word the whole trip. Just thinking. And neither had Audrey. He gave her hand a final little squeeze. They were quite different, but in some ways, birds-of-the-feather. He smiled slightly, emotionally remembering a childhood shared.

Then quite suddenly, from a completely different direction, he asked himself, *why in the hell was somebody trying to kill Neil?* It couldn't be THK, that just didn't make any sense. But another explanation just might make sense and fit with the inkling he had about Rociana. He'd have to think on that a little more.

As always, on every landing he'd experienced, his whole body was immediately filled with an all encompassing desire to jump out of the plane and kiss the ground. He never had, but it sure didn't stop Special Agent Ted Fletcher from wishing he could.

115

*　*　*　*　*

Collin Boyle was told by his lieutenant he'd probably
saved Officer Will's life last night. He didn't know about that,
but he sure was glad Gid had made it.

Gideon's hospital room, a room he'd initially only
found by following a blue colored stripe on the floor, had that
horrible hospital-disinfectant smell that made him want to
puke. Nonetheless, he was so glad to see Gid lying there in
bed still alive, he was able to choke down his nausea.

He thought the tubes that seemed to be everywhere
were unusually large, while the vital-sign piece of hospital
equipment monitoring Gideon's condition seemed
inordinately small to handle the task at hand. Collin hated
hospitals and knew very little about things medical. But he did
know, regardless of tube or equipment size, no scary beeps
had gone off, and every time the nurse had done a machinery
check, she'd smiled at him reassuringly. Most importantly,
Gideon was out of ICU, but still under watchful eyes in
Critical Isolation. One tiny step closer to making it.

Collin was off duty, out of uniform, and had spent the
last couple hours either sitting in a hard-backed wooden chair
against the wall, *or* making the occasional quick trip to the
bathroom, *or* grabbing a cup of horrible coffee from a vending
machine down the hall—which in turn caused him to again
make a trip to the bathroom. The rest of the time he was with
Gideon. Watching, and waiting.

Several other officers had come and gone, and he'd
been told Gideon's parents were driving over from
Albuquerque. A full day's drive, but oddly no longer than
going through airport waits and flying into Ontario or LAX,
then driving out to the High Desert.

Collin wasn't sure what he was waiting for. But when
Gideon raised his head an inch or so, opened his eyes, landed

116

him in what looked like his-line-of-sight, he bolted up out of his chair and rushed over to his fellow officer. He wanted to grab his hand, but stopped short. "Gid," he said.

Gideon smiled and answered, "Glad you stayed." His voice was rough, hardly audible or understandable. "THK..."

Collin waited, oblivious he was holding his breath.

"THK. New MO."

Again, Collin needed to wait.

"White Toyota. Hand gun. S&W maybe. BOLO." He reached out in an attempt to grab Collin's hand, but he clearly didn't have the strength and dropped his hand on the bed. Gideon's eyes closed.

"Gid, Gid," Collin said leaning in closer to Gideon's mouth. But his friend had fallen back into unconsciousness. A quick look at his vitals on the monitor didn't show any aberrations Collin knew about, and no nurses came running down the hall like in the TV shows. Gid had just fallen back asleep. A healing one he hoped.

He found his cell in his jacket pocket.

Fighting the urge to drop in on Hugh at Joey's after landing, Ted instead drove to his *new* favorite spot to continue thinking. *New* in that before transferring to Southern California, wherever he'd been assigned, Ted eventually developed a "favorite spot." A place where he could park, sit unnoticed and unbothered by the world. Even in the city. A place to think. Even on a day like today where it seemed like he'd done nothing but think.

Outside his SUV he could see dust-devils dancing along the ground. *Dust devils, always dust devils.* He glanced quickly at his dashboard to check his outside ventilation was closed off.

117

In the early days of his career, his favorite spots were places to grab a smoke unnoticed, even kick back a couple shots. He'd quit smoking at least ten years earlier, and never drank on the job anymore—but the need to get away continued to pull at him. Primeval in its source? He certainly thought so.

Remembering back-then as he sat enjoying the quiet and solitude of his SUV's interior, Ted smiled to himself and at what he now called his smoking stupidity. The humor was caused by his past hubris and delusional perspective that no one knew he smoked. *Of course they did.* If nothing else, the permeating smell in his clothes was probably enough to announce his addiction to anyone who cared to pay attention.

He knew he wasn't an overly introspective and soul-searching type like Champion, but Ted wondered what in his current life he might also be clueless about. *Or want to ignore.* For example, where were his true feelings about Rociana going to lead? And was he reading correctly what *she* felt for him?

Okay, he did love her, and certainly wanted to *protect* her—one of his first instincts in life it seemed—protecting those who couldn't protect themselves. A main reason why he was an agent. *Protect and serve.* For a millisecond, Paul Hovsepian's gentle face flashed across his mind's eye. Dead now, killed in a jewelry heist back east, but Hugh had helped bring those bastards to justice. Maybe that was the affinity he felt with the man. *I owe him.*

Ted ran his hand along the long ridge of his Suburban's sleek, digitized, and straightforward dashboard, and exorcised those old painful memories from his current thoughts. There'd be plenty of time for that in those early morning hours—*hours* that Hugh had confided in a rare moment his shrink called the human body's twilight zone.

118

To help move his thoughts on, Ted took in and exhaled a long deep breath, trying to let the horizon wash over and mellow him. He wasn't the type to go tromping around the landscape—*touchy feely* nature stuff he called it. No, he was wonderfully content to sit in the comfort of his loaded and super quiet FBI issued Suburban and take in his latest "special place" as an observer. Not a co-participant with nature—but he certainly could be appreciative of nature's effects.

"Nice," he said aloud and startled himself. He'd been in "think" not "talk" mode for so long today, the sound of his own voice hit Ted as an intrusion into his conversation with himself. "Jeez." He spoke even louder, wanting to reaffirm his status as a speaking human being. "I'm becoming as crazy as Champion." He laughed lightly.

His new Mojave special spot was simultaneously close to Joey's, and very far away. He'd found out after several long drives down seemingly endless "short" dirt roads the desert was like that. He was off Yermo Road, east of Harvard Road before it joined I-15—somewhere near the Mojave riverbed with views of both the Cady mountains and Cave Mountain—then around the back of one hill, and halfway up another.

From what he could tell, the "road" had only been used by an intrepid homesteader many years earlier. But that ingress claim was clearly long abandoned; it was now barely more than a motorcycle track. All that remained of the house itself was an eight by ten foundation, remnants of two corner posts, and two rows of what had been a fireplace. Iconic and lonely monuments to humanity subsequently moved on.

"Probably someone's dream turned to dust," he again said aloud, his voice this time firmer, more sure, and seeming to reverberate around the cavernous quiet of his SUV. He was voicing a thought he'd had more than once, gazing at more than one set of Mojave ruins. *The Mojave, a good place to start a life.* His smile turned to a sigh. Or—a place to end a life—on purpose. His FBI mind quickly moved to the "desert cold-case" tales he'd heard about at headquarters. Several bodies were suspected of being buried in the Mojave. *Who would ever find them?*

Unbidden, and just for a moment, his own former cold-cases insinuated themselves into his reverie. All unpleasant memories, memories of the ones that got away, the ones that never paid for their crimes. The victims who never received justice. Cases still in VICAP, or local data bases around the country—unsolved. But for the officers concerned, not forgotten.

He wondered how many of those cases would be solved by exhuming the whole darned Mojave Desert? *So many secrets out here.* He shook his head, exorcising memories, recriminations, and what he considered silly thoughts.

In front of Ted lay a rolling moderate vista of hills, rather sharp peaked and inconsistent in their arrangement. There was growth, but not lush. A landscape, he speculated, experienced from his unique "favorite spot" perspective by very few humans before him—if any. It gave Ted an odd feeling of pleasure to be one of those few.

As he expected, the peace brought by sitting quietly in his favorite spot brought his thoughts—and emotions—back around to Rociana Bustamante de Reyes. *Yes,* he did love her. But he would not tell her. *Not yet.*

This afternoon, Murphy weighed heavily on Della's mind. Her duty to her cousin would call—soon. First though, before unpleasant reality demanded her attention, she would take a few moments to herself on her deck, with her best friend Jazz.

Strangely in the desert scheme of things, there usually weren't any pesky flies driving her crazy on this side of her house, and the panorama from her west-facing deck was one of Della's favorite viewpoints. She liked the thought of looking down across Route 66, imagining the hopes and dreams of the many who made the journey before her. She especially liked taking in the world from her deck in winter when the sun started its descent early in the afternoon. She liked how it hung on the southern horizon, seemed like the more muted sunset colors were also more varied, more multifaceted. And at this point in her life, she was comfortable with being alone, mostly only listening to her own thoughts, her only audience, Jasmine.

Indeed, from Della's elevated location along National Trails before it rolled into Victorville, she'd come to think of Jazz and herself as living on a Mojave desert island of sorts, with the occasional "shipwrecked" visitor like her cousin, Hugh.

This afternoon, she'd ensconced herself outside in a deck chair, bundled in a fleece-lined hoodie and tucked herself underneath a deep-pile, multi-colored throw. On the side table next to her, golden-crème colored French Vanilla-bean ice cream was piled high in half of a generously sized and pre-chilled soup bowl—while extra dark triple-chocolate partnered in the bowl's other half. This was not a "casual" dessert. *No*, Della called this treat her "half and half," and considered the vanilla and chocolate combination the ultimate in dessert pleasures. Nothing fancy, just delicious. And it didn't make any difference it was winter. By her way of thinking, ice cream was welcome year round.

Della took a modest spoonful, slowly savoring the complementing and contrasting flavors. She wanted a few dedicated moments of culinary pleasure to think—and plan. Her cousin Murphy, Hugh's sister, was about to put her in a bind she not only dreaded, but feared mightily. *Like* her ice cream, Hugh and Murphy were quite different; but *unlike* her ice cream—definitely not enjoyable when in the same dish. Murphy might be the CEO of some hot-shot Wall Street firm, but in Della's mind, oblivious to some items of common sense—and in her least charitable moments, she thought Murphy a mean person.

Intellectually bemused, she indulged herself and carried her analogy even farther. Here she was, enjoying a beautiful, albeit chilly afternoon and her luscious ice cream— while at the same time, plagued with uneasy misgivings for what the afternoon and eventual evening held. *The vanilla and chocolate of life?* She almost laughed aloud at her forced comparison. She did smile.

Then the phone rang. A portable landline handset in her pocket.

Her smile morphed into an audible sigh, but Jazz didn't bother to look up. She had given her canine companion two dog biscuits and a chew-stick as guilty over-compensation for not being able to share dairy and chocolate with her. For the time being, Jazz was foregoing the immediate pleasure on biscuits, for the more lengthy experience of gnawing on rawhide.

Della let the phone ring for several annoying more rings—trying to savor another spoonful of chocolate and vanilla before having to face the inevitable.

"I should have muted the ringer and let everything go to the machine," she bemoaned to Jazz.

After licking the last touch of sweetness and flavor from her lips, she placed her spoon on the deck table next to her Adirondack chair, a chair, she knew was almost identical to the one on Hugh's deck. Begrudgingly, she pulled the receiver out of her jacket pocket.

"Oh good," Murphy said from somewhere across the miles. New York still? Some hub on the way? Her tone, Della thought, expressing her habitual irritation.

"Hi, Murphy." Della forced her voice to remain calm, trying not to let her visceral distaste for Hugh's sister rise to the surface and spoil her ice cream moments. "Is there a problem?"

"Of course, there's a problem. There's always a problem flying these days."

Della felt her jaw tightening. "How true."

"My connecting flight in Houston is delayed. I'm sitting in the airport."

"Oh, no." Is Murphy actually worried about me sitting at Ontario waiting? She felt a pang of guilt. *Murphy was thinking about me.*

"Wanted to make sure you'd wait for me, and not go home." Murphy sighed so heavily, Della pulled the receiver back from her ear in reaction. Murphy continued, "Doubt I could get a taxi or limo to take me to that..." she hesitated then finished in a more diplomatic tone, "to your area."

"I'll be there," Della reassured her in a level and measured tone.

"See you then." With that, Murphy disconnected abruptly.

Della looked over at her ice cream dish. A little had melted and morphed into a discolored and unappetizing puddle in the middle of her bowl.

She wasn't scheduled to pick up Murphy until seven — plenty of time to get to Ontario. Murphy was probably forgetting the time changes. Indeed, it would be a long day for Murphy—with no direct flights, and the time change. She needed to put on a "happy face." Prepare herself for Murphy. But the issue of her Aunt and Uncle was so distasteful, compounded by having to deal with Murphy's personality.

"Ugh," she allowed, while trying to salvage some solid clumps of ice cream.

Her desert island was about to be befouled, and she couldn't stop it.

"To Melony," Audrey led their toast raising her coffee cup.

"To Melony," Ted and Neil chorused almost simultaneously. Ted had a Coke can, and Neil a cup of coffee.

Hugh was last with his can of soda, "To Melony," he said, and an unexpected catch in his voice surprised him. Late afternoon had caught Hugh by surprise, and by the time he joined Audrey, Ted, and Neil in her office, it had already been the longest stretch of hell—with no discernible sleep. *Not since those early days after Lewis's murder.*

Indeed, Sunday night had been awful, then last night with the attempted theft and sniper piled on top of grief. Now after this morning at Griffith's house, Hugh's mind and body were in overload. *I still haven't slept since Monday night.*

Gabe finally returned him home after talking to Griffith and Baddon. After checking his gone fishing sign was hanging on Joey's front door and gone across the deck to his doublewide, Hugh managed to stumble through feeding Hobo and Black-Jack. When he was finally about to strip and fall into bed, Neil called. Then Audrey called. And finally, Ted.

He knew he'd driven himself to Yermo in response to their calls, but couldn't actually remember the deed itself. Now in her office as summoned, slumped in one of her criminally-hard wooden chairs, he yawned, then took a deep long breath. Oxygen was needed to get his brain back in gear.

After their toast, Audrey started talking, Neil and Ted seemed to be listening intently, but Hugh felt numb. He was trying to absorb, *understand* if that was possible. But it felt like midnight in more ways than one. He squinted, tried to focus his eyes to focus his mind. The three of them also looked beat, worn out, worn down. *I must look even worse.*

Audrey's words of concern penetrated his consciousness, "You look awful, Hugh."

What can I say?

"Does one of us need to drive you home?" she asked.

"Drive *me* home?" Hugh laughed, probably louder than appropriate. "Should I yank the mirror off the wall in the bathroom so you all can see how you look?" For some reason, he couldn't seem to stop laughing—not over the top, but so inappropriate given recent events." *Too tired.* "Sorry," he tried to apologize through a smile he just couldn't make disappear.

Instead of criticizing, Ted also smiled and said, "Since I've come to town, it has been crazy around here." His smiled broadened. "Especially for a podunk area..." He brought his hand to his mouth and said, "Oops," in a juvenile and comical manner.

Neil picked up Ted's thought-thread. "All this gunfire action we've been involved in—you, me, and Hugh shot at on the side of the road in Hesperia, me hit and in a coma in the hospital," he said, and shook his head. "Hugh shooting that Arnie Bellows guy, Audrey shooting Toby Portson, crazy movie people at the office with loaded ammunition—" Neil cut himself off, shook his head even more vigorously than before, and also started a smile. As incongruous as it appeared, Neil was still smiling when he added, "And now Melony is killed, I'm shot at twice—the second time Baddon and Griffith also almost taken out." By the end he was laughing outright.

Hugh said, through his own continued laughter, "It's supposed to be peaceful out here."

125

Audrey covered her mouth and said, "Don't forget when Hugh and I were shot at on the side of the road." She dropped her hand, evidently no longer able to contain or hide her amusement.

Of course Hugh knew what it was. *Grief.* Communal grief. Still, he wished he could stop. He'd never gone to Chicago-style wakes because of the boozy party-like atmosphere. This was worse.

"You were in the hospital too," Audrey said. Laughter caused her arm to wobble as she pointed at Hugh like she was accusing a fifth-grader of pulling her pigtails. "We thought you were going to die, too."

Then as suddenly as it had started, silence immediately engulfed Audrey's office. A switch had been flipped—somewhere.

Hugh watched, now instantly somber, and with a surprising amount of affection, as Audrey leaned back in her chair and let her head drop back for a few seconds. When she sat back up straight, she reached down to her bottom drawer and said. "I believe this is an unofficial wake for our dear departed, Melony."

Hugh dared not look at Neil or Ted, didn't want to see their grief. Instead he kept his eyes on Audrey and watched as she brought forth from its hidey-hole, a bottle of what he immediately recognized as Jameson Pot Still Irish Whiskey. The same whiskey his father drank. *Good stuff.* She had finally poured Ernie Stapleton's rot-gut down the drain. The former Sheriff's drink of choice would definitely not be missed.

After the whiskey, four glasses—real shot glasses—appeared from the depths of that same drawer.

Well, he thought, *maybe not a Chicago style wake.* But yes, on this winter day, and as tired as he was—he would mourn Melony in the second-floor back office of the Mojave County Sheriff's Department in Yermo, drinking booze in the ebbing of the afternoon—in the company of three people he was beginning to consider friends.

After quite a few long moments, Audrey asked, "Hugh, have you heard about Gideon Will?"

He shook his head, and it felt like his brain rattled. "Who's he?"

In the end, after he'd been told about the CHP officer shot last night, and after a thorough inspection and once over by his three law enforcement friends, Hugh was allowed to drive himself home.

It wasn't a long drive, and initially uneventful. However, on the dark isolated stretch of Yermo Road around Minneola Road, Hugh had the first inkling into the character of a man he was certain was involved with the scrap metal thievery. A breakthrough.

Funny, he thought, *when and how realizations come.*

Then on the Melony front, it hit him how heavily THK's serial rampage was weighing on him and his friends. Each impacted in their individual ways; all their little "desert islands" hit and battered by the same storm. He figured today had been a day of reflection for all of them—each caught up in their own thoughts, regrets, and desires.

Once rested though, he—*they*—needed to do *something*. It was not yet clear what that *something* was, but somewhere, underneath, over, and around Melony's murder, unpleasant strings were being pulled.

And on a completely different front, he feared that for him, part of the crap bouncing around in his head and laying-in-wait was personal. He couldn't yet imagine what or how. He shivered slightly—and on impulse he pulled over on the side of the road and parked for a moment. *Isn't this the same stretch I was hit with a terrible bout of the trembles?* Only six months ago. Hugh wasn't sure, but fancied it was.

In response to a second impulse, he got out, and leaned backwards against his car door, letting his head drop back, his view, a black star-sprinkled sky above. "Mojave" skies he whispered, and thought there must be a song in there for the musically inclined.

Neil never expected to be shot at like he was Sunday night, and then again this morning. Sure he was a deputy and theoretically always in the line of fire, but being a sniper's target was not run of the mill for most cops. That shootout awhile back near Hesperia had been bad enough. Back then, during what he called "The Turner Jackson Incident," it was more like in the line-of-duty. *But this?* A sniper thing was different—he was being "hunted." Personal. Involuntarily Neil shivered while reminding himself not to let Sally hear concern in his voice.

"No, no, I'm fine," he assured her over his office phone while standing behind his desk. She'd just heard the news about Collin Boyle saving Gideon Will's life last night. "Good to have a partner like that." He couldn't help but think about Melony. How she'd died alone.

"Do you know Officer Boyle?" Sally asked.

"No, he's CHP. I'm Sheriff's department and our paths haven't crossed."

"They passed with Officer Bustamante." After a couple seconds she added, "I mean, maybe you liaisoned with him like you did with her."

Sally is jealous. He couldn't keep his voice neutral. "It was work only. I promise."

128

Her voice turned soft, apologetic. "I'm sorry to sound like such a shrew. It's just I'm looking in from the outside."

"Well," he needed to move past this topic, "never met him. Or Will."

Then out of the blue, Neil's brother popped in his head—his lay-about gambler brother. And how opposite people like Collin and himself were from Conrad. What a screw up his brother was. No way would Conrad ever put himself in danger for someone else, and no way would *he* ever be like Conrad. He hated thinking about him, and wondered why he was now.

Neil felt his chest rise, and he surreptitiously snuck in a deep breath before continuing his thought with Sally. "People like Collin," *and me*, "take our obligations seriously." He could almost feel Sally's adoration through the phone, and instead of being fearful for his life, Neil felt quite good.

Sally said, "I have to go," and quickly hung up. He knew her abruptness meant something at work had turned urgent. He sighed audibly.

After Hugh and Ted had headed out, he'd left Audrey to her work and walked down to his new office at the front of the second floor and found his phone was ringing. Sally. Now, after hanging up, he looked around his office for a moment. Slowly. He was *here* in this position, a place he wanted to be— even asked for it from Ernie. He should feel happier. *Fais attention à ce que tu demandes.* So true, you sure needed to be careful what you asked for.

Full darkness was moments away from enveloping the Mojave, leaving his office in an eerie half-light, with the only illumination entering from the hallway—where fluorescent panels cast a shadow-of-light through the doorway and across his desk. A winter-fresh evening breeze flowed in through his slightly open window. If he *had* to live in the desert, winter wasn't that bad, and for a fleeting few seconds, Neil actually felt in sync with the High Desert. A phenomena he seldom experienced.

Still, nice breeze or not, something was bothering him, and he wanted to figure out what. Since "The Turner Jackson Incident," when he'd recognized Malcolm "Mel" Tap as the dead jewel thief hanging in the overturned semi-truck, Neil's interest in actual detective-type police work had steadily grown.

Besides, his mentor Ernie had left, and it was silly to continue pursuing politics as his main goal—at least not with the same vigor as before. And truth be told, *et pour dire la vérité,* Sheriff Boyes treated him with more respect than his brother-in-law, "Honest Ernie" Staples, ever had.

He looked around his office again, and smiled, realizing his French was also coming back. Then Neil walked forward into the darkness steadily engulfing the front of his office and stood at Champion's favorite spot at the window— looking down into the world of Yermo. He could barely make out the outline of Audrey's loaner patrol car in the parking lot. The Sheriff's Department sign lights had switched on, but in the half-light didn't seem as effective as they should.

The memory of recognizing Mel when he was in a coma-like state, once again washed over him in a flood of joy just like six months earlier. It was a most wonderful experience. At that moment back then, everything had been so complete. He'd figured out who one of the jewel thieves was, and blurted it out to Champion.

It hadn't made any difference if Boyes and Champion would take credit—which they hadn't. Just knowing was enough. It was the first time he didn't even care about a promotion, or his political aspirations. And the best part of all, Sally Madison had come to see him. *And we're still dating.*

His heart jumped, surprising him—but Neil's smile broadened nonetheless, and he whispered her name out loud.

"Sally." It felt good. It had also felt good talking to her on the phone—sharing. *How can she possibly be jealous?* They were their own little island in the sea of the world's humanity. In that he'd almost been killed three times—earlier in the day Neil decided to call his mother and father in Palm Beach. He hadn't made the call yet, and tonight—in this moment—changed his mind. Sally was enough. The thought of just the two of them up against the world was oddly romantic. *I'm mellowing.*

But as Neil continued to gaze down into the Mojave Sheriff's Department parking lot, this morning's event circled back around into his consciousness—full force, and with vividness that wasn't there earlier. *Yes,* he'd seen something at Griffith and Baddon's place. Actually, more like he'd "felt" something. An emotion between Griffith and Baddon? *No,* more like from Baddon—directed toward Griffith.

And something else physical he'd seen. *It'll come,* he told himself. Just like six months ago. A coma hadn't stopped his mind from working, so a little thing liked being shot at—*twice*—wasn't going to stop him either.

Was it something on Griffith's workbench? *No,* more like something about the two men. And clarity arrived. It was Griffith's height—tall and thin, Gabe had said.

It took Rociana all afternoon into evening to get back to Southern California—even at interstate-cop-speed. Indeed, even though she *could* do ninety, traffic, safety, and clueless civilians made it darn difficult to speed. In theory interstate-cop-speed, ICS she called it, was a cool perk, but in reality seldom panned out as expected. Besides, letting the Southwestern sky lead her home, she wasn't in a particular hurry. Contrary to her impulse to speed, it was time well

131

needed and useful. Time she could spend thinking about her relationships, and what to tell, do, say—or act upon.

A time to emotionally face up to the fact she loved Ted Fletcher. The feeling had come as a surprise, sneaking up slowly, then jumping up out of nowhere and slamming into her heart. The love-bug bit her so suddenly and so sharply, she missed noticing the Mercedes-Benz enter Highway 99 traffic, then with abruptness and stealth, slip in behind her two cars back.

Maybe there is a happy ending in the cards for me after all, she half thought, half wished. An ending where she didn't end up a miserable old lady, with a thousand cats her only companions. Rociana knew all too well she'd been an island unto herself since the divorce. Living by herself, fending for herself. *Alone.* And she didn't like it, and in her heart wanted someone to love. That someone had appeared—and his name was Ted Fletcher.

Rociana was introspective enough about how her mind and emotions worked to know she needed to close unresolved past issues before attempting to embrace her future. She blew out a long stream of air before officially acknowledging and accepting the singular unpleasantness from her past. Roberto Reyes was back stalking her. She could feel it. He might officially have a residence in Puget Sound, but he was *here* alright, *here* in the High Desert. Maybe it was time for her to just kill the bastard before he killed her.

And for the countless time since Sunday night, the almost unbearable adjunct question reared its evil head. *Had Melony died in her place?*

Unconsciously she shivered, while intentionally wiggling in her seat. *No,* she wasn't ready to accept Roberto would want to kill her. *No,* it was THK who had snuffed out sweet Melony Dibbs's life.

*   *   *   *   *

For Hugh it was the longest of days. A day that would not end.

"Really sorry if we're disturbing you, Doctor Champion." The sad-faced man at Hugh's front door gave his wife standing next to him an anxious look before taking a deep breath and continuing. "But we need you. You being a psychiatrist and all."

He couldn't refuse entry to Melony's parents out at the gate, and now up close, it didn't take a psychologist to see Mrs. Dibb's eye sockets were swollen, or recognize the sadness overwhelming Mr. Dibb's face. *His whole body.* Out by the gate, looking through their car window hadn't told the whole story. Their overwhelmed expressions combined with their dejected postures raised an unexpected and huge lump of emotion in his throat—and for a second Hugh wanted to hug them both. Reticence and decorum held him back.

"Come in, Mr. and Mrs. Dibbs," Hugh mumbled. Then quickly added, "I don't go by Doctor." He didn't bother trying to explain the difference between a psychologist and a psychiatrist. *Doesn't make any difference anyway.* Their daughter was dead, and they thought he could help. Unfortunately, psychologist or not, Hugh didn't know what to do or say.

What he really wanted to do was step back, pretend they hadn't come honking at his gate and he'd gone out and let them in. Instead, he just wanted to retreat to his bedroom and curl up in a ball under the covers. Escape and end this horrible day through sleep. Nonetheless, and of course, he'd let them in his yard, then waited at his door patiently for the Dibbs couple to slowly get out of their car, traverse his deck, and reach his front door.

Now, he opened the door wider and motioned politely for the couple to come in. Hobo had watched the whole event

133

from an alert, but sympathetic sitting position as if he knew what this sad event was about.

The Dibbs looked older than Hugh would have guessed—*grief for sure has stooped their demeanor*. And to Hugh's eye, both were rather nondescript—medium height, thinning white hair, and age and weather matured skin. Still, elderly or not, they garnered a certain presence.

"I'm Margaret," Mrs. Dibbs said as she carefully stepped in and walked by Hugh. "And I'm, Oscar," Mr. Dibbs murmured in a dead-man-walking tone as he followed his wife, head down. "Thanks for coming out and letting us in."

Even Black-Jack seemed to realize this wasn't an occasion to be pesky and both critters quietly retired to favored spots while Hugh eventually settled the Dibbs on the sofa in his living room. Hugh chose to sit in Grandmother Todd's Victorian—"Grandfather" titled and sized—burgundy and dusty-rose upholstered armchair. He knew it's provenance, and remembered Ethel Todd every time he sat his butt in it. Even tonight. *Grandparents and parents—are not supposed to see their children go before them.*

Before seating himself, Hugh offered coffee, tea, Cokes, knowing refreshments were clearly the last thing on their minds, and accepted their refusal without fuss. He tried arranging an *"I'm here for you"* look on his face—not that he didn't genuinely want to help them. But it was an affectation he'd worked on in front of a mirror for hours in younger counseling days. He knew from clients and his own personal experiences, how much an inappropriate facial expression could unwittingly give away—in just a fleeting millisecond. The right look or body language could make the difference between building a bond, or creating irreversible alienation. In the past, effective masks were required tools-of-the-trade.

After a couple moments of silence and a few deep breaths by both husband and wife, Oscar finally began, "Are you parents still alive, Doctor...I mean Mr. Champion?"

Hugh nodded, and inexplicably felt himself warm. "Please, call me Hugh." He noted the slump of Oscar's shoulders simultaneously conveyed relief and uncomfortableness. He was a large man, still tall and broad despite the effects of age, with a deep voice which Hugh guessed would be stronger under different circumstances. Margaret was also tall, but thin, and tonight she sat looking overwhelmed by grief on the couch next to her husband— almost leaning on him. Even sitting, and in their current misery, their presence, though diminished, was still formidable.

Hugh guessed they were both in their seventies—and thought Melony must have been a late-in-life gift.

"You're not supposed to outlive your children," Oscar continued, mirroring Hugh's thought. His voice caught, and he looked away.

"We want you to find her killer." Margaret picked up her husband's thread, her voice surprisingly strong, *despite* her swollen and red eyes, *despite* the fact she was wringing her hands, *despite* her labored breathing, *despite* her clear need for support from her husband—*despite* her overall aura of grief.

Strong woman, Hugh thought. But he was mystified she thought he could help find Melony's killer. *Grasping for straws?* He averted his eyes a few seconds, trying to figure it out. *I'm supposed to be some kind of healer-detective?* Hugh cleared his throat, straightened his back, returned his gaze to Margaret, and aimed for his most professional voice—knowledgeable and comforting. The Dibbs needed to be dissuaded from the notion he could do anything special.

He said, "I know for sure the sheriff's department is doing everything they can to find Melony's murderer." *Yes, murderer.* "In fact, I believe law enforcement across the country are hunting this guy day and night." Maybe not all, but with the I-40 interstate connection, the hunt was certainly national in scope. *And after the shooting last night.*

Silence ensued for several more long moments before Margaret said, "You helped LoraLee Jackson." Then she stiffened and made piercing eye contact with Hugh. In a soft and knowing voice, she added, "And Marsha Portson."

It took all the will power he could muster not to physically react. "You and Marsha were—are—friends?"

"Yes."

"Good friends?" *Confiding friends?*

"Yes."

Surprising, given the circumstances, Hugh found himself wanting to smile. Of course Marsha needed to confide in someone. *Well,* so what if she knew Marsha had been Turner Jackson's killer and he hadn't turned her in. But how Margaret was logically connecting LoraLee and Marsha's circumstances with Melony's murder was another question.

Again, a long moment passed, one of those moments where you can hear the silence—then from somewhere on his property, Hugh couldn't tell if from front or back—but the super loud screech of *"Krawk, krawk,"* pierced the solemnity of his living room. A solitary raven, with solitary advice.

The Dibbs acted like they hadn't heard his raven harbinger, *or was it counselor this time?* She looked at her husband, and he nodded; which Hugh took as Oscar's indication Margaret should continue doing the talking.

After yet another deep breath, she said, "Marsha thinks you're a god." She actually smiled fleetingly. "We're not fools, Hugh. But we want...*need* your help."

"Grief is causing—"

"Please," she interrupted. "Let me get it out while I can."

Hugh clamped his lips tight and forced his empathy for Melony's parents into the background—right next to his aversion for getting involved. He gave a slight nod.

"Marsha had given up all hope." Her eyes found his again and were pleading for him to see into her mind. "She had given up on happiness, life, everything." Another deep breath followed by a slow stream of air. "You gave her hope, Hu gh. You gave her *hope. Hope* that her life could—*would*—be better." She paused, for a moment, as if she wanted to make sure her words, her emotions, were adequately transmitted to him. "And at the end, you gave her freedom." Her final words were barely audible. "Not just freedom from prosecution and all that surrounded that—but freedom of the heart, freedom of the soul." Then with a breath that bordered on being a sob, a single tear rolled down her cheek.

Without thinking about what he was doing or what was happening, Hugh got up, walked up to his living room picture window, and looked out into Tuesday night darkness. *Just two nights ago their daughter was alive.* What he saw was himself reflected back in the window glass—clear as a mirror image. Hugh did not like what he saw. Indeed, the reflection was of a beaten man, a retreating man—not a psychologist. Not a helper. *But I haven't been that for years now,* he rationalized.

Yet, Marsha had told Margaret he was a god. He laughed—but not hearing any sound or seeing the expression on his face change, he realized he was laughing inside. *Thank goodness.* He was still a mentally injured man, stronger than a year and a half ago, but still making his way on crutches—but not completely loony yet.

He did not think himself a coward, and the Dibbs had hit upon something at the core of his very being. Something he had to re-find, bring back to full life if he was to ever walk

137

whole again. *And something else?* Something he couldn't yet put his finger upon.

He tried to turn around, and speak to Margaret and Oscar, but he couldn't seem to make his body respond to his wishes.

Again, *"Krawk, krawk,"* from somewhere in the night.

Finally, Hugh was able to turn and face Melony's parents. "I will do whatever I can to help find who killed your daughter." He could hear the conviction and sincerity in his voice, and see the looks of relief on Margaret and Oscar's faces.

This is the longest of days. From *somewhere*, strength of *some kind* edged its way forward. Margaret and Oscar had come to him for help—and in the process, he fancied he'd helped himself.

Hugh looked down at his hands. No trembles.

Chapter Four

Wednesday morning

THK's night had been quiet. Another good "target" never materialized even though he'd monitored his scanners all night out of habit. Ludlow to Needles was a nice central stretch, easy driving east and west—mostly not too busy—but busy enough for him to get an initial handle on the CHP cops patrolling the area.

He decided not to pay any attention to Arizona—he'd stay in California this hunt. THK also decided this morning to change to daylight "hunting." Overnight preparation, then hunting at first light. His mission was just and right—no need to hurry, and no longer need to hide in the darkness of night.

It wasn't quite light yet, but he'd completed his breakfast at the diner, now all he had to do was to go looking for a "special" spot, monitor his scanners, wait, and at the right time, "break down" on the side of the road. But first, he had to make sure his target was righteous. In his mind, time spent on research was never wasted.

Yep, today would be great. Looking around, taking this section of the Mojave as he found it, making it his own. *Yep*, he liked Route 66, and this would be his little desert island hunting ground—the rest of the world be damned.

Yep, yep, yep.

He turned on the radio, and as if a sign he was indeed doing the work of the just, the first song was a tune he liked a lot. THK started to sing.

* * * * *

Hugh sat straight up in bed, determined, *and for once,* he thought, with a clear goal. However it happened and whatever the key ingredient, last night, seeing, talking to, and "feeling" Margaret and Oscar's pain had "put the final nail in the coffin," as his father was want to say. This coffin in question, was of the *I want to do something* variety.

First though, he needed to order his thoughts, clear out the emotional cobwebs so he could develop a reasoned and accomplishable plan of action. With that as his immediate goal, Hugh looked out his bedroom window and unconsciously shook his head, as if that act would bring order.

To his surprise, huge bolts of lightning were shooting through what should have been plain old pre-dawn semidarkness. The lightning impact was quite dramatic—the flashes of electrical energy were discharging in rapid succession, slashing through the horizon at an almost perpendicular angle from sky to land. Hugh had never seen anything like it before, even during the August monsoon his first summer—which supposedly wound its way up from Mexico, or was it up from Baja? *Doesn't matter.* The light display brought him to full consciousness quite quickly. Even though Tuesday had been the longest of days.

Where's the thunder? He hadn't heard any rumbling— but didn't know what that meant, except maybe the lightning must be quite a distance away; still, he thought a downpour was heading his way. One of his senses was warning him about impending moisture, though he wasn't sure which.

While Hugh's body was reacting viscerally to the show outside his window, his urge to figure out what was going on with THK and help bring him to justice also continued to build. *Yes,* he had woken up with purpose. An emotion he hadn't felt in a very long time.

On top of that, there were the additional pesky little items of the scrap metal thievery, why the heck Neil was being

140

shot at, and his nagging feeling of lingering psychological distress that needed to be cleared up. He had a murderer to outwit, thieves to apprehend, and a sharp shooter to take down. He laughed at his Superman-like resolve.

Regardless of not being a super hero, Melony, Neil, Margaret, and Oscar—all did deserve his full attention. Unfortunately, shaking his head had not made the puzzle bits and pieces fall neatly together. Real and forward-moving action was needed, and for the first time in years—*since Lewis Jenkins's death*—he actually felt up to dealing with current challenges.

"I'll be damned," he told Hobo who was already up and waiting. Evidently, he also hadn't missed Mother Nature's light show. "You better not," he added in a whimsical tone and looking directly into Hobo's questioning and eager eyes, "*ever* answer me back." Hugh laughed once more. *Again,* a new feeling—a new kind of lightheartedness?

His immediate intent was to cover all his "junk" the scrap metal thief had been after from possible incoming rain, then to walk his buddy to Poe's Condo. That was if the lightning didn't look too close—wouldn't think of putting his buddy in danger. *No thunder,* he noticed, must be still safe. Yet, he still "felt" rain. With his new determination and optimistic frame of mind, Hugh showered and dressed quickly.

Ready to face the world, and as he walked through the kitchen heading toward the back door, the phone rang. Curious as to who was calling so early, Hugh picked up the receiver. "Hello," he said, expecting to hear either Gabe or Audrey's voice. Hobo sat down and whined.

"Sorry to call so early." It was Rociana Bustamante. "I wanted to know if I could come by sometime today and talk to you?"

He was surprised. "Ah, sure."

141

She laughed lightly. "It's not something horrible." Then she sighed loud enough Hugh could hear it over the phone. "I'd like your opinion on something..." Her voice trailed off.

"No problem," Hugh said, while wondering *what the heck now?* He remembered it was poker-night. "Are you coming to poker tonight?"

"I forgot. So much happening."

"I know. But I'm thinking, maybe you could come by early, and we could talk before everyone else gets here?"

"Great." Even though he couldn't see her face, Hugh thought Rociana sounded relieved and grateful. "See you tonight," she concluded and his call went dead.

She had come to several poker games—by now a bi-weekly ritual—the first with Ted, then more on her own as a member of the "gang" in her own right, and Hugh was familiar with her direct and decisive mannerism. He smiled, re-envisioning her and Ted together, not knowing at the time they were "an item." *They make a good couple.*

Once finally out his backdoor, the lightning show looked more distant—but oddly, even more dramatic. He stopped in his tracts. All his building supplies that had been leaning against his bedroom wall were gone. *When, how?* His firewood was seemingly untouched.

Hugh cursed, almost stomped his foot like a child, then cursed again. What made it even worse, he knew Gabe was going to rub it in. Oddly though, before he could really get worked up about the thievery, Hugh noticed how clear and enticing the air felt and smelled. Air that told him a storm was coming.

"Hell with it." *Just material things.* Walking Hobo was more important at the moment. "I still think we can squeeze in a walk." He knew how ridiculous it was talking to his dog, and even more, asking Hobo questions. But their relationship

142

was going more and more that way—heading down the path, he thought, often frequented by sappy and indulgent pet owners. "What do you think, Hobo?" So be it, he *was* a sap when it came to his buddy. The energetic head motion Hobo responded with, Hugh took as a "Yes."

With Hobo at his side, they'd only made a couple hundred yards of progress along his fence line before Hugh found his mind returning to their "wake" in Audrey's office last night. A gathering of people that only a year plus ago were complete strangers. *Now, almost family.* He thought of John Donne, wondered at his familial conclusion, and murmured, "Not an island anymore."

Eventually, man and dog sat in the protection of Poe's Condo for a bit—Hugh's mind vacillating between catching Melony's killer and his stolen supplies. Indeed, he'd just purchased that new soldering torch set from Home Depot last week. He'd opted for the pricey one—now gone. He sighed, emotionally trying to let his building supplies and tools go. *Just junk,* he told himself again.

His internal clock said it was past time for dawn to break, but the eastern horizon remained dark and ominous. Lightning continued, and rolls of thunder were now also audible. He'd been so engrossed in his inner thoughts, it wasn't until he got up to walk back home, did he notice a significant wind laden with dampness had found them—and was building. He shivered, for with the wet wind, the temperature had dropped significantly. Hugh had put on his jacket, now he zipped it and told Hobo, "Let's make this fast."

I waited too long, he chastised himself.

Indeed, within several moments, what had been a building wind turned into shingle-shaking gusts—producing all around them ominous whirlwinds of sand. Rain followed. Large heavy drops at first, and in what seemed liked only seconds, morphing into sheets of rain like he hadn't seen since the Midwest.

"Thanks for meeting so early," Ty Redlin said, cradling a cup of tea brewed with teabags he'd brought along with him.

Ted thought Ty's tea smelled like burnt swamp grass, causing him to want to rub his nose and ask his friend why he was drinking that crap. Instead, he clasped his hands together and said, "No problem. I needed to come into the office to clean out some paperwork." He leaned forward across the table. "But I am surprised you were able to get something for me so soon. And I'm glad we could talk in person about this. Not on the phone."

Ty smiled knowingly. "The fewer electronic footprints, the better."

"I sure appreciate it." They were sitting across from each other at a two-person table in the break-room closest to the office Ted shared with another Special Agent in FBI LA headquarters. They were alone—nonetheless Ted felt like a pre-teen school boy sharing "girlie" cards and trying not to get caught. "On your way from Sacramento to San Diego you say? Long drive." Then Ted dropped his eyes for a second and said, "You know," he quickly looked back up, "I owe you one on this."

Yep, he'd asked Ty to do something unethical, maybe even illegal by some interpretations, no matter how far he pushed his rationalizations. And Ty had not only willingly done the research, but had also been quick at it. His friend needed to know he appreciated his support.

Ty laughed, the same easygoing laugh Ted remembered from undergraduate days. "You owe me *several*.

144

And big ones." He laughed lightly, "And I expect to collect—one day."

"When I least expect it, right?"

"Right." Ty leaned forward like Ted had and lowered his voice. "To tell you the truth, it was easy. Reyes was easy to find. Really hasn't been trying to hide anything."

Ted straightened and leaned back in his chair with an accompanying sigh. "You mean he's still in Tacoma." He couldn't keep the disappointment out of his voice. *I was so sure.*

"Not exactly." Ty smiled slyly. "What I mean is he's still doing all the resident kinda things, like DMV vehicle regs, paying his rent and utilities. But nobody's seen him in several months."

"Not going to work?"

"Took a voluntary layoff with a nice little severance package." Ty smiled. "Two pensions now, Marine for twenty-plus, now defense contractor for ten."

I'd thought him a little younger. Ted let his head drop back and stretched his neck. "He's here. Here in the High Desert." *Stalking my Rociana.*

"Can't tell you that with certainty." Ty pulled a crumbled piece of paper out of his stylish tan colored leather jacket pocket. "But," he said and handed the paper to Ted. "Here's everything I got. Including a plate number on a rental."

Always well dressed, Ted remembered. But the crumbled note-taking was something new. Not like the methodical Ty he'd known. His facial expression must have given away some of his thoughts, for Ty continued, "This is crumpled like trash on purpose. It's to remind you to either burn or shred."

"Leave nothing behind." Ted nodded once, then reached for the piece of notepad paper Ty was handing him. "A R. Reyes showed up on Irvine FasTrak® records."

145

"He got a ticket in Southern Cal?"

"Well not exactly." A self-satisfied looked spread across Ty's face—accompanied by knowingly raised eyebrows. "Technically, a rental car with those plates was cited."

Ted finished, "And you got to the rental agency via his driver's license number." Ted smiled and looked down at the paper. The car, make, and renter's hotel address were scribbled in ink. "Your penmanship hasn't improved."

They both laughed.

After Hugh dried Hobo off and changed clothes, he pressed a carafe of coffee, then collapsed in a chair at his kitchen table hugging a steaming mug of fresh brew.

He'd thought one of his ritualistic walks with his best friend would have cleared his head. Instead the micro-burst with its tornado-like winds had sent him mentally spiraling back into a place he thought he'd just climbed out of. It was like being on an emotional roller-coaster.

Over the last few months, Hugh found himself warming to the Mojave esthetic—especially when the sky was blue, and the air clear and calm. Occasionally he'd found explanation, inspiration, even spots of mental clarity from his broad panoramic views. The physicality of exercise—his daily walks with Hobo—he knew, was also part of it. Add to that the solitude, Hobo's companionship, the uncompromising desert expansiveness—and of course, the ravens. *My* ravens. This morning, however, with the theft, the downpour—he thought the edge of depression could be laying in wait.

Indeed, all of a sudden he was now having the darnedest time marshalling his thoughts into any kind of coherent pattern—much less develop theories he was hoping

146

for just minutes earlier. Hugh knew he wasn't Mensa-level smart, but he also didn't consider himself a complete dummy—particularly when it came to logical thinking. Wasn't that how he'd helped his patients—thinking clearly when they couldn't? Maybe his own craziness was now keeping him from putting the pieces together. It couldn't be just because it started to rain.

He got up slowly, went over, and stood for a couple minutes at his kitchen window—his mind vacillating between mental clarity and a vague feeling of disconnect. From nowhere, a memory flashed—Mrs. Steinberg, a client of his for awhile in Chicago. She was recovering from what at the time was called a "nervous breakdown." Not really a psychiatric term—but for Lilith, it meant she had been overcome with severe anxiety, and for a few weeks lost her ability to cope. If he remembered correctly, her own mortality had been a key ingredient in her collapse—and oddly enough in her recovery.

Looking down at Hobo sitting at his side in front of the sink, an inquisitive look in his canine eyes, Hugh explained out loud, "Well, I don't have time for a breakdown." If he was going to figure any of this out, getting his thoughts ordered was crucial.

And I owe it to Melony to try.

He looked down and saw his hands were tightly gripping the sink edge, then felt the accompanying tightness in his forearm muscles. He breathed deeply and forced his hands and arms to relax. Another memory came, but this was more like an apparition; his father and mother looked back at him in the reflection of his kitchen window. They smiled, and for several long seconds, Hugh felt a wave of heat encompass him—just like last night when Oscar and Margaret mentioned his parents. Then just as quickly, Hugh felt normal, the heat and his vision-like memory evaporated. What had he just experienced? *Fever?* First queasiness, then heat. Wanting an

147

explanation, he quickly accepted the supposition he was fighting a cold or flu.

A couple aspirins and mindless activity was needed. He didn't feel up to driving all the way down to Oro Grande and cruising his favorite section of 66. Besides, if he drove down that way, he probably should stop and see Della. No, he wasn't up to visiting his cousin. Not this morning.

Still, a stretch of mindless driving might be perfect. In fact—it felt like a little interior voice was pulling him to the open road. *The lure of Route 66, that must be it.* Just not Della's section.

He heard his stomach growl, and that additional impetus pushed him to a decision. Within minutes, and with surprising conviction, Hugh patted Hobo on the head, grabbed a jacket and his gun. In a few more minutes he wanted to be in his Altima heading south through Newberry Springs toward Route 66 and I-40.

With that goal in mind, he stopped for a moment to freshen Black-Jack's water dish and check he was okay. *Yep, asleep in the guest room rocker.* But before he could hit the road, the landline in his kitchen rang. He ignored it, just wanted to get going. He'd parked out back, but before he could get out the kitchen door, he heard Julian Bogard's unmistakable voice—cultured, well modulated, and kind—starting to leave a message on his phone.

He stopped and picked up the receiver. "Julian?"

"Hello, Hugh," Julian said. "Thought you might want to know how Marsha and LoraLee are doing."

Hugh was quick to answer, "I would," and felt himself smile—simultaneously at himself for using the word "would," and from pleasure at hearing LoraLee and Marsha's savior's voice. "I do," Hugh amended his response. *Not on the Upper East Side anymore.* Or living with a father who took pride in correcting his grammar. Everyday vernacular and present tense were just fine.

Last year when the Turner trouble all began, they'd first met in Audrey's office, and at the time, he'd guessed Julian to be in his mid-fifties. Hugh's smile broadened, remembering what had first caught his eye—the bald spot running straight down the middle of Julian's skull.

"LoraLee has a tutor," Julian said. "And she and Timothy have bonded better than I'd hoped."

Hugh was sure Julian's voice reflected pleasure and parental pride. "That's really good to hear." He waited a few seconds, then asked, "And Marsha, how is she handling New York?" He chuckled lightly. "Or should I ask, how is New York dealing with Marsha?"

"She's taken the Upper East Side by storm. *And* TriBeCa, from what Jefferson says."

"How are you capitalizing that?"

Julian paused a second. "Capitalizing?"

"Spelling. My father says it should be T-r-i-*B*-e-*C*-a." Hugh tried for a moment to remember the last time they'd had that discussion. A few years now. "I argue it's T-r-i-*b*-e-*c*-a." Hugh grunted, remembering their continuing disagreement on this minor point. "As if anyone really cares." Hugh's voice turned thoughtful. "I think I asked you before. But you've never met him, have you?"

Silence.

"Are you there, Julian?" *Maybe the line has dropped.*

Finally, Julian said, "Don't know what happened there. Seemed to have lost you for a moment." He changed the subject. "Are you still associating with that Sheriff?"

Associating? "Actually, there's been another murder," he answered, ignoring the fact Julian was asking a rather personal question; instead, he explained about Melony and THK.

149

"That's awful," Julian said. "Are you sure it's this Highway Killer psychopath? Not someone local?"

"Everyone seems to think so." Truth was, he wasn't sure—but he didn't yet know why.

They talked longer than Julian expected, and Hugh had sounded genuinely pleased he'd called. Without paying attention, Julian pressed the off button on his hand-receiver and replaced it in its cradle. He didn't do it correctly, and the receiver fell forward onto the surface of his massive desk.

There were no accoutrements on his desk's gleaming surface except for his antique styled but deceivingly modern telephone, and a leather Horchow desk blotter with woven-side-panels; its leather, like his desk, was also wax-polished. In the center of his blotter lay the pictures Hugh recently mailed to his mother, Eloise Todd Champion. The pictures were taken in Joey's back office. One was of a round-faced black and white schoolhouse clock on the wall above what Julian remembered was Hugh's "window" into Joey's. And he was pretty sure the clock had been a grand-opening present over a year ago from Eloise. It was made of cherry wood with a small pendulum, big Roman numerals, and ornate hands.

He had neatly laid out the snapshots in a rectangle—four in total—so he could see them all at one time. The moments, the memories, the pictures—and most importantly, the dilemma they represented was monumental.

Julian's study in the back of his Upper East Side Manhattan apartment was expansive. Easily able to accommodate his desk, wall-to-wall bookcases, a walnut antique bow-front bar, and a companionably styled fireplace mantel that fronted a massive fireplace. Now, a small fire was burning behind the grate—warming the room and producing a mild fruit fragrance. He guessed Marsha had ordered mixed hard-woods and cherry. *She's a wonder,* he reminded himself.

His study, desk, books, fireplace—all of it—were snobbish affectations he knew, and bordered on excessive. Nonetheless, he liked the aura of old-world ambience surrounding him. His study was a place—admittedly an indulgent place—where he was able to escape from the demands of New York City, a city he loved. But a city always awake—snatching his time and emotions.

Here, this moment, and for a few more moments, he had the precious time to sit and think. In his own private world.

Indeed, Julian also loved his "Old New York" 10021 zip code building. Not because of money or prestige, in fact there were wealthier neighborhoods these days in Jersey and California. It wasn't the swanky-cache either that came with the area—no, for him it was the history. He wasn't so naïve as to think New York represented all that was unique and exciting about the United States—and even though he often traveled to the District of Columbia, neither was he a typical "Beltway" world-viewer. But Julian did consider the East Coast a treasure chest of American History.

Rubbing his hand slowly over the highly polished and smooth surface of his impeccably restored 1885 Victorian styled American Walnut desk, he could almost feel the presence of its designer, William S. Wooton; Julian even fancied a piece of America's history passed from the desk into his palm.

And for a fleeting second, a smile washed across his face.

Then from a different direction, he remembered Marsha Portson asking him, "To happily be a gentry-man, now aren't you?" She'd posed her question-cum-pronouncement when she and LoraLee had first stepped into

151

the foyer of their new home. Marsha's eyes had been large, unbelieving, maybe even bewildered—but definitely happy. Over the following half year, he'd quickly learned Marsha had a predilection for infinitives--split or otherwise. And occasionally, she would surprise him with mild curse words. Marsha also had an interesting and uncanny way of positing a significant truth, hidden behind something not so important. A fact Hugh had first alerted him to.

Well, maybe there had been gentry way back when— his family coming from England to the colonies—cherished family heirlooms in tow. He murmured, "Doubtful," then sighed—his smile fading. *More like escaping debtor's prison.*

Quickly, his thoughts jumped back to present interests, such as Marsha and her introduction into *his-world,* and the night he pulled into the parking lot of the Oak Tree Inn in Yermo, California with Timothy. Both were still bright in his mind. *Insane, what I did.* Yet, that introduction to *her-world* and the Mojave Desert had started a whole new chapter in his life. Especially after calling Jefferson, *then* things started happening, *then* events moved fast, *then...*"

I should have told Hugh right off. "But how could, I?" he asked his museum-sized office. His smile had completely evaporated into the artificial quiet of his study. *Of course,* he should have told Hugh last year. When Turner Jackson had been murdered. But Charlotte was running the show—then and now—and she knew best. It was her job, after all—*she* was Hugh's shrink, not him. But what about just now, *I should have told Hugh just now.*

No, not over the phone. *Always an excuse.*

Julian sighed with regret—forced upon him, he thought, by the complexities and hard choices in life. He stood up, and went over to his bar. Only late morning, nonetheless, he wanted—*needed*—a drink. An opened bottle of Jameson "15 Year old Pot Still" Irish whiskey awaited him. Hubert James

Champion Jr. had kept him supplied for many years. Unopened bottles stood in two neat rows on his bar's bottom shelf; Julian was an infrequent drinker. A minor smile again overtook his face. He would never forget the sight of Hubert Champion Jr., Hugh's dad, downing three Jameson shots in a row—as he often did. *An amazing man.*

Still, he liked his son infinitely better. And sometimes wondered... *Yes,* he definitely needed a drink.

Then there was Junior's daughter, Murphy. Now that was a completely different story. "A nasty piece of work," he said aloud.

Despite his words and distaste for Murphy, Julian's smile lingered as he remembered Yvonne, his long deceased, but never to be forgotten love and mother to Timothy and LoraLee. It was a phrase she had been fond of using. "A nasty piece of work," he repeated in homage to Yvonne. Oddly, it was a phrase he heard Eloise Champion, Junior's wife and Hugh's mother also use.

Yes, Murphy was possibly about to do irreparable damage. And there was nothing he could think of to stop her.

With all my power and money—nothing I can do.

"Events will have to play themselves out," he informed his beautiful, warm, and grandiose study.

He liked hearing the sound of his voice seemingly bounce around the room, from one cherished item to the next—touching history in the process.

Julian's call had stopped Hugh long enough for him to realize he needed to do something about Joey's before he left. Hang his sign, or get a minder. Thankfully, Ruthie was able to come in and watch Joey's, Hobo, and Black-Jack. Both of his critters were fond of her dog, Whiskers. "And yes," Ruthie

153

had said, "I'll call Gabe for help if Leon calls that he's doing a tour bus today."

Ruthie was a jewel, and Hugh tried not to ever forget how much his survival depended on her help. He'd asked her how Margaret and Oscar were doing, and she said she'd heard something about Oscar not feeling great. She would check, and leave him a note. "You're free to go wherever you want," she offered cheerfully. "I have keys, you know. Hobo will be fine."

Hugh made sure Hobo had water, then headed out guilt free. Route 66 and breakfast were in his near future. And a drive definitely would help his mental and emotional processes move along another step. *Yep*, he needed to drive.

Valley Center was a paved road that ran East and West through Newberry Springs, and for many locals, the closest paved road to get from Minneola Rd to the West, and Newberry Road to the East. Which meant access to the Post Office and places to get gas and minimal supplies. The road wasn't a necessary thoroughfare for Hugh, but sometimes, he just drove down the road for the heck of it. Like the town of Yermo, there was just something he liked about this road. There was a "feel" he never experienced anywhere else.

To Audrey, much like when he'd told her his predilection toward Yermo, his Valley Center enthusiasm was also inexplicable. "Just another dusty desert road," she'd said, clearly mystified.

"But, it's paved."

"Still dusty," she'd countered. "And doesn't really take you anywhere."

Hugh now half-smiled remembering that discussion and rolled his window down farther. Early morning was getting away from him, but it was still cool, with impending rain tantalizing his nostrils. *Winter in the Mojave is not that bad.* And Valley Center was just as he remembered the last time

154

he'd driven across Newberry Springs. He didn't think it much over a five mile stretch, but he liked the view into the community it provided. Reminding him, there were people who chose to live in the area. People *coming* to the High Desert *on purpose*, not just lost souls like him, running away from something.

Then out of the blue while cruising along, Hugh was hit with the wish his parents would visit, come see and experience the Mojave. It was the same he'd experienced driving Route 66 near Della's—but never so near his own turf. *Who am I kidding?* They'd never visit him here. Sure, his mother loved him, but she'd always in the end bow to Junior's wishes in those kind of things; not that she wasn't a strong willed woman. But she believed the man should lead the family.

In a clarity that was painful, he realized Eloise and Junior would never see his Mojave, never experience its diamond-in-the-rough allure. Neither would his father deign to make the trip out to see any part of Route 66, no matter how much Hugh fanaticized. His mother's clock and Grandmother Todd's antiques would have to suffice as his "familial connections." *So be it.* He, *Hubert James Champion III*, needed to adjust his thinking, grow up, for Christ's sake. Included in that growing up was to find out who killed Melony Dibbs, not fanaticizing about his parents.

Fortunately, driving along Valley Center, his resolve returned. That pleased Hugh. Hiding out in the desert was one thing, but not letting a killer of innocents get away with it was definitely not acceptable.

And for the first time, he *knew* going to Griffith's was essential. Whether to solve Melony's murder, or Neil becoming target practice for some reason, or scrap metal thievery—he wasn't yet sure. But today was the day. It had taken him a while to bring justice for Lewis Jenkins, Della's Ex, but with Melony, justice would come sooner. Hopefully, by his hand.

First though, he'd have breakfast. And on a whim, Hugh decided to head to Ludlow and the café there. Hadn't eaten there in ages, and he loved their pancakes.

"This really is a coincidence," Hugh said, thinking the concept *coincidence* hardly did justice to this type of luck. "I seldom come here." When he did eat out, he tended to frequent the restaurants accessible to I-15 and in Barstow.

"Worth the trip, though, isn't it?" Griffith said.

"Yeah," Hugh agreed, taking a moment to look around. As on his few previous visits, he still found the Ludlow Café cozy, warm, and exuding an atmosphere of comfortableness. "I always like it here. I should drive out more often." He smiled at each man. "And it's nice having company," Hugh added, tipping his head in acknowledgement. "Thanks for asking me to join you at your table."

Griffith "G-Man" King and Baddon "Don" Giles were sitting across the table from him in a booth at the front window. They'd seen Hugh enter and waved him over almost as soon as he'd walked through the door.

Several other booths and tables were also occupied. Hugh was now ensconced comfortably with Griffith and Baddon, and continuing to take in his surroundings, he noticed at a large table close to them a group of six were excitedly speaking French; though he couldn't make out what they were talking about. *The international "call" of Route 66.* It was a nice *thought*, a world connecting *thought*. Unfortunately, not a *thought* that would progress his agenda—solving the mysteries facing him and his friends.

156

With a wave of his hand, Griffith caught their waitress's eye across the café. "We just ordered," he said as an aside to Hugh. To the waitress, he half-called and half-mouthed, "We have a new member."

She smiled and nodded she understood, then headed for the coffee pot before actually coming toward their table. Her congenial manner, smile, and assumption *"Everyone wants coffee,"* caused Hugh to relax a bit—take in the moment. The wonderful breakfast smells of bacon, butter, coffee; a comfortable temperature inside and out; a now clear and beautiful sky staring back at him through the window; and a chance encounter with two people he very much wanted to talk to.

Hugh didn't bother with the menu, he already knew what he wanted. There'd been plenty of time to think and salivate on the drive out. Coffee, orange juice, water, pancakes, eggs, and bacon. And maple syrup, of course. He gave the friendly waitress his order efficiently and with anticipation. "I'll bring everybody's food at the same time," she assured them, and with pad in hand headed directly toward the kitchen.

"Ha," Baddon said right after the waitress left their booth. "Same thing I ordered." His intonation suggesting to Hugh, his duplication of his order was some kind of validation.

Then Hugh caught a side glance Baddon gave Griffith, which started his mind to speculate even farther about the two men's interaction. He wasn't sure exactly *what* their relationship was, but he was sure it was more complicated than sharing a workshop.

"Pretty lucky, us bumping into you out here," Griffith said.

"Yeah." Hugh hoped he wasn't staring, but he couldn't help to notice this time around, Griffith wasn't that bad

157

looking of a man. Mid-forties to mid-fifties, he had that rugged rather craggy look about him, without looking too "rough." Funny, it was different taking in the man "up close and personal" in this relaxed and intimate surroundings. When he'd bought the first feeder in the early days, there was no reason to appraise Griffith fully—just that his presence under the tree had been so striking. Then yesterday morning at the shop. *So much happening so fast.*

This morning, an instinctual nudge-like feeling told him he needed to know more about this man, and to know more, *I'm going to have to pry.* And pry he would. Too much was at stake to care about being thought of as nosey-parker. Besides, he was a psychologist, and psychologists ask questions—though he didn't know if Griffith knew anything about his past. *Small town, though. People talk, especially Gabe.* In addition, somewhere within his being, Hugh knew this breakfast was about to tell him something. And that knowing caused a slight queasiness in the pit of his stomach—but his desire to get answers and move forward was most powerful.

"How long have you two been friends?" Hugh asked, smiling first at Griffith, then at Baddon.

Griffith laughed lightly, and congenially. "Seems like forever, doesn't it?" he asked and turned his head toward Baddon. "Actually, it's only been a couple of years." Then he turned back as if to speak directly to Hugh, instead, Griffith squeezed his eyes shut for a few seconds, and made a sigh-like clicking sound. "Maybe longer than that," he said reopening his eyes and again turning to Baddon. "Can you remember?" His tone was one of interest. "Mr. Champion's got me thinking about this. Time flies by."

"Call me, Hugh, please." He nodded his agreement with Griffith. "I know what you mean. Can't believe I've been here in the Mojave almost two years now."

Back looking at Hugh, Griffith's expression turned even more thoughtful. "Two years you've been here—*Hugh*?" He shook his head "That long?"

Looking down at his table mat, Baddon said softly, "Five years. It's been five years since *I've* been at your place."

"Jeez," Griffith responded, and Hugh thought he looked genuinely surprised.

Hugh said lightly, "You know what they say about when you're having fun." He looked at Baddon directly — wanted to engage him—wanted to know more about him. Insight of a sort had come; *the key to prying into Griffith was through Baddon.*

"What do they say about fun?" Baddon asked, his tone serious.

"Ah," Hugh hesitated a moment to try to garner from Baddon's face if he was pulling his leg. *No,* his facial expression said he'd never heard of the phrase. "Maybe, you've never heard of the phrase," he said carefully, "that time flies when you're having fun."

Baddon smiled, "Oh yeah, actually I have heard that." Then he looked to Griffith, his smile broadening. "I guess we have been having fun."

Neil hated hospitals. Nonetheless, he inhaled deeply and kept walking.

As he made his way down the corridor to Officer Gideon Will's room—he experienced a feeling near to *Déjà vu,* but not quite. He knew the French phrase translated to "already seen." But he'd been unconscious when last here, near death, and being rushed to an operating-theatre on a gurney.

The corridor walls were painted "hospital-cream," to calm anxiety supposedly, but never quite accomplishing that mission. And there were many fear-enticing double doors, anxiety producing elevators that opened on two-sides, and a myriad of overcrowded wards and rooms that you didn't want to look into, too afraid of what you might see.

He shivered, remembering, but kept walking. CHP Officer Gideon Will's room was near. *I don't have much farther to go.* But it wasn't just his personal memories, but the universal hospital ethos that summoned up his physical reactions of nausea, light headedness — almost revulsion. All reactions and emotions that made Neil very angry. Angry at himself. *Not manly.*

Most importantly, he knew he needed to be here today. Compelled to be here actually. "Why" was not yet clear. But there were answers in Will's room, just like there had been answers in his coma-state six months earlier. Patience and fortitude were needed. *Yep,* he'd become a *real* cop, and *real* cops didn't get squeamish walking down hospital corridors.

A nurse, he thought — though the multi-color scrubs she was wearing didn't tell him anything about her role in the hospital — stepped into the hall from behind an unmarked and consequently scary looking door.

Initially she smiled at him, but after a few seconds, her expression changed and she tilted her head a tad, and asked, "Are you alright, Sir?"

Neil immediately realized his aversion to everything-hospital must be translating to his face. To counter-balance the impression his face must be giving, he squared his shoulders and forced a smile. "I'm fine, thank you."

Her smile returned and she laughed lightly. "You have that 'Oh my god, I'm in a hospital!' look on your face."

He had to laugh too, even though he didn't want to. Indeed, he reminded himself, this was the same hospital and

160

the same staff that had saved *his* life—if anything he should be rejoicing to be there. "I'm Deputy Neil Knight, and I'm looking for Officer Will's room."

"Follow me." She made a come-on hand gesture. "He's in Critical Isolation. Would have been closer if you'd come in through emergency."

Of course, I should have known that. A man doesn't just hop up from a blast in the chest that quickly. Probably a miracle he even survived. It seemed like an eternity longer and miles away down innumerable cream-colored halls before the adjunct to ICU finally materialized—and Neil stepped into the world of tubes, round-the-clock nurses, and constantly beeping and flashing machines.

Remaining alone in their booth, lingering over a third cup of coffee, Hugh watched as Griffith and Baddon both gave him jaunty goodbye waves from the parking lot, then got in Griffith's car—heading home they said.

Hugh had tried to pay attention during breakfast. Trying not to miss a clue or insight. *Instinct and training returning?* He knew from experience, understanding sometimes came from rituals, reactions, and body language—not just from verbal answers. But regardless of his abilities and psychoanalytic skill, at some point during breakfast—and he certainly couldn't pinpoint that actual moment of insight—Hugh came around to Gabe's thinking. *Well, once part of his theory.* Griffith might possibly be part of this scrap metal thievery stuff.

"More coffee, Dear?" asked their waitress who seemingly appeared from nowhere.

Startled, it took Hugh a couple seconds to react. "Ah no," he finally said. "I mean, no thank you." He smiled. "I'll be heading out soon, freeing your booth."

"No problem," she said, and moved on.

He looked around, and the place wasn't packed, but during the hour or so they'd sat talking a couple more groups of "roadies," had come in. He made his identification based on Route 66 outer-wear and the fact they were speaking foreign languages, this time ones he couldn't identify except to say they were probably Eastern European.

Despite what he told the waitress, Hugh took his time—finishing his coffee, and gathering his thoughts and trying to formulate some conclusions. He'd asked a lot of questions, heard their words, and watched their reactions. And even though Hugh's intent had been to pry, hopefully his questions had come off as the trivial trifles of normal and mundane social conversation.

He turned his head to take in the café's parking lot again, National Trails Highway, and then a little farther beyond, the freeway overpass for I-40. It was an odd moment—the aromas of good cooking still permeating the air, the sounds of excited voices telling tales about their American journey on Route 66 in languages he couldn't understand, and the fading image of Griffith and Baddon waving good-bye to him.

Bits and pieces of their breakfast conversation jutted in and out of his thoughts. When he'd asked Griffith if he did his welding alone, he said, "Of course," in a manner and in a tone that for one to think otherwise was in fact, unthinkable. Hugh had simultaneously seen disappointment wash across Baddon's face before quickly looking away. Hugh remembered from his visit to their shop, Baddon worked with wood, but he couldn't quite re-visualize the pieces he'd seen in his corner of the workshop.

He *did* remember the almost finished raven mounted on a huge birdfeeder, how grateful Baddon had seemed for Griffith's friendship, and how he'd thought Griffith rather a philosopher type. The two men's relationship, he finally concluded, was not an "easy nut" to crack.

The group of French tourists were standing up, getting their things together. Also a nondescript rather thin man he hadn't noticed earlier stood up and headed toward the counter to pay his bill. *Doesn't want to wait for the waitress,* while I'm in no hurry to move on. He sighed, feeling he was on the verge of "solving" something and wanting to prolong these moments to bring all the pieces together.

He savored the last still warm and aromatic dregs of his coffee.

Outside a tour bus was coming across the overpass; Hugh sighed again. They'd need all their tables soon. Time to move on.

One last look into the parking lot confirmed that, *yes,* a not unexpected small wind and accompanying dust devils were starting to swirl, and *yes,* the tour bus was headed to "his" comfortable little restaurant. "Nothing lasts," he whispered to himself.

But still no rain—just the smell of it.

Hugh noticed the thin nondescript man heading toward an older white non-descript Toyota sedan. The man was quick—Hugh figured he wanted to get out of the parking lot before the bus pulled in. And as the Toyota first backed up, then pulled around to exit Hugh noticed several antenna wells on the little sedan's fenders. He almost laughed out loud. Most probably another Route 66 enthusiast with several CBs, not wanting to miss a thing on the route. He'd seen it before— even on motorcycles. *The call of the road.*

Hugh left the coffee shop with regret. As expected looking outside from the comfort of the restaurant, trademark

Mojave winds whipped lightly at his pants and jacket, stirring up small swirls of sand. The air was still cool and damp, it wasn't cloudy—the sky still blue, but a bit pale.

A sensation engulfed him, one he'd experienced more than once recently—the feeling the desert beneath his feet and the skies above were infinite. The rest of the world did not exist. And he almost felt good. *Almost.*

Melony's murderer was still out there. Hunting.

"I'm sorry," Neil said. "I didn't know someone was here already." Expecting Officer Will to be alone, the uniformed female CHP officer sitting by his bedside caught Neil by surprise. "Guess I should have known there would be a guard." Then he felt his face warm. *Will's girlfriend.* "I'm Deputy Sheriff Neil Knight. Mojave County."

Even though circumstances didn't call for it, he felt his body take a parade rest kind of stance on its own, and he just caught himself before actually putting his hands behind his back. "Wanted to pay my regards."

It was hard for anyone to look good in a hospital bed, but Gideon Will looked horrible. His face was swollen, and his darkish skin was splotched with off-putting yellowish-blue patches. *Besides being shot, he must have hit the ground hard.* Tubes were connected to his arm, his right hand, and into both nostrils. Neil could see the top edge of bandages peeking above the neckline of his hospital gown, and he was certain those edges foretold of a chest covered in bandages. His eyes were closed. And seeing Gideon Will up close, Neil had a flash of residual emotion from his own time in a hospital bed. He was able to move past it immediately.

The female CHP officer stood, put an official looking folder she was holding in the chair, smiled, and offered her hand. "I'm Kathie-Marie Hoffman. Gid's partner."

Her grip was firm, her handshake short, and any embarrassment Neil had felt disappeared. "So you were there too?"

Clearly caught by some emotional remembering of her own, Kathie-Marie caught her breath, then released it with a long and full breath. "Yeah," she said, "I was there when it happened." There were two chairs against the wall, and Kathie-Marie pointed to them. "Wanna sit?"

"Yeah, sit and stay," a surprisingly strong, but mush-mouthed voice said from the bed.

Neil immediately went to Gideon's bedside. "You're talking already?" Again, he remembered his stay—in particular, the fact he'd succumbed to a coma. "I'm mean, you've had a bullet dug out of you."

"Several," Kathie-Marie rushed to point out. "He's damn lucky to be alive."

"You can say that again." Gideon's voice turned hoarse by the end of his short sentence.

Neil held up his hand, "Officer Will, don't over exert yourself." He almost added, *pas de zèle*, hold back on the zeal, hotshot, but caught himself in time. Some frank introspection since his promotion had resulted in the conclusion his foreign phrases—gibberish as Gabe called it—didn't necessary put him "a cut above," but more often than not, put him on the outside. Sure, they still popped out, but less frequently with people he didn't know.

"Deputy Knight is right, you need to rest."

Gideon looked like he was about to object, then his eyes closed—almost simultaneously with a nurse coming into the area, smiling at him and Kathie-Marie, fiddling with the IV

165

pack, reading, then nodding at Gideon's monitoring meters. Then she was gone.

"Wow, that was efficient."

Kathie-Marie chuckled. "She's been on duty about an hour or so. Fast, efficient, and from what I've seen, quite competent."

This CHPer is easy to talk to. "Well, at least you know your partner is in good hands." He'd thought it might be hard to get information from the recuperating officer, but his partner should be able to tell him.

Neil was turning from the bed when Gideon's eyes popped open and he said, clear as a bell, "KM and Collin saved my life." His eyelids fluttered. "Saved my life…"

Neil took a quick look at Gideon's monitoring-machines, as far as he could tell, nothing had changed. "Drugs?"

"Yeah, he's in and out."

"I noticed we passed a little waiting room on the hike here. Do you have a couple moments?"

"I'm doing my report now." She picked up the folder from the chair. "No problem telling you what I just faxed in." Her pleasant countenance turned sour. "The sooner we get the info out on this bastard, the better." She lifted her chin and looked Neil in the eye, direct and fierce. "I'll never forget all the blood gushing out of Gid's chest and Collin throwing his jacket over him, pressing down." She inhaled deeply. "I hope I'm the one taking him out."

"You mean arresting him?" Neil knew exactly what she meant. But he wasn't going to say it.

She chuckled, "Sure, Deputy Sheriff Knight. I mean arresting him." Her smile returned. "Want to go sit and talk a bit like you suggested down the hall?" She tapped the folder in her hand. "Got it all here." But before moving toward the

166

hall, Kathie-Marie added, "And no, I'm not Gid's girlfriend. We're partners. Partners as in 'work together.'"

Neil half-smiled while clearing his throat, and hoped his face wasn't giving away any more information. *I jumped to the same conclusion Sally had about me and Rociana.*

Hugh was standing by his Altima's open door when he got Neil's call. The Deputy's name came up on his phone's screen and he immediately accepted his call while turning his back to the door and leaning against it. He didn't yet feel like accepting the confines of his car.

"Listen, I think I have an idea about Rociana and Melony," Neil said without preamble.

Hugh was close to I-40 and fairly frequent cell-tower transmitters, so reception was good—not always the case in the Mojave. "I'm all ears," he said. Hugh could tell by Neil's tone of voice he was excited.

"Is Rociana coming tonight for poker?"

"I think so." Hugh didn't mention her earlier call and her plan to come early.

"Good. I need to talk to her if I can." Then changing the subject, and again without preamble, "I just heard Bob Thomas had a heart attack. He's at Barstow hospital."

"He's alive?" *Damn.* He hadn't known the man, but after seeing Bob and his wife Cleo at the Community Café, he felt like he did.

"Yes."

Hugh 's next question was thoughtfully slow in coming, and in delivery. "You think the stress of this scrap metal stuff caused the attack?"

"Yes."

Hugh cursed again, aloud this time.

167

Once again Neil quickly changed the subject . "I just came from Will's room. He's still in intensive care area, sort of."

"Because he's getting better? Going to make it?" Hugh held his breath.

"Looks like it." Neil paused, clearly for effect, "And—"

"And—"

"And he got a look at THK. I've already called Audrey and Ted."

"A description?"

"Sure looks like it," Neil said, elation and pride edging his words. "And the car. He paid attention to the car."

Hugh could barely believe this break, and he expected Audrey, Ted, *well heck*, all law enforcement along THK's hunting grounds were putting out APBs. "That's great news. Maybe they'll be bringing him in soon." And Neil had gotten the information, while everybody else was running around looking for THK, Neil had done an "act of charity" and gotten them some information.

"Thin, wiry-looking according to Will."

Hugh's world shifted, and a shiver slithered down his back. "And the car?"

"Older white Toyota." Neil chuckled lightly. "Gideon Will is *some* cop. Even noticed there were a bunch of antenna-wells on the the rear fenders."

Hugh pushed his car door open wider and dropped backwards into the driver's seat, feet remaining outside. He didn't drop the phone, but he did drop his head between his knees, trying to ward off an immediate swell of nausea. *I was so close.* He took a long deep breath.

"Champion? Champion?" Neil demanded wirelessly, "are you there? What's going on? I can hear you breathing."

Several more moments of misery passed before Hugh was able to tell Neil about breakfast.

Chapter Five

Wednesday night

Hugh parked his car inside his yard at home, then quickly walked through the house from front to back, forcing himself to ignore Hobo and Black-Jack vying for his attention. Hard to do, but he needed to get his Joey's responsibilities taken care of before he could wallow-away the afternoon in manufactured-guilt-driven misery—complaining to his canine and feline friends what a dope he'd been this morning. Indulgent self-pity would have to wait.

He felt like he was on autopilot, and knew to some extent, he was—making his body keep moving, *step after step, task after task*. Out his kitchen backdoor, across his deck, and into his office at the back of Joey's.

Home.

Even though his office-cum-window into Joey's felt like home these days, where just being there brought a modicum of equilibrium and alertness, he didn't linger. Hugh proceeded quickly out into Joey's proper where Ruthie and Gabe were "watching the store," drinking cokes, and enjoying Mounds bars. He told his wondrous multi-tasking housekeeper, and his one-of-a-kind friend to lock up and hang the "Gone Fishing" sign whenever they'd had enough of storekeeping for the day. He also made each take a twenty-spot for pizza, and didn't accept refusal from either. It was a token anyway. Hugh was well aware he owed them a lot more. *Joey's wouldn't even exist if it weren't for their help.*

Gabe assured him he'd be back for poker later, "Wouldn't miss tonight for nothing." He wagged his finger. "Too much we need to talk about."

Hugh almost laughed at the now rather beloved desert-rat caricature Gabe insisted upon presenting—but he didn't. *Too* tired to make the effort, *too* kind to tease, *too* accepting to object. *Gabe is Gabe.* And most importantly, now a friend. Among all the other things circling and rattling around in his head, those few seconds of realization were a nice wave in a sea of anger, sadness, and apprehension.

Hugh said, "Same time as usual." He smiled, and looked to Ruthie with raised eyebrows. "I've got plenty of snacks." He'd asked her several times if either she or her husband, Justin, an engineer at Fort Irwin, wanted to come. His house was big enough to accommodate several tables. She returned his smile with her usual quick shake of the head that Hugh had always read as "Thanks, but I have a lot more important things to do than play poker with you old geezers." He often forgot how young Ruthie was, but moments like this reminded him. *Moments like this* that made him feel old as dirt.

Gabe said, "Ruthie made you a platter of deviled eggs, and a cheese dip." He smacked his lips like a cartoon character. "Tried 'em both."

"It was supposed to be a surprise." Ruthie made a disparaging face and rolled her eyes at Gabe.

Another friend, this young woman, Hugh thought. "Thanks," he said, hopefully in a non-emotional tone.

"No, problem. I made them while Gabe watched the register."

"Friends," Hugh found himself saying out loud—but not thinking of Ruthie and Gabe. His mind had jumped to Griffith and Baddon, and was once again wondering at what kind of relationship they had.

"What?" Gabe asked.

170

"Oh, just grateful for both you guys," he sidestepped. *No*, he wasn't ready to speculate out loud about the two men. Tomorrow though, he'd pay the birdfeeder-welder another visit. "If I haven't said it enough, I'm saying it now—thanks for covering my butt."

Ruthie and Gabe smiled. But Hugh knew, smiles or not, and happy moment withstanding, there was unpleasantness still waiting for him before this was all over.

THK was still out there. He'd actually seen the man—but not well enough to give a description. *Damn.* He looked down at his hands, no trembles. But his stomach lurched, and he had the oddest sensation he'd mentally been at a similar place six months or so earlier. A point where bits and pieces started falling into place, filling in a puzzle picture that he didn't like one bit.

Joey's obligations taken care of, Hugh walked through his office, across the deck and into his doublewide via his back kitchen entry. As he passed through the house, he "apologized" to Hobo there'd be no afternoon walk today, and patted Black-Jack on the head—who didn't seem to care. *Cats.*

Once in his bedroom, Hugh pulled off his jacket, then fell across his bed shoes still on—shutting off his speculations, emotions, apprehensions, fears—everything rumbling through his mind and body.

Sleep was quick to come, and deep.

Hobo jumped up from his guarding-position under Hugh's dining room archway and ran barking to the front

171

door—but halfway there, he stopped barking and slid to a stop as quickly as he'd started—his tail going into super-wag.

Hugh had awakened feeling surprisingly fresh and ready for tonight even though he knew their *regular* poker game was not going to be very *regular*. But he did think it would be a turning point of some sort.

He'd showered and dressed quickly, almost eagerly, and by the time Hobo was charging the front door, Hugh was in the kitchen, busily putting together poker-night snacks. He was positioned to see his multi-paned double door entry through the archway between his dining and living rooms. The "fancy" doors were an upgrade he'd recently made at Della's request and signaled a milestone passed in his Mojave sojourn—at least that's what Della told him. "Upgrading and remodeling meant something," she'd said accompanied with a knowing look. For a few seconds, he smiled, remembering.

Who he now saw through his front door's window-lites was Rociana Bustamante. In uniform, including sidearm. S&W 4006 he guessed. *Another useless piece of info in my brain from Quantico. A zillion years ago.* He almost laughed, or maybe Ted told him what CHP standard issue was. Not likely they would have mentioned it at Quantico.

He went to let Rociana in thinking Ted was lucky to have found her. Not only was she good looking, but she had a way of standing that said, *'I'm proud of who I am.'* He wondered how Hobo knew she was friend, not foe? *Smart dog?* Or was it just because she was a woman. Hobo was putty in female hands. He decided, *no,* Hobo was sensing the same sense of "place in the world" Rociana generated.

Behind Rociana, he could see a horizon washed in yellows, oranges, even gold—the beginnings of the sun setting. Early, by his body clock. *But it is winter.* In a matter of moments, he expected various hues of red would first touch the edges of gold, then encompass all the lighter palette

172

shades into a mass of streaked red's, even touches of blue. Then in subsequent few moments, he now knew from experience, the horizon's brilliance would vanish into darkness. *So quick.*

"I'm in the kitchen." He opened the door, waved her in, and stepped aside. "Come on back if you don't mind talking while I get stuff together." He hoped his voice didn't betray any of his juxtaposing emotions.

"Nice colors," she said by way of greeting. "Your view, that is. Never get tired of desert sunsets."

"Yeah." He wondered why she was in uniform, thinking maybe she wasn't staying.

The wailing, then chirping of sirens on I-15 indicating more than one cruiser had just sped past his exit. *Eastbound.* The piercing sounds stopped both of them, physically and verbally for a couple seconds. Hugh turned his head and gave Rociana an inquiring look.

She said, "Not after our guy." She gestured toward her patrol car parked inside his yard, and close to his deck. "Just heard the call. Accident at Afton Road exit. No injuries. Traffic control needed." She added in an offhanded mumble, "Eleven eighty-four."

"Are you on call?"

"Yep, pretty much everybody is—at least it seems like it." She tapped her holstered pistol. "They don't need me on this one."

Taking the inference from her gesture and words that if the call had been about THK, she wouldn't be standing there talking to him. Hugh didn't comment, thinking for the time being, it was wiser to hold-his-peace.

"I can help with food prep." She seemed eager, but also a little nervous. "Deputy Knight called to make sure I was coming."

173

Hobo trotted doggedly behind her all the way to the kitchen—almost under her feet. Once in the kitchen, Rociana, squatted and gave Hobo several long minutes of petting and baby-talk. By the time she finished, he was on his back, legs in the air, clearly turned to puppy-mush.

Hugh chuckled. "He's putty in your hands." He made a wry clicking sound, "You don't want to have dog hair all over your uniform."

She stood and looked around, her gaze landing on the sink. "Better wash my hands before I help with food. Should I wash here, or in the bathroom?"

"Here's fine. Towels are in the second drawer on the right."

They were dancing around getting started. So be it. Whatever Rociana wanted to talk to him about was worth the wait. He'd been peeling avocados for a popular guacamole kind of thing he made and picked up a fresh one and started pulling the skin off.

"You know," she said looking out his kitchen window, "I've been here for several poker nights. But I've never been in your kitchen."

"No need really. I've tried to lay everything out before you guys get here." Then he remembered the first time, with Gabe and his cousin Travers lugging their huge cooler up on his deck. Hugh added with a nostalgia that surprised him, "I have to admit, though, if it hadn't been for Gabe that first time around—well, I don't think I'd be having poker nights."

She seemed to be only half listening, her gaze still fixed out Hugh's kitchen window. "Sure didn't realize you had a rose garden out back."

"Yeah, surprised me too. That I liked them." He stopped peeling avocados, squeezed a little lime juice in their bowl to hold the ones he'd already skinned, then walked the

174

few steps to stand next to Rociana, his gaze following hers. "Are you a 'rose person'?"

"No, but my mother is." Her voice had turned contemplative.

Hugh waited.

Rociana continued, "Funny, roses. So beautiful. But with thorns so severe they can draw blood."

"A metaphor for something?" He held his breath.

Rociana sighed, and said, "Unfortunately, yeah."

Hugh again waited. But after several long moments passed, he said, "This is a brand new window, you know."

She turned her head enough to look at him and made a questioning face.

"This is where the sniper took his first shot at Neil," he further explained, then shook his head remembering that incredible night again. "Monday night." And not sure if he was completely past the sound of that humungous bullet whizzing by, and the thought of what could have happened, Hugh left it at that. *Amazing, I can still almost see it.* Of course he knew he didn't actually "see" the bullet come towards them and shoot by Neil's head. But the sensation had been so real; still was.

He heard Rociana catch her breath as if reading his mind, but her words were mundane, conversational chatter, not clairvoyant empathy. "You got it fixed quick."

"Neil's doing." *Quite remarkable actually.* "Can't even tell." The fifty-caliber hole in his wall though was going to have to wait until Forensics gave the word. "I owe Neil one."

Without a blink, Rociana switched topics. "Once a shrink, always a shrink, right?"

Hugh didn't have any trouble following her topic shift. "Well, you certainly don't forget everything you've learned," he said, hoping to keep the conversation light for a bit. He didn't bother telling her he wasn't a psychiatrist.

175

Rociana turned toward him, her holstered gun bumping, then resting against the sink rim. "I need someone to confide in." She said it like wanting to talk was a guilty weakness. "You're like a priest, right?" She squinted her eyes and nailed him with an intense and penetrating stare.

"Well, not exactly. But," his tone turned serious to match the intensity of Rociana's glare, "but under most circumstances, whatever we discuss stays with me."

"The circumstances where it doesn't?"

"Well, if there's something criminal involved?" He left the end of his statement open.

She sighed heavily. "Can we sit?"

Outside his kitchen window, a single raven landed on the chair back rim of one of his rose-garden wooden deck chairs. Unlike his Adirondack chairs out front, these were Home Depot specials.

"Krawk, krawk!" the raven counseled.

By six, everyone had arrived. Evening came earlier in the Mojave in Winter, and as the days shortened, their game start time moved with daylight. Fortunately, Hugh and Rociana had plenty of time to chat and get everything ready. Now they were seven in all, Audrey, Neil, Gabe, Leon, Ted, Rociana, and himself. Neil and Leon only arriving before the current hand of Draw. On the next hand, with so many, they'd have to switch to Texas Hold'em.

Card tables hadn't seemed appropriate for tonight, so they were sitting around Grandmother Todd's expansive dining room table. Hugh wasn't sure why he decided that, but guessed it had to do with their number—and Melony. A poker wake for Melony required a more formal setting. Besides, he had food help from Rociana and Ruthie. On top of the deviled

176

eggs, there were several dips and crackers, a veggie platter, and a shrimp ring, so they were using his card tables for a modest buffet-like setup.

Actually, Hugh mused behind a surreptitious sigh of relief, everything had come together easily, and he felt okay — given how miserable he'd felt earlier. He was still beating himself up for missing THK, but the realization wasn't quite as painful.

Poker-wise, he'd just folded with a pair of deuces, and a six-of-hearts high. While Hugh waited and watched as Gabe and Ted, the only two left in the hand, tried to bluff each other out — he took time to appraise anew his little band of would be high-rollers.

Ted was now on the other side of the table to Audrey's right. Hugh hadn't missed that Ted was dressed up for the occasion, a departure in that *this* Special Agent usually took poker-night as an occasion to dress down. In the past, Hugh figured it was part of Ted's relaxation strategy. Looked like tonight, for Ted too, was different. His dressing up was an action in line with congregating around Grandmother Todd's dining room table. Hugh again thought, *a poker wake.*

In addition, this change in habit and attire presented an added facet to "the Ted" Hugh had developed in his mind. For even though he'd become accustomed to wearing Walmart-issue jeans, sweats, T's, and workout hoodies himself, he could still spot designer sport clothes. Especially shoes. *Inherited from Father, no doubt.* And with his next thought, *Junior would probably start foaming at the mouth if he saw my current wardrobe,* Hugh came near to smiling. Inexplicably, his next thought jumped to Julian Bogard. The New Yorker had claimed he didn't know his father, and they certainly wouldn't have played poker together. Maybe Julian was still lingering in his emotions from the telephone call earlier. And for a few

177

fleeting seconds, the sight of an impeccably dressed Julian flashed across his visual memory.

Hugh didn't mean to speak, but unconsciously asked out loud to his friends, "Remember Jefferson Washington Adams?" Once his words were in the world, he felt extremely foolish.

But Audrey, sitting directly across said with a smile which Hugh read as a shared remembrance, "I liked him." She chuckled lightly. "And so, so, East Coast."

"New York City," Gabe added, sounding almost like the iconic salsa commercial, while peering at the back of Ted's cards like he could see through them.

Hugh guessed Gabe hadn't meant his words as comical, but Leon jabbed back, "Nothin' wrong with New Yorkers."

He liked the two cousins. *Yes,* friends.

With the disappearance from his thoughts of Julian and Jefferson, he found himself, once again despite his earlier resolve, entertaining the fanciful and unrealistic thought his mother and father would come out to the Mojave one day. He'd thought early on that Della's presence would have drawn them westward to see California—but it hadn't. Besides, if he wanted to see his parents, all had to do was make the trek back to New York. *Will I do that soon?* Doubtful.

Gabe folded, and Ted swept the five-dollar pot his way with flourish.

Suddenly lightning cut through what had turned into a particularly black night. From their different perspectives all around the table, all heads snapped to look through back, front, and side windows. So startling was the flash, Hugh thought everyone must also have jumped. With the passage of only seconds, thunder next rocked his doublewide enough to rattle windows.

"*Merde,*" Neil cursed under his breath.

"I told you a storm was coming," Gabe puffed.

Hugh didn't remember that conversation, but let it slide. *Typical Gabe.* And for some reason, his thoughts rolled back to Ted and his spiffy wardrobe. He guessed his Special Agent friend had been to Cabazon, near Palm Springs, and done some shopping at their upscale designer stores. Or maybe LA? *Certainly not here.* It was a weird picture for his mind to grasp, Ted shopping like a regular human being. He'd had the same type of reality and persona disconnect when running into Gabe once in the 99¢ Store in Barstow. Gabe Travers was a being of his Mojave world—neighbor, gossip, mentor, friend, shopkeeper—all the things Gabe had become over the last year and a half. *Not a shopper.* Which unfortunately took his mind back to THK. He certainly hadn't looked like a murdering bastard this morning.

Back to Ted, he recognized his shoes from their distinctive silver buckle—Gucci Horsebit Loafers. Ted's looked to be rubber soled—style and comfort. *Fit Ted's personality,* he mused, then immediately wondered why. Ted didn't tromp around in the desert, did he? There were things he'd *guessed* about Ted, but nothing he really *knew.* Hugh wasn't sure about his jeans and chambray shirt, but guessed Ted's jacket was Armani, no less. And somehow, from some corner of his brain, he knew his guessing at Ted's mind and methods was part of bringing justice for Melony's murder.

Gabe was sitting next to him, to his right, but he felt his friend staring at him. *Probably squinting as usual.* Hugh ignored him.

Funny, he returned to his mental ramblings about Ted's attire, how some things stuck, some didn't, and where insights came from. In particular, *why would he be able to recognize designer clothes for Christ's sakes.*

He sighed, blew out a large and noisy breath of air. Another bolt of lightning flashed, and as if professionally chorused and choreographed, right before the sound of rumbling thunder rolled through his dining room, Hugh said, "I think I saw THK this morning."

Everyone fell silent and looked at him.

Finally, Audrey said, "I know. Neil called and told me."

"And I know that he did." Hugh smiled wryly, and gave Neil a glance. "Had to."

"We've already BOLO'd him." Audrey and Neil both said, both using the same words, and speaking almost in unison. Audrey added alone, "You know CHP officer Kathie Marie Hoffman and Neil also got a firsthand description."

Hugh sighed again and repeated this morning's events in Ludlow for the rest of his poker-pals.

"I didn't know you'd seen G-Man and Don this morning?" Gabe said, sounding offended. "You do remember, you did see Ruthie and I earlier, don't you?"

Hugh wasn't sure if Gabe's displeasure was genuine— he thought it was, and apologized. "I knew I'd be seeing you tonight. Besides, I didn't want to upset Ruthie."

Gabe wasn't easily sidestepped. "I'm telling you," he leaned forward, "He's the thieving bastard that caused Bob's heart attack."

"And let off some shots at all of us?" Neil asked incredulously. "He was diving to the ground like all of us." Hugh didn't miss Neil didn't point the sniper-finger at himself, and guessed it was to avoid the fewer people knowing, the better.

"Could have hired somebody," Gabe grumbled.

"And killed Melony?" Rociana asked, and Hugh thought he heard hope in her tone.

180

Hugh said, "You don't know if what you're saying has any truth to it."

"I know what I know." Gabe's tone was firm, and seemingly untroubled by his unsubstantiated conclusion, Hugh's objection, and Neil and Rociana's questions. "G-Man is running a thieving scrap metal ring." Hugh heard him toss a chip on the table. "Are we playing poker, or not. And," he repeated with emphasis, "*Remember* I told you it was going to rain. And remember I told you G-Man is having financial problems."

Most suddenly, what sounded like gargantuan rain drops could be heard pounding on what Hugh considered his flimsy mobile roof. *The prophetic Gabe Travers has spoken.*

"Whoa," Leon said. He was sitting next to Gabe—both ends of Hugh's long dining room table were unoccupied. "That was weird." Then like a yo-yo, Leon switched gears. "What game are we playing?" He gave his cousin Gabe an intense look. "This is serious. Draw or Hold'em?" Leon huffed and made a face. "And it ain't only gonna rain tonight. It's gonna' pour." He jabbed his cousin in the arm, "And *I'm* the one who told *you* it was gonna' rain."

"Did you know it was coming from the east this time?" Gabe shook his head and rolled his eyes.

Hugh turned to actually look at Gabe, let him see he was smiling. The "why" in *why* their weekly poker game had become a pleasant habit was instantly clear to him. *The answer is Gabe.* He was the key, he made the whole thing work.

For example, the last six months had taught him Leon was a darned-good poker player and prone to talk "poker-trash"—but without Gabe, who would appreciate his feigned looks, comments, and poker-lies?

For himself, without Gabe's outrageous pronouncements, *well,* the game would probably be rather dull. Of course Neil brought his own particular twist to the

181

group, but Hugh was pretty darned sure Neil actually enjoyed Gabe's jabs at his pretentious habits and outlook on life.

"I'm with Leon," Ted urged from the other end of the table. "I think Gabe's just a damn sore loser." Then he winked at Gabe.

Yep, Gabe makes this poker-thing work. The lynchpin for their little poker group. And for several fleeting seconds, the "lynchpin" concept triggered a connection of some sort in his mind—but before he could grab hold, the thought and deductive linkage was gone.

He'd seen Ted wink at Gabe, even though his FBI friend seemed unusually far away at the other end of the table next to Audrey. The feeling of distance was probably because they were usually crowded around his kitchen or card table.

Yep, his thoughts had come full-circle. Unspoken among them, but Hugh knew it was understood without exchanging words—tonight was a wake of sorts—*a poker-wake for Melony.*

He looked over at their buffet-like food arrangement. Enough for three-times their number. *Food enough for a wake.* Gabe and Leon always brought beer, but tonight they brought a couple cases of Melony's favorite, Dos Equis.

Tonight, *was* special, and he'd intuitively felt it from the start. That's why he'd also brought out two bottles of B&B from the bottom shelf of Grandmother Todd's hutch.

Audrey knew too—arriving with two bottles of Beaujolais.

And stylishly dressed Ted, had come with a brown paper bag wrapped bottle of Tennessee Honey Whiskey.

With his eyes coming to rest on his bottle of Benedictine and Brandy at the end of the table, Hugh said aloud what had been jumping in and out of his thoughts all evening, "A poker-wake for Melony." A lump rose in this throat as soon as he got the words out, and he had to fight down a swell of grief.

Melony had come to several poker-nights, and he'd thought she'd taken a liking to B&B. He forced the picture of her smile after her first taste from his mind's eye. Too painful. He couldn't even raise his eyes to meet his friends'—but figured they were doing the same.

He heard Audrey say after clearing her throat, "If everyone has a drink of some kind," then heard her swallow hard before continuing, "maybe we could raise our glasses to Melony?" He looked up, and smiled meekly at her. *The humbling effect of death.* He'd seen it in others before, felt it himself before.

There was an empty chair next to him. *Melony's chair.*

For several long moments a heavy silence engulfed them, somberly orchestrated by the pounding of rain drops on his roof. Then he had the oddest sensation, almost in time with the rain drops, he could hear Maurice Ravel's *Bolero*—the tempo and volume low, but definitely starting to build.

"The cop brotherhood is pretty tight you know." Ted said to Rociana sitting to his right. Then to Leon, "I raise you."

Watching Ted, Hugh saw the twinkle in his eye and figured he didn't have squat—probably a pair of deuces. You never knew with the Special Agent; he was a loose but savvy player. Hugh figured Ted would drop out after the flop.

Switching to addressing Rociana, Ted's tone turned somber while he waited for Leon. "It was clear to me in Sacramento, we're going to get this guy."

Hugh had to avert his eyes from Ted and Rociana sitting only inches apart; Ted's adoring looks and demeanor were just too sappy for him to want to retain in memory. A love smitten FBI Agent was simultaneously ludicrous and endearing. Especially since Rociana hit just the right note of fondness and public professionalism. Hugh wondered if he looked the same way at Audrey, while she retained her dignity and acted with decorum. *Jeez.*

Hugh's intuition told him there was something else Ted *wasn't* saying. And when he looked over at Neil, he saw the deputy was also eyeing the love-birds. He remembered Neil's call after his hospital visit, wanting to talk to Rociana. He hadn't paid enough attention tonight, and wondered if Neil had gotten the chance.

"And CHP knows their folks have big targets on their backs," Audrey said. She leaned forward to look around Ted and directly at Rociana. "Are you on two-officer car patrols?"

"Started today." Rociana gave Ted a look. "So you can stop worrying."

Unsaid by all was the fact Gideon Will was still laying in a hospital bed.

As usual, Gabe was quick to jump in with his take on the situation. "See, Champion, I told you. Cops are gonna be after this b—" he caught himself and rephrased, "this slime-bag. Nope, he ain't gonna get away." He clicked his teeth definitively, shook his head, and repeated, "Nope ain't gonna get away." He'd also dropped out of the hand and took the opportunity to open a fresh bottle of Dos Equis, and take a hefty pull. "Yep, cops stick together and that's a damn good thing."

Hugh wasn't sure who the slime-bag Gabe was talking about—Griffith, THK, or someone yet unknown—but he heard more thunder and the rain wasn't showing any sign of letting up. Gabe and Leon were clearly right on the rain front. He felt a sudden chill, and realized he'd visibly shivered.

"Temperature must have dropped," he mumbled. He rubbed his long-sleeved shirt covered arms. "Anyone else cold? I can turn up the thermostat." Everyone else seemed fine temperature wise. Hobo, however, had chosen to sit quietly at Rociana's side all evening. Now, he barked, once and emphatically, as if he'd understood Hugh's temperature question and was voicing his opinion. Everyone laughed, and any edge left after Audrey's toast to Melony seemed to fade.

"Okay, Hobo," Hugh said standing up. "I'll turn up the heat."

Once back at the table, he said aloud, "A brotherhood," while wondering how good a "thing" that was. In Melony's case, he was one-hundred percent behind an all out hunt for THK.

As if reading his mind—which he hated—Audrey said, "Well Gabe, I'd agree, it's a good thing. Most of the time." She blew out a whiff of air, "And my cards are crap." She turned them over flat on the table. "I'm out too."

Neil had been unusually quiet all evening, and had folded during the first round of betting on this particular hand. Now he said, "We have a lot of power and weapons."

Hugh caught a sadness in Neil's tone that he hadn't expected. *I continually underestimate this man.*

"And Leon's been hot all night," Neil added in a much lighter tone, tapping the backs of his turned down cards. "And, he's tricky. Watch out Rociana."

She laughed lightly, and said, "I thought it was Hugh you told me I had to watch out for."

Their knowing each other enough to talk about poker was a slight surprise to Hugh, and he asked before thinking, "You two know each other?" He was trying to ask, besides from their poker games.

Neil looked at him strangely and squinted his eyes rather thoughtfully. "We've met in Yermo several times for lunch. I think you were there once?"

I was. "Jeez," Hugh said, then sighed. "I'm getting old." For a reason he was not yet able to pull together coherently, he knew their exchange was important. *But why?*

"Neil's right," Audrey continued with her police brotherhood line of thought. "I've known, well, actually been involved in several investigations where a "brethren" forgot the oath he'd taken." She sighed as if significant pain was associated with her comments. "Like Neil said, we have a lot of power and weapons, which doesn't seem to help sometimes with known bad-guys. But 'beat downs' on civilians that we *think* might be bad-guys..." She shook her head. "Or don't like."

It was Ted's turn to surprise Hugh.

"So where, dear sister, do you put "justice" in your cop ethics scheme of things?" Ted's tone was quite deliberate and somber, and he was looking most pointedly at his sister.

Hugh caught Rociana quickly looking down toward her lap—but not before he caught the look on her face. *Fear? Embarrassment?*

Gabe inserted himself again. "And what are you guys gonna do when you find the guy?" He squinted his eyes like he often did, shifting his gaze dramatically around the table, one by one, from Ted, to Rociana, to Audrey, to Neil. "Bring him in?" He fell back into his high-backed and formal dining chair and folded his arm across his chest in his typical manner. "Or just take him out."

The looks Hugh saw on all their faces were unanimous, causing Hugh to almost feel sorry for THK when he was caught. But not really. In his heart of hearts, if asked for his vote, he would probably come down on the side of saving taxpayers a lot of money. His mind and sense of right, wrong, and justice, however, said that was not the cop's job. Yet— Marsha Portson had killed Turner Jackson—and *he'd* made a

186

judgment call. Would he do it again—opt for justice over the rule of law?

Looking at his friends around his Grandmother's elegant dining room table, and remembering Melony—he wasn't sure what he'd do if he came across THK again. The Mojave had changed him, and he was not yet ready to make a call on what that change encompassed.

For some unknown but compelling reason, Hugh looked back at Ted, and caught the Special Agent in *a moment* of private contemplation. *A moment* in time Ted most assuredly thought no one else saw, *a moment* in time that revealed to Hugh what Ted knew, and most importantly, what he was planning on doing.

Both women were momentarily silent, and Della hoped Murphy might be sensitive enough to have enjoyed the last few moments as much as her. Sunsets and sunrises— Mojave calling cards. Maybe a common appreciation they could share? *I can only hope.*

She'd heard thunder in the far distance and seen lightning slice across the Eastern horizon earlier. In Hugh's area, she'd speculated then. Now they were standing at her dining room French doors looking out toward the *Western* horizon, almost touching shoulders, but not quite—watching the dregs of the day's light dissolve into blackness. And thunder and lightning were now filling *her* skies in all directions.

Somehow Jasmine had managed to squeeze between them, and Della fancied her loyal companion was mimicking her interest in the world outside and thoughts about Murphy. *Of course that's silliness.* More likely, Jasmine's interest lay in trying to see the occasional darting rabbit in the darkness, and anything   else—but   she   preferred   her   own anthropomorphizing of her canine friend.

Murphy shifted her weight, moving a *bit away* from Della, and Jasmine wedged herself in a *bit closer* to Della.

Unfortunately, it had not been a spectacular sunset. *In fact,* Della thought, *rather disappointing.* Still, there had been blotches of peach, even a couple spots of red insinuating a touch of vibrancy into an otherwise bland blue pallet. Della put her hand out and touched a door-glass pane. *Cold.* Following suit, Jasmine touched her nose to the glass, then quickly pulled it back. Murphy didn't seem to notice. *In her own scheming world,* Della uncharitably thought.

Her day had been long and emotionally straining. And now, this evening, Della knew what was hanging in the air between her and Murphy was coming to a head, and had to be resolved.

Nonetheless, she tried for the moment to keep her thoughts focused on the now very dark vista, still savoring the last moments of sunset over her little piece of the Mojave. *Past my hills,* she mused, *as the eagle flies, civilization awaits.* Indeed, unseen and beyond her little patch of peace and tranquility, I-15 cut northeast and southwest through the desert—to and from Vegas and San Diego, moving hundreds of thousands of cars through multitudinous southern California clusters of suburban humanity.

So different from her tranquil little piece of Route 66.

Indeed, for the moment, all was quiet outside, and inside. But she knew another "storm" was gathering clouds within her own little home. She could feel the lightning-like electricity building even in the air around them.

Murphy was the one to break the silence. "So, he's not talking to Dr. Lincoln anymore?" her voice was low and rather nasal—her tone accusatory. Della was always amazed how petty and immature Murphy often sounded, given her stylish wardrobe and demeanor. And she was such a pretty woman, almost model-like in her features and body sleekness.

"No," Della said. *It's starting.* The inevitable discussion they couldn't sidestep any longer was at hand. "And I'm not surprised." Della laughed quickly and lightly, trying for a mood that didn't exist. Her tone rang false even to her own ears. "Hard enough keeping any kind of relationship going over so many miles, much less between a shrink and her client." Ironic words, she knew. Hadn't she tried using miles to escape from her murdering ex-husband Arnie? *Didn't work, did it?*

Murphy reached out to pat Jasmine on the head, and she growled—causing her to jump slightly, pull her hand back, and say, "I guess we aren't friends yet."

"Sorry," Della murmured. "She's very protective." *Oh dear.*

But Murphy unexpectedly said, "It's good she protects you."

Silence again for a moment.

Then Murphy asked, "Have you tried to tell Hugh?"

"No."

"And Julian Bogard and Jefferson Adams? They didn't tell him either?"

Of course not. "It wasn't their place, Murphy. You know that." Della could hear an edge of irritation in her voice, and forced her tone calmer. "If his shrink couldn't get him to face reality, how could they?" Surreptitiously she sucked air in through her teeth. "What they did is what we've all been doing. Been told to do. Pretend. Wait until Hugh realizes himself what actually happened."

Murphy partly has a point, Della admitted to herself. Julian Bogard was the Champion Lawyer—and had fiduciary responsibilities. She knew he also had a lot of discretionary power and was consulting with Charlotte Lincoln, Hugh's

189

shrink. Hubert Jr. had put Julian in the middle. Della knew Junior never really "liked" either of his kids, and didn't want to deal with them directly.

True enough, maybe Julian and Jefferson should have forced the issue when they were in town. But it had been so clear Hugh had repressed everything—didn't even recognize them for Christ's sake. Besides, LoraLee had been the number one issue at the time; Hugh's dealing with reality had to go on the back burner. Looking back, she thought Julian came close to telling Hugh. But she knew he was a nice man. *A kind man.* Would have been hard.

"But maybe that's what he needs," Murphy's tone and delivery turned colder, "to be pushed." She took a few seconds for a dramatic deep breath—long, slow, and implying a need to turn justifiable impatience into long-suffering patience. "It's been a long time. At some point, my brother is going to have to face the fact our parents are both dead." Her voice caught for a second. "Over three years now for Father, and one with Mother right after he opted out of life and fled out here to this god-forsaken—" Then her voice lowered, became calmer, softer. *"Mors vincit omnia."* Her Latin pronunciation and delivery rang pompous. "Death conquers all. Hugh needs to face up to reality."

Mors vincit omnia. "How true," Della reluctantly agreed. "Even for the great Hubert James Champion Jr." She closed her eyes for a second and saw a picture of Hugh's father. A picture from the time when she'd left New York for Chicago. Tall, self possessed, controlling—she hadn't liked him as a child, or as an adult. *Too bad Murphy's so much like him.*

"Yes, even for Father," her cousin agreed.

It was a minor and fleeting moment of agreement. Della straightened her shoulders, and said, "Listen to me." She turned to Murphy. "I think I need to be clear on my position."

190

Time for firmness. She was sure if left unchecked—and like her deceased father—Murphy would attempt to control the situation. "Hugh will face the truth when his mind and emotions are ready to handle it." She took a breath of her own, then forced her tone harder. "Why do you think it's *your* duty to make him face their deaths, here, now, and on your timetable? Your reasoning escapes me." She softened her expression. "What difference does it make if he takes his time accepting their deaths?" *It's his craziness.* She added, "Who is he hurting?"

Murphy jerked her gaze from the blackness outside, took a step back, and turned to face Della. Her eyes were narrow and her top lip quivered slightly. "Some things can't just be ignored. Just because you're too chicken—"

"No." Della didn't want to rise to Murphy's level of animosity, but she couldn't let her get the upper hand. And this issue needed to be dealt with, firmly. "*Because* I care about someone I love not being hurt, or mentally damaged permanently. *Because* the truth is not always the right answer. *Because* I don't have your level of self-righteousness." Della stopped, hoping she hadn't gone too far—then she recognized something else in Murphy's expression. "You want something. Or need something." She couldn't stop now. "Hugh's facing the truth will get you something you want, but I just don't know what it is. Yet." She caught herself in time. Suddenly and clearly she did know what Murphy wanted. She wanted Julian Bogard to settle the Champion estate. Greed was motivating Murphy. However, Della held her tongue. Maybe too much truth for this moment.

"Now it comes out." Murphy laughed harshly. "You think I'm responsible for Serena dumping Hugh." She scowled unattractively. "That was hundreds of years ago. *Someone* needed to tell her what a goofball he was."

191

"What the heck are you talking about?" Della heard blood pounding in her ears, and her heart felt like it had jumped into her throat. "What does Serena have to do with anything?" A swell of nausea grabbed at her stomach. She wanted to stay in control, stay calm, act like nothing had happened. *But it has.* To this moment, she hadn't known why Serena and Hugh broke up. *Murphy.*

A long moment passed, then despite her physical distress, Della said with deadly calmness, "You?"

"Of course, *ME*. You don't think I'd let my best friend ruin her life, do you?"

"Hugh is your brother."

"So?" Murphy sighed impatiently. "The point is, sometimes you have to tell people things if you want the right outcome."

Jasmine evidently received some kind of message from her mistress and growled, louder than earlier, and bared her teeth slightly.

Murphy took another step back. "Maybe I better pack."

"Maybe you better." Della's better side added, "But maybe you shouldn't leave until in the morning."

Murphy's voice was hard, dismissive. "I can get a redeye out of LA tonight. I can call for a rental and drive myself to the airport you know." She turned abruptly and walked away toward the guest bedroom.

Della admonished Jasmine to stay at her side by the window as she listened to Murphy moving through the house, gathering her things. Of course she would have to drive her wherever she thought she was getting an overnight flight. Ontario? LAX? John Wayne? She shook her head and felt a smile born in irony curling her lips. Most likely *she'd* be dropping Murphy at a hotel where she'd book a morning flight. "Well and good," she informed Jasmine. "I don't care where she stays. As long as it's not here." She did want to

192

make sure Murphy got on a plane and the hell out of her desert without going to Joey's. Uneasiness in that respect weighed heavily on her heart.

"Murphy certainly brings out the worst in me." She looked down at Jasmine. "You and I are going to have to go see Hugh tomorrow." *She* needed to tell him—not Murphy. *And maybe Audrey?*

Hugh was right—Della concluded with new-found wisdom—*not* to open Murphy's Christmas card.

"Thanks for meeting me so late," Della said taking a sizable gulp of coffee. "Coffee's good." She smiled and pushed the small empty plate in front of her away. "And that pie was *far* too good."

"Yeah, I don't come here as often as I'd like." Audrey returned her smile, and pushed an identical looking plate away from her. "I'd gain too much weight."

Audrey finished the last of her glass of milk. It had been a long day, but these moments of relaxation with Della were nice. Though she already knew there was a catch— something serious was behind all this. Della called her at the office in Yermo, and miraculously, she'd stopped back in after Hugh's poker game to pick up a couple files. Their discussion about cops, power, and abuse had rankled a bit, and started her thinking. She hadn't left for home yet when the phone rang. *A very long day, indeed.*

Audrey had caught something in Della's voice, a neediness she hadn't heard before from the seemingly quite self-sufficient woman. Audrey was past tired, but suggested a late night snack at Penny's Diner—*if* Della felt like driving up in the dark to the little Airstream-styled diner attached to the Oak Tree Inn. She certainly didn't feel like driving down to

Oro Grande—*no*, she just wanted to go home in the opposite direction—and crash for a few hours.

There would be no true rest until THK was dead. *Well, or behind bars.*

Pulling herself back into the moment, Audrey thought, *Della has a nice voice,* It was a recognition that surfaced every time they got together for something or other, not that often actually, but often enough for her to come to like this ethereal looking cousin of Hugh's. It was good to like his relatives, and for the first time since what she called "their seriousness" began, Audrey wondered if she'd ever meet his mother and father.

The waitress came to remove their dishes, fill up Della's coffee cup, and dispense friendly banter. As Audrey waited for their conversation to resume, her overriding emotion morphed from relaxation to apprehension.

After their waitress left, she turned her gaze directly toward Della and noticed Hugh's cousin was looking at her most intently, like she was searching for something; oddly, she didn't find Della's scrutiny uncomfortable. Audrey did however, turn her head for a second, to the South, and glanced out the window. It was dark, no stars really. She couldn't tell, but felt the sky was probably still cloudy. Indeed, she could still hear rumblings of distant thunder. *Vegas by now?* She already knew the air was after-rain-fresh, and the temperature pleasant.

If she could keep awake when she got home, she might like sitting on her hilltop deck for a bit. Look down on I-40, be mesmerized by traffic headlights, imagine taking THK down.

Della said, "I thought this couldn't wait." She took a deep breath. "You know who Murphy is, right?"

Audrey brought her attention squarely back to Della, and Della alone. She'd been caught off guard a bit. *Murphy?* Then she remembered, maybe. "Hugh's sister?" Then she

194

watched as Della's face turned sour. *This isn't going to be good.* How bad, she was yet unsure, but felt herself straighten her shoulders, preparing for the worst.

"You probably didn't know Murphy was in town."

Audrey felt her eyes widen. *All this going on, and Hugh's sister is in town.* "We'll have to—"

Della held up her hand. "She's gone now." Her following sigh made Audrey even more concerned. Della finished, "But it isn't over yet. If I know Murphy."

"What are you talking about?"

Della reached out and opened her hands, gesturing for Audrey to accept the embrace of sorts. "Will you go with me tomorrow to Hugh's?"

"I—" Nonetheless, and though still confused, Audrey willingly and easily put her hands into Della's.

"Please." Della gave her hands a little squeeze, then released them.

"Well, of course." Audrey wiggled in a child-like fashion in her chair, but she couldn't refuse Della. "What's going on?"

Della sidestepped. "You know the Oak Tree Inn is where Julian Bogard stayed. You remember him, right"

"How could I forget?" Indeed, it had barely been six months earlier. She remembered him as a kind, generous, and cultured man. And quite well dressed, even according to East Coast standards.

"He's Junior and Eloise's lawyer."

All Audrey could do was ask questions of ignorance. "Who's Junior, who's Eloise?"

"Murphy wants the Champion estate settled now. She's tired of waiting."

"What estate?" Audrey held her breath. While one part of her couldn't wait for Della to reveal to her secrets about the most secretive Hubert James Champion III—who she'd just

195

recently admitted to herself she loved—another part of her dreaded hearing whatever Della was about to reveal.

Whatever it was, Della certainly did not have a poker face.

Della let Audrey leave first, content to sit a bit longer. She had a long drive home, and wasn't eager to hit the road. She even ordered a pot of tea as a coffee and pie chaser—hoping it would soothe her before having to face I-15 drivers at night. Being with and talking to Audrey had certainly gone a long way in lessening her anxiety and apprehension. But still, Della's stomach remained in knots. An unusual and uncomfortable circumstance for her.

She'd called Audrey after dropping Murphy at The Double Tree by Hilton, only minutes away from Ontario Airport. Two airlines had early morning flights out to New York with only one stop. Murphy stated emphatically she planned to be on one of those flights, last minute or not.

"They'll fit me in, especially if I go first-class," Murphy had stated with haughty assurance. "I certainly don't expect you to put-yourself-out and drive me all the way into LAX."

Looking down into her tea cup, Della smiled—remembering. Murphy, she thought, had expected her to insist. She hadn't. For once, disdain had overcome her innate since of graciousness and hospitality.

A nasty piece of work. She repeated her earlier mental refrain. Then forcing herself to also recall their drive to the hotel. Della wanted to be firm in her mind that Murphy deserved her ire. Indeed, it wasn't a difficult task to reaffirm she was on the side of righteousness. Just replaying her cousin's departing statement made her angry all over again.

"And if you think I'll continue to let slide Hugh's oh so convenient 'not remembering,' you are sadly mistaken, miss-holier-than-thou." Murphy's words were edged in such palpable venom, Della had been compelled to take her eyes off the road—*in airport traffic no less*—to see, if only for a second, Murphy's accompanying expression.

It was at *that* moment, with *that* vision of Murphy indelibly edged in her brain—Della disowned her cousin, and vowed to do whatever was necessary to protect Hugh from his own sister.

PART THREE
Mors Tua, Vita Mea
Your death, my life

Chapter Six

Thursday morning

> *No more mistakes.*

THK found his new "perfect" waiting-spot somewhere between two and three in the morning—a little earlier than he'd expected. It was a time between night and day he considered special. Little traffic, quiet, still dark—a time to wait, plan, then hunt with the coming of light. He was excited. *This Thursday morning I will be fulfilled again.* The death of another—renewed life for him.

On the side of National Trails, he'd found a little gulley in the hard packed sand and gravel in front of a slight rise. The closest on-ramp to I-40 was to the west toward Newberry Springs.

Actually, his new spot was more like a trench—but whatever the car-sized hole should be called, it almost completely hid his Toyota from the road. Several other spots he'd considered were flooded from last night's storm. But not this one. And in the darkness of predawn, he could monitor the bans unobserved, know when a CHP cop was within striking distance.

Perfect. His spot was also in a section where the dirt was oily-black, looking almost like lava to him, even in diminished light. *Weird*, he thought, but great. All he had to do was wait and listen to his police band for shift change or codes, or maybe just let his instincts take over. This morning the ideal target *would* be coming his way. And it would only take a couple minutes to drive up and out of his little hidey-hole, hop on the interstate, then park on the shoulder when he sensed the time was right.

Yep, *perfect*. He could even call nine-one-one, if nothing good popped up. Then just wait for a black-and-white to come-a-calling his way

THK felt like singing.

Ludlow Cafe was not only a thirty-minute-plus drive east out Route 66, but also in the opposite direction of Audrey's often wind-battered hilltop home—which would add about ten miles to the return trip getting to her Yermo office. And after last night—what with Melony's poker wake, then Della's revelation and plea for handholding—she was darned tired.

Sometimes, however, Audrey liked treating herself to a stack of their pancakes. *This morning,* was one of those times. In fact, she craved their light fluffiness, stacked high, saturated in butter, and dripping with syrup. Of course there'd be bacon too. And orange juice. Just like at Penny's Diner last night, her body was begging for indulgence. So what if she'd have an abnormally long drive back to her office? Besides, this morning she was still driving a loaner CHP black-and-white— wouldn't have to go on her own expense report.

Leaving her office last night before heading to Penny's, Audrey found that Neil's cruiser had "gained" two flat tires. *Unfortunately,* not for the first time. To her mind, Mojave dirt roads were land-mine obstacle courses for tires. Could have been a slow leak. *Or,* could have been a "friendly" local. *Fortunately,* Transportation would be towing his cruiser off this morning, but that wasn't scheduled until ten or so.

Funny, she thought in remembering her call to Neil late last night, he wasn't that upset he'd have to drive his Audi around until his cruiser's tires were repaired—probably two days considering the paperwork involved. He did ask, "Were our cars parked where they usually are?"

She had to think for moment, revisit. "I think so."

When Neil didn't immediately respond, she asked, "You think the tires were personal? I mean, to you, not cops in general."

He made a noncommittal sound and thanked her for the call.

Consequently, knowing she'd be spending several extra hours getting another cruiser sorted out, Audrey got up an hour earlier than usual. Darkness was still heavy upon the morning sky, but by the time she showered and headed out, Audrey expected there would be a wonderful dawn light flooding her octagon home from all sides. Early morning was one of her favorite times of day—even when driving east into the sun.

And for some reason, this morning it was her fancy to "dress up" again like yesterday. Even after all her years as a cop, it was still special wearing a uniform. Audrey also liked wearing her hip holster better than an underarm one. Admittedly, she wore her uniform fewer and fewer times since Ernie promoted her. To this day, she still found it hard to believe he'd quit and moved to Baltimore, promoting her in the process. One day Mojave County would probably evolve to elections. But not yet.

Actually, since Melony's murder, she hadn't left home without a holstered gun. In her mind, a sidearm was definitely justified. Not so much for her own protection—but for Melony's sake. *I will find her killer.* Ethical concerns from their conversation last night at poker wanted to insinuate themselves into her thoughts, but she dismissed everyone's comments. Her own in particular. Rightly or wrongly, she *wanted* THK. In fact, when Audrey first woke up in the

203

twilight hour between night and dawn, she told Melony's spirit—real or imagined—as much.

Now, preparing to leave her hilltop home, Audrey smiled, bringing back a particular memory. Hugh had confided with her during one emotionally intimate moment, that his old shrink—she couldn't remember her name—had called that speck of time, the "human body's twilight-zone." A time when and where the ordinary pace of life suspends itself. Stops, almost. Hugh hadn't shared much about his inner past lives and inner "hells." His sharing this tidbit from his former life had pleased her immensely. And now, in her own twilight time, she fancied she'd spoken to Melony.

The mind does funny things.

By the time Audrey got in her borrowed cruiser, her desire for pancakes was so great, she was not only salivating, but her stomach was also starting to ache from hunger pangs. So, as she headed out on I-40, a section she preferred to think of as "Route 66 express lanes," her heart and stomach obsessed over a stack of pancakes. It was also a perfect time to figure out how to nail THK—Melony's murderer. *Pancakes and justice, a perfect combination.*

Okay, she admitted to herself as she navigated the curves down her hill, for her, right now, justice was just another word for revenge.

First though, she checked in with Barstow CHP, letting them know she was still using their cruiser.

The mind does funny things, Hugh thought sitting on his bench under Poe's Condo. Hobo was stretched out at his feet; but he knew his dog-buddy was actually on alert—keeping an eye out for rabbits. Hugh also knew from experience, rabbits were far smarter and faster than Hobo. Nonetheless, Hobo

204

was on a loose leash so he wouldn't have to worry about chasing down a dog under rabbit-scent control.

Even though the previous few days had been long— grueling actually. And *even though* grief, instead of becoming lighter, was weighing-in heavier and heavier which each day, Hugh was trying to put the bits and pieces in place. So could then develop a strategy to catch who he thought was a particular type of bastard. One, whose egocentric selfishness claimed victims.

He didn't know Bob Thomas, actually only saw him once at the Community Café, but there seemed something extraordinarily wrong about a man's home being invaded, his wife scared to death, and him having a heart attack because of the event. The immoral act of taking another's property didn't mean much these days, Hugh realized. But these particular set of thefts weighed heavy on his psyche and emotions.

In his past life, he'd looked into more evil minds than he'd ever wanted to—or even imagined he could tolerate. In some ways, he'd even grown inured to the reality of such people—but it still made him angry. Outraged, in fact.

"Funny," he told Hobo. "Beautiful morning. Bad deeds."

Krawk! Krawk! An unknown raven somewhere in Poe's Condo voiced counsel.

In response, a mosaic of happenings, players, and events stored in Hugh's brain all moved around, shifted, and formed a brilliantly colored, and to his mind, accurate and complete picture. Hugh wasn't sure why he was seeing this mosaic in Technicolor. Maybe because his mind had fashioned this last week's happenings in an ornately patterned tile-like puzzle? Impossible to tell, but he didn't fight the imagery his mind's eye was putting together. To the contrary, he was very pleased.

All the pieces fit. Now, all he had to do was get Griffith to talk to him again. No matter his instinctual liking for the man, it had to be done.

It was still very early, but he thought desert dwellers were in large part early risers. He flipped open his cell-phone to call Gabe to get a phone number for Griffith "G-Man" King.

Somewhere along the stretch of road where Audrey could see the Amboy Crater and Lava Field, her body revived its culinary excitement—pancakes took center stage and she would be eating them soon.

It was a unique section of Route 66—the desert floor covered with black rock left from an ancient eruption. There was a crater, but she didn't remember exactly how old it was reported to be, but thought it was in the thousands of years. She did remember the claim the last eruption was about five hundred years earlier. There was a National Natural Landmark with a parking area and view point. And for a fleeting moment, Audrey thought she might go off, take a moment to enjoy the morning light. But she was too hungry, and decided to keep going.

Then, before the Ludlow exit, she saw a little white Toyota parked on the side of the road on old Route 66, its emergency blinkers flashing. Her CHP black-and-white had a Mobile Data Terminal, and she glanced at the communication system looking for an alert, bulletin, or call-code. *Yep*, 10-46, motorist needing assistance.

She cursed, "Damn." then laughed. *I can't be that hungry.* She fumbled around the console a few seconds before finding the light bar switch and flipped it on. *Duty call*s. Her stomach would have to wait.

Won't take long to take the exit and backtrack a quarter mile or less.

As soon as she was on the "old road," a swell of nausea rose in her stomach, but she didn't pay attention, attributing it to hunger. Once pulled in behind the Toyota, but before getting out, Audrey made sure she was "loaded," Glock and taser. Also before exiting her cruiser, she called in the stop — code 10-28 for an out of state registration check, and almost as an afterthought, a 10-29 check for a wanted person or vehicle.

As Audrey exited her cruiser, she instinctively noted several things. *Illinois plates,* though the driver was heading East. *Maybe heading home?* And all the antennas — *a CB and short wave enthusiast.* But driving an old Toyota.

"An old white Toyota," hadn't Hugh said while beating himself up yesterday? *Yes,* the BOLO on her desk, and probably accessible on her console if she knew how, had said "white Toyota."

Audrey felt her fingers twitch when she touched her holster — and this time, paid attention to what her body was doing.

Had Melony done the same things? She wondered. Melony was so new. An innocent. *Murdered.*

Next Audrey had the oddest sensation. *As if Melony's hand was on her shoulder.* She stretched her neck and pulled her back and shoulder erect in an attempt to exorcise her deputy's psychological ghost. But out-of-the-blue, she remembered for the first time in decades — a wintery afternoon in grammar school when Sister George had insisted the class all slide over in their seats a bit. Telling them to make room for their guardian angels. *Well,* she might not actually *believe,* but Audrey knew herself to be a woman who covered all bets — if she could.

Funny, even in those seconds of reflection, the early morning air, fresh, dry, and familiar registered with her senses. She was in tune with the Mojave—born and raised in the desert, and here is where she planned to live out her life. It was a philosophy she and Melony had shared and talked about.

Our desert, she thought and came near to smiling. So beautiful in the morning. The sky, the sun touching the Eastern horizon—the smell. A wisp of breeze brushing her cheek. Especially after that horrendous rain storm. It was insane to think she was about to confront THK, more likely she was on the verge of helping this person. Being broken down in the desert was not fun. And if the driver was from out of state, probably didn't have adequate water. Well, she knew all the tow numbers by heart, the closest tire-jockey—

Audrey stopped. And time also seemed to stop—though she knew it hadn't. Initiated from somewhere in her psyche, Audrey dropped and rolled back toward her cruiser door, almost as if something or someone pulled her down and away. Her chin scraped the ground, and she tasted, then swallowed sand.

Two, three, *no*, four shots whizzed through the air where she'd just been standing.

Then with expertise and speed born in practice and experience, Audrey un-holstered her Glock, and from her position on the ground, her elbows and forearm forming a tripod, aimed for the heart of a tall thin man rushing toward her with a handgun pointing directly at her head.

Her magazine held nine bullets. She emptied it.

Hugh hadn't expected the opaque looking window in Griffith's shop to refract stilted winter morning light as it did. He was familiar with the phenomenon—calcium in his well water clustered in, around, and on most surfaces it touched.

208

Griffith's window, though clouded as it was, infused the areas it illuminated with a halo-like quality that paint brushed the entire room with an *Impressionist* feeling—causing a particular memory to return. A pleasant memory touching all his senses. Right after graduating from college, compliments of his parents, he'd spent an idealistic and romanticized two weeks in Paris. During that time, he ended up spending several days at *Musée d'Orsay, Musée Marmotan,* and *Musée de l'Orangerie.* He still retained that impressionist lens somewhere in his mind's eye. This morning it was in the forefront. *How important, your "life-lens" is,* he reflected—thinking particularly of Griffith and Baddon.

His Paris remembrances also prompted his heart to send a little mental thank you across the miles to his mother and father. He wouldn't nominate Junior for anyone's father-of-the-year award; but there were many things his parents did he should be grateful for. *I'll call soon.* Oddly, he couldn't remember if he'd actually called his mother Eloise since his thank you note for his school-house clock in Joey's. Sent pictures? He just couldn't remember. But he *did* remember Paris.

Hugh certainly hadn't prepared himself on the way over for experiencing Griffith's shop in this manner. To the contrary, he would have wished for a harder edged environment to accomplish what he needed to do. Indeed, the welder's clouded shop window and all it represented surprised him, nearly throwing him off balance.

"You can see," Griffith was talking, pointing, and walking toward Baddon's area of their large workshop, "his bird houses are quite nice." He smiled. "You can't get workmanship like that anymore. Uses pegs for joining, you know."

Hugh nodded, and smiled himself. But despite the surprising scene he found himself in, and his initial liking of

209

Griffith, it was time to get down to business. Of course he knew timing was all important. This would take all his skill as a psychologist, skill he wasn't sure he still possessed.

"Interesting you and Baddon are able to amicably share a work area," Hugh said as a first real volley into the two men's relationship.

Griffith was still walking around, now as if appraising anew his own workshop. "He prefers Don, you know." He looked to Hugh, like a man drawn in abstract with a few brush strokes.

"And do *you* prefer 'G-Man'?"

Griffith laughed. "No way." He walked toward the window, becoming even more part of what was beginning to feel to Hugh like a tableau—with some mysterious artist off scene putting them down on canvas. "A little late now, however, to disabuse everyone from using it."

"Disabuse," no less. Hugh had to admit he liked the man. At least, he liked the man's language.

Griffith turned around abruptly, and said, "Come over here, will you, Hugh?" His voice betrayed excitement. "Have something I want to show you."

Hugh had been standing since he arrived, not following Griffith around except with his eyes—still reconnoitering for the best way and spot in the workshop to confront him. Now he followed him to one of his work benches.

"You've finished the raven." Hugh couldn't keep the wonderment out of his voice. "He looks like he's actually in flight." For several seconds, he forgot all his intentions and was at a loss for words. "The way you've expanded his wings—" His voice trailed off in appreciation and awe. Hugh reached out and touched the raven, asking as he did, "Does Don help you design? Or is this raven from your mind alone?" The metal was cold and smooth.

210

Griffith reached out and touched his sculpture himself, and smiled. "Let's sit, Mr. Champion." He extended his hand toward a small table and two chairs tucked in the far corner of the workshop behind Don't birdhouses. "Let me tell you about Don and me."

Just like on his last and only previous visit, the air inside Griffith's shop smelled clean and fresh. This time, the welder's particularity regarding his work area, especially his desire for order and cleanness told Hugh something about the man.

"Don was lost when I ran into him at the ministry," Griffith explained, peering intently into Hugh's eyes. Seemingly trying to *will* him to understand.

Hugh nodded.

"I was teaching a class on welding." Griffith paused and looked away as if remembering.

Hugh took the moment to indulge in his own thoughts. A little over six months earlier, in the dark of a starless night, Hugh had silently crept down the driveway at the Jackson household—he could still feel how a wayward current of cool air had brushed his face. He was on a mission to rescue Marsha Portson. He still had the aged black jacket he'd worn as camouflage that night—his .45 Redhawk in his right pocket, and a halogen flashlight in his other. This morning, he had no emboldening sidearm. Just his mind, his training—and his desire to set things right.

Griffith's shop became eerily silent.

That night on the Jackson driveway had also been eerily silent—no owls, no trains, no ravens. The silence before a storm. Just like right now, in the brightness of morning. One could have heard a nail drop in Griffith's shop. *That night*, he'd

211

continued to move forward, soundless footfall after soundless footfall until he'd finally made it to the driveway and caught his first snip of Toby's voice.

His mental footfalls this morning would also have to have that same stealth. His weapon this time—only himself. His training, his brain, and his determination.

This was a duel of the minds—not of firearms.

Had he finally come back around to being a psychologist? Indeed, for the first time in several years, Hugh's feet felt on firm ground, not sinking in the quicksand of self recriminations, guilt, and doubt.

Hugh said, "So, you knew Don for a couple years before you offered him a spot to plunk his trailer on?" Hugh thought he remembered Baddon claimed five years at breakfast in Ludlow.

Then he broke Griffith's intense stare and leaned forward—not toward Griffith and not away. As if he was engrossed in his own thoughts. In truth he was trying as best he could to watch Griffith's every expression, his every move.

And this was not just another faceoff. Griffith King was not Toby Portson. He was a good man, a smart man. Still, Bob Thomas was recovering from a heart attack because of scrap-metal thievery, and it had to stop.

Audrey had rescued him that night. This beautiful morning, in brush-stroked light of day, Hugh was on his own.

He turned his head, leaned forward a little more, and tried to catch Griffith's eye—this go-round, he would be the aggressor. "Please hear me out, Griffith." But he still needed to exercise a balanced professional tone—a tone he'd perfected in his earlier days as a psychologist. Something was missing now—he could hear it. But Hugh quickly realized what was absent in his voice, his demeanor even. *Communication of my own caring.* That piece of himself that said, *"Trust me, I'm on your side.'* Clearly, this moment was as much about him, as it was about Griffith and bringing a killer to justice. "You need to do the right thing about Don."

Griffith returned Hugh's stare, defensive unkindness now hard in his eyes. "What are you getting at?" Even the blurring affect of impressionist brush strokes couldn't hide Griffith was now on alert.

"You need to do the right thing," Hugh repeated simply. "You know that yourself. I'm just the conscience you'd rather ignore." He took a deep breath. "And everything I've guessed at, you've known all along, haven't you?"

"What are you talking about?" Griffith asked — calmness *and* challenge lacing his words.

"You say you helped, Don, helped him find an interest in life. Something he's good at. Something that needs his full attention." He looked around the shop slowly, accompanied by a low-key but sweeping hand gesture. "You brought order and meaning into his life."

"Yes."

Hugh couldn't stop now. He needed to get Griffith to see what he saw. "You also gave him a private place to stay of his own."

"Yes."

"A place "to be" in the way of the world."

Griffith didn't respond this time.

Hugh's thoughts about Gabe from Melony's poker wake returned. "You're the lynchpin in his life."

Again, Griffith was mute, and Hugh felt himself warm. But his hands weren't trembling. He needed to push on. "He wants to help you, garner your praise. He wants—"

"You're going too far." Griffith's voice turned hard, offended.

Hugh took a surreptitious fortifying breath, letting a moment of silence hang between them. Finally, he said, "Don loves you, and wants you to love him in return."

213

Griffith started to stand, but Hugh was quick to wave him to sit back down. "I mean 'love' as in a father or brother's love." He sighed. "You're his family."

"But, but," Griffith said, suddenly seeming confused. "I still don't know what you're trying to tell me exactly."

"I think you do," Hugh smiled, wryly, but kindly he hoped.

Oh yes, Baddon "Don" Giles was stealing scrap metal and using the proceeds to make the final payments on Griffith's land, and he could see in Griffith's face he understood. Hugh had also noticed a brand new soldering torch on Griffith's work table. Baddon probably gave it to him as a present. He decided not to mention it.

What he did say was, "You must have suspected he faked the robbery here to divert suspicion?" He paused a moment, giving Griffith time to assimilate everything he was saying. "That shot at Neil, though, must have really surprised him." *Surprised us all,* he remembered. He'd wouldn't get them off track by explaining who the sniper had been.

Griffith didn't answer.

The shop door opened abruptly and Baddon, tall and thin, almost leapt into the room, one hand clutching a fist full of bills. "G-Man, I just had a lotto winner, enough to pay this month's—" Then he saw Hugh, and stopped in his tracks.

"Where's your car?" he demanded of Hugh, seemingly without forethought, but assuredly with accusation.

"Out back," Hugh answered calmly and with a smile. He didn't know what was going to happen next. Baddon coming home was not an eventuality he'd prepared for. "Next to your dark-blue pickup truck." Hugh knew he was looking at the man just Monday night he yelled at from the inside of his bedroom. The man he'd been ready to shoot if need be. His own words returned and reverberated in his ear, *I have a gun, and I WILL shoot.*

214

For a moment, Hugh felt a pang of sorrow for Baddon, but that emotion was fleetingly pushed aside by an imagined picture of Bob Thomas in his hospital bed, trying to survive a heart attack. Stemming from a medical condition Bob probably already had, but most probably helped along by Baddon's thievery.

He doubted Baddon would get very long jail time, if any. But he needed to be charged, and hopefully convicted — whatever the sentence.

Griffith stood, and once again Hugh was struck with how impressive a presence this wrought iron sculptor exuded. Not hard to accept Baddon looked up to him, thought of him as the ideal father. For a fleeting second a memory of Junior holding his hand as they walked through Central Park overwhelmed him. *Yes,* it was past time to call his own parents.

"*We* need to talk, Don." Griffith stepped toward Baddon as if he was going to embrace the younger man, but he didn't, stopping short of invading his personal space. "Then we need to talk with Mr. Champion. Then all three of us need to talk to the police."

Hugh expected Baddon to object, run, start a fight — something in that vein. Instead, the young bird-house builder said, "Okay, G-Man," He even halfway smiled. "Whatever you say."

It's over.

He'd succeeded as a psychologist, persuaded a good man to do what was right. An event that hadn't happened to Hugh in a long time.

A piece of what was Hubert James Champion III returned to life.

* * * * *

215

Ted Fletcher sat a long time at his favorite spot, his bucket seat tilted back slightly, yet retaining a clear view of his favorite mini-peak almost straight in front of his parked SUV. He'd become quite fond of that particular out-cropping—finally accepting Mojave hills as "mountains"—and had dubbed this little one, Rociana's Peak.

He smiled thinking about her, but a frown quickly followed when his train of thought uncontrollably reverted to thoughts of Melony Dibbs. Nothing would bring back the young deputy, but as far as he was concerned, justice would be served. His smile did return at the thought his sister Audrey took down THK, Melony's *presumed* murderer.

He relaxed his shoulders and neck, sliding down a little into his seat and forcing his attention back to the desert landscape in front of him. It was amazing how isolated some Mojave areas were. *No sign* of human intrusion for decades. And for the third time since arriving here this afternoon, he forced his eyes and accompanying attention to travel up every inch of the trail in front of him—as far as he could see.

No boot tracks, no evidence—if anyone ever came looking—of man and desert interfacing. No reason for anyone to ever follow that trail until it eventually faded seamlessly into Mojave dirt, dust, and sand. Last night no longer existed.

Outside the cocoon of his car, the wind was building, blowing to the East, Vegas bound. On the seat next to him was bag of finely cross-shredded documents, including pictures, a manila envelope, and Ty's crumpled note. He'd used the high-tech special shredder at headquarters and was tempted to let the prevailing wind carry the illegally obtained reports and pictures onward. But no, he'd take them home and burn them in his condo's fireplace. Hadn't used his brand new fireplace yet; obliteration of Rociana's past with her Ex would be its inaugural burn.

216

He ran his hand along the ridge of his dashboard — slowly, almost lovingly. *Yep,* all was right in Ted Fletcher's world. Robert "Roberto" Reyes was no longer a problem.

For no discernible reason he could come up with, Ted next wondered if Neil would like to have a beer with him — and thought he might.

Out loud he said, "Odd friends to have, Champion and Knight." Of course he'd never tell Champion about Reyes, neither would he ever tell Neil he'd almost been killed because he'd liaisoned with Rociana. Though he thought Neil might have figured that one out himself. *Hell,* and Champion was a head-doctor — might even have guessed about him and what he'd done. But whatever they thought, it would always be a guess. No evidence. Ted had made quite sure of that.

Out of the blue, he remembered the only French phrase that had stayed with him over the years, *le malheur ne connaît pas d'ami.* Adversity does indeed make odd bedfellows. Champion and Neil had both influenced him. *Who would have figured?*

He laughed. For a long time, the tempo growing louder and more urgent, before finally fading. A release, he knew.

Then, Ted wept for Melony. Softly.

Finally, after swiping his eyes with his shirt sleeve, he said to the world in general, "I hope you went gently into that good night, Deputy Melony Dibbs. And you, Robert Reyes, I hope you rot in hell."

He'd laughed, he'd cried, and now he smiled.

Neil hadn't forgotten how much he hated the Mojave just six months earlier — especially when he was driving down to Victorville — which he was doing today. Supposedly, it was his day off and he and Sally were going to try to spend the rest of the day together. Of course he was still on call, everyone was until THK was taken down, and since his cruiser was out of commission, he could drive around all day in his Audi.

Audrey was going into the office, planned on being there all day, and said she'd call if he was needed.

He tried to relax. Anticipating seeing Sally still made him nervous. Or excited. He hadn't quite figured that particular emotion out yet. But a jittery feeling was building in his stomach, so he took a deep breath—then sighed. Neil didn't like feeling emotionally vulnerable, but these days seemed to be filled with change.

All around him, scenery wise, nothing there had really changed—he'd still have to endure another half-hour of mind-numbing dirt, dirt, and more dirt—accentuated by minor topographical bumps the locals had the nerve to call mountains. And they still weren't even hills by his way of thinking. Yet, something was different now—even with the boring desert scenery.

Something significant. But like with Sally, he wasn't yet sure what he was experiencing.

Yep, to his sensibilities, the Mojave was still a God-awful yellow-colored dustbowl one had to survive to get to Nevada highlife. No trees, no water features, no nothing. And Las Vegas was the place where there was some "action." Lights, people, even lakes. Folks there fixed their places up. Grass, trees, all that regular stuff.

Somehow, someway, all those things—once negative and almost unbearable—were now preferable. *Good things*— even with the heavy weight of Melony's death on his shoulders. A weight he'd carry forever. Indeed, Melony's kindnesses to him would always remain with him.

Still, he couldn't push down the new buoyancy of spirit he was feeling. *Is it because I now have friends? Champion, Fletcher, Sally.* He thought there might be a French phrase that covered what he was thinking, doing, feeling. But none came to mind. But a Latin phrase did, *Mors Tua, Vita Mea.*

His cell phone rang. Audrey. *"Merde,"* he cursed. Despite his nervousness, he didn't want to miss seeing Sally. Then he heard Audrey's voice. At first, he thought it must be a mistake. *But no,* she repeated them. "THK is dead. I killed him."

"Alléluia," he responded louder and with more jubilance than he would have wanted.

"I want you at my side, Neil." Her tone rang earnest, true—and so sweet to his ear. "You're my right hand man."

He swallowed hard. "I'm on my way."

As soon as Neil disconnected with Audrey, he rang Sally with apologies. She'd heard the news too, and sounded as excited as he was. Then he flipped the switch on his portable after-market siren and flasher, both magnetically mounted on his Audi's rear deck.

Audrey needed him.

After exchanging hurried cellphone sound-bites with Audrey about the day's amazing happenings, she had quickly ended their conversation with, "I've got to talk to an FBI bigwig right now." Her voice lowered, "He's heading right toward me. At least he's smiling." Her voice lowered to a whisper, "I know you're tired, but don't go to sleep on us. Della and I will be there as soon as we can."

Hugh could envision her—still at the scene, she'd said—surrounded by cops of all persuasions, several districts, and several states. Strobes flashing, uniformed cops from all over, news media swarming with their vans, cameras—eager news anchors and assistants. Being bombarded with questions from all sides. He felt sorry for her for a flicker of a second,

219

then reassessed his initial reaction. *No,* he was glad she'd be in the spotlight, if you could call it that. She deserved all the attention she could get. Audrey had taken down THK.

For a moment, he thought he might drive over there. It wasn't far away, and it was still only mid-afternoon.

He was dying for her details, on both her shooting and Baddon's booking—he'd been shooed away far too soon—"Go home," the arresting officer, a Barstow City policeman had insisted. *Must have drawn the short straw,* Hugh thought. The scene of the THK takedown, or the grilling of a local scrap-metal thief? Hugh knew which action he'd rather be involved in.

He was told they'd take his statement tomorrow. Right now, they'd get everything they needed from Griffith and Baddon. Hugh even guessed, that by tomorrow morning, maybe even tonight, Baddon would be out on bail. Probably bail up-fronted by Griffith. *Their bond is deep.*

No matter how monumental his own mental and emotional turn around, Hugh's heart raced back to Audrey. *His* Audrey had taken down THK, and *his* heart swelled with pride because of what she'd accomplished. And love? *Oh yes, I love her.* At this point, it couldn't be more obvious.

She'd phrased her coming over later as a celebration. However, a little cautionary bird somewhere in Hugh's psyche flashed a warning light. But, he'd just have to wait and see, wouldn't he? *This moment is a time for relief.* THK was dead and no more CHP officer's lives would be cut short in the line of duty.

And my Audrey took him out. He couldn't revisit the thought and emotion enough.

Right before Audrey's call, there had been Della's. Waking him up, actually, from a post-Griffith stupor. Della informed him Murphy had been in town, and now she was gone. Offering no details, even though he'd pressed. All he'd known was a visit was planned—and now it was already over?

It took him a few moments, however, to fully encompass what Della was telling him. His sister had come all the way out to California, didn't see him, and was already gone. Maybe he should have opened her Christmas card.

"She needed to get back to New York," was all Della would say.

He'd become a little angry, insisted she tell him more; Della, however, remained as tight-lipped as he'd ever known her. Certainly not her regular informative and helpful self. *Another warning light. Yep*, something was up.

He didn't want to think about it. In fact, his brain suddenly felt fatigued and he returned his attention to the horizon, where just the earliest edge of sunset was developing. *Later than I thought.* Well, it would be a good one tonight—made particularly special because Melony's murder had been avenged—and Audrey would get the credit for it.

He inhaled deeply, and his head felt a little clearer. Winter desert air—fresh and crisp.

Truth was, he'd become rather fond of Mojave sunsets, terrain, and air. The winds, he could do without. But the sunset colors were quite unique. Appreciation had been slow in coming. Desert sunsets were much different from Chicago or New York's city pallets—now, seemingly quite dull and narrow in comparison. Here, the horizon seemed to stretch forever. And the colors, far more saturated—deeper yellow, orange, and red.

Over the last few months, his "artist eye" which he considered minimal, also had come to "see" how unique the sunset's backdrop-color was—even dubbing the shade of blue, "Mojave-evening-blue."

Hugh didn't expect tonight's show of colors to disappoint. As he stared out into the Western horizon from his front deck, ensconced in one of his Adirondack loungers with a quilt over him against approaching nighttime chill, letting his mind take over and ramble wherever—"hither, thither, and yon"—from Della's call, Audrey's call, THK, Baddon and G-Man, and how he felt about himself professionally. *Moments for remembering? For taking stock?*

He found several memories from his recent past demanded center stage—pushing out the extraordinary happenings of the day. He sighed, surprising himself at how loud. But he was alone—who was to hear? Hobo was taking a late afternoon nap, stretched out on "their" bed. Black-Jack, evidently taking his cue from Hobo, was in the second bedroom on "his" rocker asleep.

Nonetheless, "The longest of days," he said aloud as if they were at his side to hear.

"Krawk! Krawk!" Hugh was quite startled, enough to physically jump. Clearly, he was not alone. Somewhere out there, a raven friend, like him was anticipating the approaching darkness.

And advising?

He smiled at himself and his fanciful raven thoughts, and let himself return to mentally floating. Back six months or so ago, yet, he could still visualize and "feel" *that evening* so intensely—*an evening* he believed started "whatever" was still going on now—*the evening* he first saw LoraLee Jackson. *Her cherub face surrounded by long corkscrew red hair, and her luminescent gray eyes so vacant—looking into space.* He even remembered surmising at the time, that LoraLee saw and visited places most humans knew nothing of. And for a moment of other-worldliness, he felt connected to Julian, Marsha, and LoraLee. And Timothy too.

Tonight's sunset was building, and an inner tempo of some kind was getting stronger, just like in Maurice Ravel's *Bolero*. That shouldn't be—Audrey had taken out THK, and

222

he'd talked G-Man into turning Baddon over to the police. *It's over.*

His mind easily returned to LoraLee and re-visited the vision that had confronted him that night—her hands in her lap, clasped tight, as if she were a child being forced to sit quietly in church. Her yellow cotton sundress, styled to recall a much different era with its puffed sleeves and ribbon sash, was covered in blood. And even in the muted light of his dark living room, the dry blood covering her dress had been a vulgar brownish-red, and even now, painful to see again, even if only in his mind's eye. Most probably, he'd never lose that vision of LoraLee Jackson.

He could also hear her words most clearly: *"The nuns at Holy Trinity believe all good Catholics go to heaven when they die,"* she'd said, her voice low, soft, and accepting. *"Their souls live forever. Eternal."* Then she'd smiled—*oh, do I remember that smile*— before adding, "The nuns also said pretty much everyone has to go to purgatory first." And that was it.

Without thought, he shook his head in a clearing-the-cobwebs manner. That night had been a beginning marker of some sort. *For what?* Instead of answers, however, the questions kept coming. *Murders, shoot-outs, betrayals?* Indeed, his Mojave sojourn had not turned into an escape—more like a journey.

He jumped again, this time not because of a counseling raven, but because lightning shot across a sky that somehow had turned dark and brooding without his noticing. Thunder followed quickly. *Another storm, two nights in a row.*

"Jeez..." he murmured. For sure, he hadn't seen any clouds, but in an instant the horizon had become black and ominous. From inside he heard Hobo howl plaintively.

* * * * *

223

It was well into evening in New York, but the city "lived" after sunset, even in Julian's tony neighborhood. He and Marsha Portson were sitting in matching armchairs gazing into the tall flames flickering healthily in his "game room."

LoraLee and Timothy were listening to audio books he'd chosen for them while simultaneously playing video games they'd selected on their individual tablets.

"To blindly not know," Marsha stated in her inimitable way, "seems to be mightily strange, indeed."

Thank you, Hubert James Champion III—Julian mentally sent his gratitude across the continent. In six months, LoraLee Jackson and Marsha Portson had become staples in his and Timothy's life that he didn't think he could do without. "He just couldn't accept that reality," Julian tried to explain. "With Della's husband's murder," he paused, it *was* hard to layout without wading into psychological mumbo jumbo. "And with the type of work he did."

As she often did, Marsha brought into the light of day what an "education snob" he was. "Takes a toll on a man's soul, taking on the troubles of another." She shook her head. "Besides, his head-doctor probably held everybody off."

He smiled. "Yes, Dr. Charlotte Lincoln advised us all to just wait."

"To patiently wait until Mr. Champion remembered himself."

He doubted Hugh would ever "remember." Murphy had called him, and Della's call had followed quickly after. Yes, tonight, Della and Sheriff Boyes were going to tell Hugh before the conniving Murphy did. As the flames danced and warmed his little family in his comfortable Upper East Side flat, Julian Bogard couldn't control the fear grabbing at his heart. He wasn't a praying man, but tonight he wished he were.

The amazing Marsha Portson read his mind. "I'll be a praying for Mr. Champion tonight. To happily be, is what he deserves."

Black-Jack was fearless when it came to storms, but Hugh knew Hobo hated thunder to the point of actually cowering and shivering. A part of him wanted to stay, take in the lightning light-show, feel Mother Nature—admittedly emotionally protected under his quilt. But Hugh folded up his coverlet and pushed himself up from his deck chair to go inside and offer comfort to his canine friend. As he did, he touched the wooden deck table Julian Bogard had given him, and another memory flashed—dramatic and vibrant. It was an afternoon when Julian explained he'd brought him a table, and Hugh tried to imagine how Julian and Jefferson Adams could have possibly wedged it in the trunk of a Mercedes-Benz.

And as he, Jefferson, and Julian had gone outside to see the Mercedes-table-miracle, Julian fell behind Hugh, and touched him on the back. "Thank you," Julian had said. And Hugh had felt *something* pass between them then, and again now. *Something* he hadn't quite understood. But now—he still wasn't sure what, but *something* was starting to stir in the back of his mind. He and Julian, were certainly connected. *How, though?*

As several more electrifying bolts of lightning shot across his Mojave's western sky, Hugh headed inside to comfort Hobo.

"Jeez," he said again, and wiggled his shoulders before looking down at his hands. *No trembles.*

* * * * *

It turned out to be not much of a storm. A starless black sky now hung over them, and the air was so fresh he could almost taste it. They were outside on Adirondack lounge chairs on his front deck. Audrey arrived before Della, and now, with a glass of wine in hand, she was stretched out next to him. He would have rather stayed inside, but she'd insisted.

"A lot of 'sound and fury' about nothing," Hugh quipped.

"Bulletin on my MDT said it's pouring farther east on I-15. Worried about flooding through Primm Valley," Audrey said. "Moved on around and past us."

Julian Bogard's deck-table gift held a remaining half bottle of Beaujolais. Hobo had chosen to take a chance the thunder was over—or—Hugh speculated, Hobo wanted to be with Audrey and had screwed-up his courage. For now, he was laying at the foot of Audrey's lounger; Hugh could also feel Black-Jack eyeing them from his front French door.

The lightning had moved eastward, no more drama on the horizon, and his solar deck lights had switched on. The storm may have moved on, but the temperature had dropped, causing both he and Audrey to wrap themselves up in hoodies.

Another Mojave winter almost survived. "Every year is different," he said.

"You're talking about the weather, right?"

"Yeah, the weather." *And more.*

She released a long slow breath before saying, "Pretty soon it will be spring. And—" Her voice caught slightly. "Hopefully, we won't be having anymore tragedies for awhile."

"Tragedies are your business." It was a melancholy statement, he knew. But so true.

This time her release of a breath was more of a sigh. "So true. Glad I still have Neil."

He knew getting past Melony's death—forefront in her psyche, would take awhile. For himself, too.

"I'm glad you have Neil, too." Hugh drained his glass, and when he reached for the bottle to refill, out of the blue he saw Jefferson Washington Adams's face yet again. The thought of Julian's high priced New York lawyer wanted to release a familiar chain of New York and Chicago memories, hurts, and regrets—but he pushed it all back. Instead, he smiled, seeing again Julian and Jefferson unloading his table from the trunk of their rented Mercedes-Benz. Indeed, *that* was a most pleasurable memory.

He said aloud, "What's with all this New York stuff?"

He heard a sharp intake of breath from Audrey, but when he turned to look at her, she smiled, and asked, "What New York stuff?"

"You didn't say anything about New York just now?"

She shook her head.

He laughed at himself and his internal conversation. "I was thinking about Julian Bogard and Jefferson Adams." He heard Black-Jack meow loudly behind him—and his mind leaped to her brother Ted. He closed his eyes for a moment— deciding. When he opened them, Hugh looked apprehensively at Audrey—then in a split second—he decided to hold his tongue.

He'd *known* since their poker game, from the look on Ted's face. All the other bits and pieces of information were just confirming facts. The smallest of which, was the doing in of Neil's tires—he couldn't prove that of course, and it was such a nit in the way of evidence. He'd waited already, and *now*, he would not break his silence and voice his supposition Robert Reyes had killed Melony—and her brother Ted had killed Robert.

227

THK was an evil bastard, but he didn't kill Melony. Everything pointed to Robert as the murderer, and Rociana as his intended victim. Poor Melony got caught in the cross-hairs. While THK only wanted to kill CHP officers, and would have realized Melony was in a Sheriff's department white with gold-insignia cruiser, not a CHP black and white—even at night. But he doubted Reyes would know the difference between one or the other—just that it was a cop car with flashers and sirens. Even if he did, he wouldn't have cared as long as he was taking out Rociana, or the man he thought was her lover.

Hugh had so wanted to take revenge for Melony himself—but in the end, Ted had done the deed. And Audrey would get credit for doing the deed. Hugh was good with that outcome.

Oscar and Margaret's grief stricken faces were still very vivid in his mind's eye, and truthfully, what Ted had done would not bring Melony back. But at least the Dibbs had received their pound of flesh. *And that feels just fine and dandy with me.*

Reyes also tried taking Neil out—the man Reyes had erroneously identified as Rociana's new lover. Hugh was sure neither he nor Ted would ever tell Neil that Reyes had tried blowing his head off. Of course, Neil was no dummy—maybe he'd figured it out himself. Hugh even thought Reyes checked *him* out as a possible lover.

That was the craziness stalkers were made of. Rociana's little talk with him before poker night had set his logic wheels in motion regarding Reyes. In the past, Hugh had counseled two stalkers, and looking back, he thought both his engagements were failures. Both men were serving life sentences, at least they were last time he heard.

Hugh went so far as to speculate Neil and Rociana though Reyes might be involved. But had either of them guessed about Ted's intentions? He doubted it. *And they will never hear it from me.*

Yep, Ted killed Reyes, and part of him wanted to smile at the knowledge. But like his words, he held his smile back. Audrey had confided she'd promised herself she'd find whoever killed her deputy. He could not take that away from her.

Audrey tilted her head slightly, but didn't speak— clearly waiting and eager to hear what she thought he had to say. *Oh, do I like the look of this woman.* What he said was, "What time is Della getting here?"

"Soon," she answered, then uncannily changed the subject. "Problem with a podunk sheriff's department is we always owe some other county for something. I just got a MISPER for a Robert Reyes. Disappeared from his rental car in Riverside County and they want our help."

Hugh asked evasively, "Don't they know *you* just took down THK? Now they want you to go looking for some missing person who's probably running away from child support or gambling debts?"

"Fame is fleeting," she said. "Especially in law enforcement." After a little pause, Audrey added in a more serious tone, "And a man gone missing doesn't *obey* county lines."

"Any signs of violence?"

"No."

"Any reason to think foul play is involved?"

She shook her head.

"Car smashed up?"

"No."

"Well, there you go," Hugh said, smiling to himself. "Probably somewhere in Vegas rolling the dice, or hopping on an airplane on the way to a new identity."

"Yep," she agreed.

229

*　*　*　*　*

Della brought Jasmine with her. "Couldn't leave her alone with thunder and lightning going on." Of course, Hobo was in heaven, acting like a love-sick puppy in Queen-Jasmine's presence; while she remained aloof, and on the surface, quite uninterested in a scuffed-up aging desert-dog.

On their arrival, Hugh asked, "Want to go inside?" The temperature was still falling.

His cousin, however, had wrapped herself in several layers of colorful scarves, wraps, and flowing jackets, and was quite prepared to sit outside with Audrey, two dogs, and himself. The storm having headed to Nevada—to his sensibilities, his Mojave sky continued to morph. He could even see a few stars daring to appear.

He opened another bottle of Beaujolais, and brought out the remains of Ted's bottle of Tennessee Honey Whiskey along with shot glasses. *Might need this later,* he thought.

"Guess I'm officially a desert-rat," Hugh said apropos of nothing. And the thought made him feel better. Yes, over the last year and a half, much had been resolved, *thank goodness.*

Yet *something* was still nagging at him, and he both intellectually knew and felt in his gut, *whatever* was lingering out there unresolved was key to his *really* moving forward. Not only in his relationship with Audrey, but also for his own acceptance and understanding of his Mojave lifestyle—and future decisions.

He recognized for the first time, in that moment of reflection that Audrey and the Mojave, now walked hand-and-hand in his mind. Without looking, he reached out toward her, and within a second, her hand slid into his.

230

Right now--all was as it should be in his world, no matter what horribleness fate was about to drop in his lap.

"Krawk! Krawk!" from the near distance outside punctuated the moment, *his moment*, and Hugh smiled. Hubert James Champion III straightened his shoulders and *waited* for what they had to say, *waited* for the veil closing off part of his mind and emotions to be lifted, *waited* for the beginning of his future in the light of sanity. And in a lightning-bolt flash, knowledge leapt forward from the shadowy recesses of his unconscious—most ironically—before Della or Audrey could tell him.

I've been living in a lie.

Maurice Ravel's *Bolero* had reached and played out its last climatic refrain, and was now over—leaving in its silent wake, finally remembered, painful, unavoidable, and irrefutable truths.

My mother and father are both dead.

Hugh not only now remembered, but the clarity and his acceptance of his parentless reality was in such sharp contrast to his previous fantastical and complete denial of their deaths—the blow to his psyche felt like a punch in the gut.

First his father Junior, then his mother Eloise—soon after she'd sent him his school-house clock.

I'm now an orphan. Have been for almost a year.

Yet—before Hugh allowed his grief, recriminations, and sorrow to engulf his emotions—*relief* flooded through his entire being. *Relief* that at last, he could finally heal.

M.M. Gornell can be visited at
http://www.mmgornell.com,
http://www.mmgornell.wordpress.com,
and emailed directly at mmgornell@earthlink.net.

Made in the USA
Charleston, SC
12 July 2013